THE DUEL . . .

"When we get to the island, I'll beach the boat. You jump out and move to the middle of the island. It's the best place to fight and I can get off the boat without having to fear that you will cut me down while I'm wading ashore.

"I don't need tricks to deal with a puppy like you," the older man replied with an arrogant sneer. "But your plan makes sense. I agree."

When they arrived at the sandbar the man stood, and looking swiftly back over his shoulder at Edwyr, said "Don't try anything. I'm ready for you," as he leaped into the shallows. Taking no chances, he quickly splashed his way to dry ground, then spun around, ready, he thought, for anything.

What he saw left him speechless. Edwyr had pushed the boat offshore and was drifting about fifteen feet from shore, grinning delightedly.

THE KOAN:
THE SWORD IN THE SCABBARD IS A TREASURE BEYOND COMPARE

Also by Dennis Schmidt:
WAY-FARER
SATORI

From ACE Science Fiction

SF

KENSHO

DENNIS SCHMIDT

SF
ace books
A Division of Charter Communications Inc.
A GROSSET & DUNLAP COMPANY
51 Madison Avenue
New York, New York 10010

KENSHO

An ACE Book

This Ace printing: November 1981

2 4 6 8 0 9 7 5 3
Manufactured in the United States of America
Printed simultaneously in Canada

This book is dedicated to
   Niels Bohr, Albert Einstein, Werner Heisenberg, Geoffrey Chew, and all the other shap-
   ers of modern physics . . .
and to
   Martin Heidegger, F.S.C. Northrup, Steven
   Toumlin, Hans Reichenbach, Fritjof Capra,
   and numerous contemporary thinkers,
   philosophers, and epistemologists . . .
and to
   D.T. Suzuki, Katsuki Sekida, Dogen, Nan-
   sen, Eno, and generations of Zen scholars,
   monks, and masters . . .
but most of all
   to my wife.

PROLOGUE

The thief crouched silently in the deepest shadows at the base of the wall.

Patiently he watched, as across a few yards of moons-lit courtyard the Brother who guarded the door of the shrine yawned and stretched. It was late and the lad was tired, bored by an eventless night and a duty that was purely ceremonial. For who would ever want to steal what lay within the shrine?

Eventually the young man braced himself against the wall next to the doorway and dozed off. As the guard's chin touched his chest, the thief flowed across the yard and through the door, moving so softly and quietly that he seemed but one more shadow among the rest.

Gently placing one foot in front of the other to avoid even the slightest creak of floorboards, the thief approached the chest that stood against the back wall of the shrine's single room. By sheer chance a tiny window set high into the wall to the right let in a mingled beam of light from the three moons that hung in the sky outside. The glow struck the left end of the trunk lid, casting fuzzy, triple shadows on the floor.

The thief reached the chest and knelt in front of it. With both hands, he slowly, slowly raised the unlocked lid so that soundlessly it revealed what lay within. Ever so gently, he lifted the long, cloth-wrapped object that was the sole occupant of the chest. Cautiously unwinding the covering, he bared the narrow, slightly curved shape of a sword in its scabbard. Placing the sword on the floor next to his knees, he replaced the cloth and slowly, slowly closed the lid again.

As softly as before he rose, then thrust the sword through his waist-band, securing the cords attached to the scabbard to hold it firmly in place. Then he turned once more and, as quietly as the moons-light itself, re-crossed the shrine.

As he passed the lightly snoring sentry at the entrance, he paused for a moment, a mischievious smile lighting his hooded features. Looking about, he spied a Ko blossom lying on the ground nearby. Two steps brought him to it and two more returned him to the peacefully sleeping lad. With the lightest touch imaginable, he drew the guard's sword from its scabbard and put the blossom in its place. Then he stuck the sword in the ground at the place where he had discovered the flower.

With a last dark grin, he disappeared into the night.

BOOK I

FATHER ANDRETTI

I

It was one of those rare, wonderful nights when all four moons rode together across a cloudless sky. Subtleties of shape and shade invisible beneath the blue-tinged glare of the daytime sun crept cautiously out to transform the world with delicate beauty, finely edged with a fairy lace of quadruple shadow.

The central courtyard of the Brotherhood on the Mountain was filled with the soft moons-light and the hushed murmur of voices. The intricate tracings cast by the great Ko tree that dominated the middle of the yard nearly reached to the open-air meditation hall that lay at its southern edge. To the north squatted the low, wood-and-adobe buildings that housed the senior Fathers, their rough textures and harsh angles smoothed and mellowed by the gentle glow. East and west were buildings dedicated to instruction and administration, quiet and empty now, their silence adding to the stillness of the night. Beyond, in all directions, other shapes were barely visible, and at the very edge of perception, more suggestion than reality, loomed the wall that completely surrounded the Brotherhood.

In the courtyard itself, on either side of the Ko tree, one could make out two amorphous but discrete groups of robed figures. The first seemed ordinary enough for a Brotherhood: the usual assortment of Fathers and Brothers, young men and old, tall and short, thin and fat, spanning the range from Tenth Frame Novices to Masters. There were at least fifty of them all told, gathered in little clumps of murmured conversation.

Standing at the edge of the first group, Burke
glared with ill-concealed hostility at the twenty or so
members of the second, arranged in a loose cluster,
separated from everyone else by six or seven yards of
empty ground. No one made any attempt to approach
them and they seemed quietly content to remain by
themselves. Talk between them was sparse, each individual seeming to be taken up with his own private
reverie, yet there was a sense of closeness and belong-
ing about them that made their mutual silence companionable and binding rather than isolating and divi-
sive.

Burke glanced at them again and shook his head.
Different, that's what they are, he thought. All pretty
much the same age, same height, same build. Look at
'em quickly and they might seem normal. But *look*
and you discover how strange they are.

Their faces, for example. Calm. Too calm. Always
that slight half-smile on their lips. Nothing ever star-
tles them. It's like they already know what's coming.

Or watch the way they sit or stand or move. Slow,
deliberate, controlled, smooth. So damn smooth.
Never a wasted motion. And always ready to lash out
with lightning swiftness. Always always ready.

Maybe some people can't tell what they are, Burke
thought. But I can. I can pick 'em out of a crowd of
'steaders, settlers, Brothers, whatever. Even without
their swords, I can smell 'em.

Deadly. Unpredictable. Different.

Burke twitched his head in their direction and
muttered to the gray-haired man who stood next to
him: "They always stay apart from the rest of us.
Aren't we good enough for 'em?"

The tense line of Father Andretti's mouth was the
only thing that betrayed his annoyance. Otherwise,

his manner was relaxed and mild as he replied. "They mean no harm, Burke. True, they stick together, but I imagine the real reason isn't so much pride as simply the fact that they haven't much to say. After all, their lives are rather circumscribed. They're totally dedicated to two things: the Way of the Sword and the Way-Farer. That doesn't leave much to talk about with ordinary people. But if you'd ever take the trouble to strike up a conversation with one of them, I think you'd find they're really quite affable. Gentle, in fact. Yes, and almost child-like."

"Talk to one of 'em?" Burke snorted. "Who can talk to 'em? The only answer you ever get is a grunt or a nod! Why, damnit, Father, even when they talk with each other they hardly say a word. They're the quietest bunch I've ever seen. I swear to the Gods, they must have their own sign language or something! Unnatural, that's what I call the lot of 'em!" He shuddered slightly with aversion, casting a black look in their direction.

Andretti's reply crackled with barely suppressed anger. "That's enough, Burke! You're overstepping yourself when you criticize the Seekers of the Way of the Sword! They serve the Great Way and all of Mankind here on Kensho, just as Jerome intended. Remember that and keep your prejudice to yourself!"

The harshness in the older man's voice caused Burke to recoil, his face momentarily blank with surprise. He had never seen Andretti angry before. Then Burke's answering anger came, creeping into his face and eyes along with an expression of cunning. "Aye, Father," he grated, "to be sure they serve. I'll not forget. And you'd be wise not to forget that we also serve, and serve right well, in a far more ticklish area! It's The Faithful who are your strength out on the

Plain, not the Seekers! We're the muscle of the Free
Council and the Great Way and the Way-Farer outside this Home Valley!"

Surprised by the sudden strength of his anger and
his loss of control, Andretti clamped down on himself,
using the mind-calming techniques every child on
Kensho learned almost before he could walk. What's
wrong with me tonight? he wondered. To lose control, and in front of *Burke*? I must be more worried
about the situation than I've admitted to myself.

Forcing a cool smoothness into his words, he
answered. "I know it well, Burke. The Faithful have
been honored by everyone ever since Jerome
founded them. They helped clear the Ronin out of the
passes. And they still protect the settlers from those
Ronin bands that survived the Great Killing.

"As for yourself," he continued soothingly, "have
no fear. We value your loyalty and services for all
they're worth. The information you gather for the
Free Council is properly appreciated, believe me."

"Hmmmm, hmmmmm," Burke nodded, mollified
by the praise and the change in Andretti's attitude.
Teach him to get tough with me, the little man
thought smugly. For a few moments he savored the
older man's apology, remaining silent as he looked
over the assemblage with his sharp, quick eyes.

"Don't see any of the representatives from the
Council of the PlainsLords here," he said finally. He
chuckled dryly, rubbing his long, thin hands together
with malicious glee. "I'll bet Dembo's really sweating
this one! Imagine! The Way-Farer calls a special
meeting in the middle of the night and doesn't invite
the representatives of the Lords!" He turned again to
Andretti, his gaze penetrating. "Any idea what it's all
about, Father?"

Uncomfortable because he had no answer, Father Andretti shrugged. How he disliked this sneaklizard of a man! Small, dark, stoop-shouldered, with swift little eyes that constantly darted here and there, spying, snooping, seeking advantage in everything. The kind of creature that steals eggs from nests. It bothered him that such riff-raff, no matter how useful, found a home among The Faithful.

But what can I do? he asked himself. I need their strength to balance that of the PlainsLords. And I need Burke's information to keep one step ahead of that devil Mitsuyama.

Father Andretti sighed hugely. A large man, well over six feet, he had a massive head with a strong, square face, surrounded by short, curly gray hair and an equally grizzled beard. In his youth, he had been powerful. But as he had risen through the hierarchy of the Brotherhood until he had reached its pinnacle as President of the Free Council, somehow his muscles had grown soft, and he had acquired a layer of fat around the middle. Nevertheless, he was still quite impressive and carried an undeniable aura of determination and authority.

So much to think about, he repeated to himself. What could this middle-of-the-night summons to Audience mean? Why had the Way-Farer called them all together? And why had he excluded Dembo and the other representatives of the PlainsLords?

"Couldn't be that you finally got through to him about Mitsuyama, eh?" asked Burke with a calculating glance. "That'd explain why no Dembo."

Mitsuyama! At the very name, Andretti felt a surge of anger and frustration. Finding ways to counteract that man and his infinite, intricate scheming consumes my every waking hour, he thought in silent fury. Mitsuyama and his cursed PlainsLords represent the greatest threat to Mankind since the Mushin nearly destroyed us at First Touch!

And now this new information that Burke had brought: did it mean that Mitsuyama was moving toward a final showdown, that the battle of rhetoric he had been waging with the Free Council was about to turn into a real battle, complete with bloodshed and death?

Andretti looked up momentarily from his internal converation and noted with pleasure that Burke had moved away and was now talking to someone else. Spies, he thought. It isn't bad enough that I've had to turn The Faithful into a para-military reserve to enforce the power of the Free Council against the threat of Mitsuyama; no, I've actually had to create a spy network with Burke at its head to find out what that devil's up to. And if this new information is true, it's a damn good thing I did!

For an instant a wayward thought crossed his mind. Was Mitsuyama really a devil or only a misguided fool? No. The man knew exactly what he was doing, carefully plotting each devious step. It took all the best minds on the Council to deal with the man's ceaseless machinations.

And even then, Mitsuyama scored victory after victory. His stand against the Council's decision to disband the Keepers and Artisans had gained him a great deal of support, especially out on the Plain. And if Burke was to be believed, there were many, even within the ranks of The Faithful, who half-believed his claim that the Free Council was subverting the purpose of the Great Pilgrimage!

What utter rubbish! he thought indignantly. Why, any fool can see that there are ten times as many men spread across Kensho now as in the days of Jerome.

And someday the entire planet would be settled. But growth had to be slow and deliberate. In keeping with the Great Way. There could be no explosive breeding, no overwhelming of the world, no conquering and subjugation. That was the way of Earth, the way that had led to the very conditions that had forced men to undertake the Great Pilgrimage in the first place. There would be no repeating the mistakes of the Home World here on Kensho. The Council was determined.

For Mitsuyama to twist this sensible caution and concern into a subversion of the Pilgrimage was the height of irresponsible demagoguery. Everything the man said and did was nothing but a ploy to discredit the Free Council. His real ambition was clearly to replace them and seize power for himself!

And if he ever succeeded? Andretti quailed inwardly at the very thought. Death. Destruction. A repeat of First Touch and the Madness. He shuddered. The Mushin, the mind leeches that fed on men's emotions and drove the unprotected mind into screaming Madness, are still with us, he thought grimly. Still very much with us. Only the Brother and Sisterhoods, following the Great Way laid down by Jerome, keep the invisible creatures under control. If the Council were to fall, who would maintain the inviolability of the Great Way? Who would continue the training that keeps the 'hoods fully staffed? Mitsuyama? He laughed ironically.

No, he told himself, there is no other way. If Mankind is to survive on Kensho, the Great Way must be maintained in total purity. And that means the Free Council must stay completely in charge of the situation. If that required turning The Faithful into an army, so be it. If it meant using spies, then they had to be used. And if it led to a final, bloody confrontation

with Mitsuyama and the PlainsLords, then that too
had to be.

From the corner of his eye, Andretti noticed a
movement to his right. Someone was approaching.
He looked up and saw Father Olson coming across the
yard in his direction. Damn! he thought. All I need is
Olson's ceaseless antagonism to really upset me.
Again he realized how agitated he was and firmly
calmed himself as the younger Father, another
member of the Free Council, walked up.

"What's it about, Andretti?" Olson asked sharply.
Everything about the blond-white man was points
and angles. There was nothing soft about him anywhere. Tough, lean, with a harsh aquiline nose that
jutted across an ascetic-looking face, cold blue eyes
that never seemed to blink and cut into one like an ice
dagger, there was no way to like Olson. You could
admire the preciseness of his mind, the keen, cutting
edge of his intelligence. But there was no way to like
him.

His very presence put Andretti on guard. Any conversation between them took on the character of
combat from the very first words. Attack, parry,
counter. "Which it!? Be more specific."

"You know what I mean. Did you tell him about the
information your spy brought?"

Andretti nodded curtly.

"And?" pressed Olson.

"And nothing. The Way-Farer responded as he
always does to our concerns about Mitsuyama and the
PlainsLords. 'My, that sounds bad, Tomas. Very serious. I'm glad you and the Council are on top of the
matter. But I'm sure you're misinterpreting things.
Surely it doesn't matter in any case.'"

"The fact that the PlainsLords are training a secret
army didn't make any difference?"

Andretti snorted. "He didn't seem in the least surprised."

Olson eyed Andretti coldly. He had known how the old man would react to the news. They all had. The Way-Farer wouldn't react at all. He never did. In that Johnston had been consistent ever since he had taken up the Sword of Nakamura from the great Coran, the third Way-Farer in the line that began with Jerome.

It's a good thing the old man's utter indecisiveness is balanced by the fact that everyone loves him so much, he thought. For everyone did love and revere Johnston. Even Mitsuyama and the PlainsLords.

Uncharacteristically, Olson sighed. "So he won't do anything?"

"Has he ever?"

"No," Olson replied, the coldness returning to his voice once more. "He's much more concerned with meditation and his hand-picked pack of Seekers," he jerked his head in the direction of the group which stood across the courtyard, "than he is with the Way or the 'hoods or Kensho itself. He never makes any decisions, not about the Keepers, or the Message, or the PlainsLords. We have to do it all," he finished bitterly.

"And what should we do about Mitsuyama and his new army?" asked Andretti, his tone heavy with sarcasm.

"You know my views. You don't respect them, but you know them."

"You've stated them often enough in Council Meetings."

"Yes, and I'll state them again. We could undercut Mitsuyama's position and destroy his credibility if we'd . . ."

"The Council has decided . . ." Andretti interrupted firmly.

"The *majority* of the Council has decided," Olson amended sharply.

"All right, damn it, the majority, the *overwhelming* majority, of the Council has decided that what you're asking, even in the limited form you propose, would harm the Way and begin the same vicious cycle that ruined Earth."

"And an armed confrontation with Mitsuyama won't hurt the Way? Bah! You're a blind fool, Andretti! You're impervious to reason and opposed to change. And determined to drag the rest of us down with you!" Olson spun about and stalked away.

For a moment, Andretti felt something akin to despair. Enemies everywhere! How could anyone sort it all out? There was so much, too much, to think about! So many factors to consider! Mitsuyama, the PlainsLords, the new army, the Keepers, the Message . . .

Damn! he cursed himself. Control! You can't control the situation until you control yourself. And you've got to keep control because you're the only one who can. Johnston's a wonderful old man, but he's useless, he's . . .

A sudden stillness settled over the courtyard. Aware of the silence, Andretti turned to see the Way-Farer enter the yard and walk slowly toward him. It hurt him to see how old and tired the Master looked. Johnston caught his gaze and held it. He's coming directly to me, Andretti realized, surprised but not displeased. What could that mean?

"Ah, Tomas, Tomas," the old man said as he embraced Father Andretti. "We've seen so little of each other these last few years. I've missed you, my son, missed your inquisitive mind, your constant doubting and searching. But then, I suppose you've been very busy with being President of our Free Council."

Turning from Andretti, the Way-Farer faced the rest of them. "Thank you all, my friends, for coming. I assure you that the reason I called is important enough so that none of you will go away feeling you have been unjustly cheated of a night's rest. Aside from sharing the beauty of the night itself, I have something very important to relate to all of you."

The old man turned half-way back to Andretti. "Tomas," he began, "one of my first disciples, one of my oldest friends, and perhaps the staunchest support my term as Way-Farer has had; I have a request to make of you."

Andretti bowed low. "You have but to ask, Master."

The Way-Farer nodded. "Ummmmmm, yes, yes, I'm sure. Tomas, please go to the shrine and bring Nakamura's Sword to me." A murmur ran through the crowd.

"Yes, bring me the Sword. It's time it passed from my weakening grasp to that of a stronger man.

"Yes, do it now, Tomas. For tonight I am going to die."

II

Despite his years of training, Father Andretti found it almost impossible to control the surges of contradictory emotion that swept through him. Deep sadness at the imminent loss of a loved and revered Master vied with exultant hope that now something might be done to stop the PlainsLords before it was too late. A new Way-Farer was bound to be more sympathetic to the Free Council's concerns!

But the strongest emotions centered on the Way-Farer's words just preceding his declaration. He asked *me* to get the Sword, recalled how long he'd known *me*, praised *my* work as President of the Free Council! Surely I'm to be the next Way-Farer! His mind aflame with speculation, Andretti approached the door of the shrine.

Bowing to the young honor-guard, he composed himself. Then, at a stately pace, he entered the shrine. Slowly, ceremoniously, he walked softly across the floor toward the chest which stood against the far wall. From the tiny window high on the wall to the right, a splash of moons-light fell on the chest, casting a quadruple shadow on the rough planks of the floor.

Reaching the chest, he knelt in front of it, touched his forehead to the floor in reverence to the most valuable thing on Kensho, the treasure of the race. The Sword of Nakamura, brought by the Admiral from Earth. Given into the hands of Jerome on board the Flagship. Passed from Way-Farer to Way-Farer since then as a symbol of the transmission of office and power. The Sword of Nakamura was the symbol of Mankind on Kensho, the symbol of the Great Way they followed, and the symbol of their eventual victory over the Mushin.

Father Andretti stretched out his hands and slowly lifted the lid of the trunk. Then, with it resting back against the wall, he reached inside to take up the cloth-wrapped sword.

As his fingers touched the cloth, a shock ran through his body. Hurriedly, he felt around. The cloth was there! But there was nothing wrapped in it!

A wave of dismay struck his mind. Jerking the trunk to him, he peered inside. The dim light of the moons fell on the empty space where the Sword should have been. Nothing! Wildly, he stared about, then again felt over every inch of the trunk's interior. Gone! Empty! The Sword was not there!

With a cry of anguish, he sprang to his feet, his gaze sweeping the empty room. Making little moans of fear, he circled about the room, ignoring the Brother at the door who stared in, utterly perplexed by his actions.

Finally he stopped, standing in despair in the middle of the floor. He stared vacantly at the young man who still watched wonderingly from the door. Suddenly, "*Gone!*" he shrieked. "The Sword of Nakamura is gone!"

* . *   *

Only two moons still clung to the sky. The double shadows in the courtyard had become so deep that torches had been brought to offer enough light to see by. The scene that appeared in the flickering brightness was a strange combination of chaos and calm. The outer parts of the yard, especially around the entrance and exit areas, swirled with nervous activity. People met, exchanged news and views, then hurried

off again to another meeting. The buzz of excited
voices permeated every corner. But the closer one
moved to the center of the yard, and the great Ko tree
that silently stood there, the quieter things became.
The rushing about ceased, and men stood calmly,
almost sorrowfully, looking at a figure that sat at the
base of the tree.

Immediately surrounding the Way-Farer were
twenty other seated figures: the young Seekers of the
Way of the Sword. They and the old man were engaged in soft conversation, seemingly unaware of the
confusion that filled the rest of the yard.

Suddenly Father Andretti thrust through the
standing throng circling the seated men. In two steps
he stood, towering over the Way-Farer and his companions, obviously bursting with news. Before he
could speak, however, the old man held up his hand
in a forestalling gesture. "Calm yourself, Tomas. I can
see you have something to tell me. Sit, compose your
thoughts. Then tell me."

With a tremendous act of self-control, Andretti sat.
But his face clearly showed both his dismay and annoyance. Gods! he thought, how can he sit there like
that when the whole structure that Jerome, Obie, and
Coran built is about to tumble down around our ears?
He shook his head in self-reprimand. He's dying, he
reminded himself. He's dying. And he's deliberately
calming his mind and detaching his awareness from
the world.

Quieted by these thoughts, Andretti's face relaxed
and the scowl left his eyes. As soon as it vanished, the
Way-Farer turned back to him and smiled. "Better,"
he said. "That's better. Now, my son, what is it you
want?"

"Master," Father Andretti replied. "We've

searched the entire Brotherhood, room by room. Nothing. The Sword of Nakamura has simply disappeared."

The old man shook his head. "Hmmmmmm. Yes. Gone, you say? My, that does create a problem. I'm about to die, and before I do, I'm supposed to pass on the Sword to my successor. But there is no Sword, so I can't pass it on. Which means I can't name a successor. What a strange world it will be without a Way-Farer!"

Father Andretti looked at the old man in shocked surprise. "No Way-Farer? But . . . but . . . that can't happen! It mustn't happen! The Way-Farer is the heart, the soul, the . . . the focus of all Kensho! Why, having no Way-Farer would be like having no Great Way."

Nodding, the Way-Farer smiled gently. "Yes, yes. Perhaps that will come to pass some day, too. But Tomas, really, if there is no Sword, how can there be a Way-Farer?"

Andretti's mind raced furiously. What the old man was saying was true! The Sword was the physical symbol of power. For everyone on Kensho, the man who wore the Sword of Nakamura was the direct descendent of Jerome, the legitimate leader of the Great Way. Would anyone, especially the PlainsLords, accept a man as head of humanity if that man did not have the Sword? The shock of that question jarred his whole system. He knew the answer: No. Mitsuyama, D'Alams, Kondori, all of the PlainsLords would look on this as a sign from heaven. It would legitimate their refusal to support the Free Council. No Sword, no Way-Farer. No Way-Farer, no loyalty. This would provide exactly the excuse they needed to break their allegiance with the Brother and

Sisterhoods, to attack the system and set up their own in its place. Andretti felt a premonition of ultimate disaster shuddering in his mind.

The Way-Farer was smiling at him. Carelessly, the old man picked up a Ko blossom that lay on the ground next to him. He looked at it, then breathed deeply of its delicate fragrance. "Lovely," he announced. "Truly delightful." He held the flower out to Father Andretti. "Here, Tomas, take it. Smell it. Beauty is so ephemeral we should never waste it when we find it. Here. Take it."

Andretti just stared at the proffered blossom. A flower, he thought wildly, a flower. The world is crashing about us in ruins. Nakamura's dream, Jerome's labor, Obie's battles, Coran's careful building, all, all stood in imminent peril of destruction. And all the Master of the Great Way can do is offer me a flower?

Tears welled in his eyes. Even now, as he offered the flower, the old man was dying. And everything Mankind had fought for for ten generations might be dying too. And now it seemed that only I care, Andretti mourned to himself. And only I can do anything to stop it. The Way-Farer offers nothing but a Ko blossom!

The tears streamed down his face as he rose. His body was shaken by great wracking sobs of raw emotion. Pity, fear, love, despair surged through him in towering waves. All he knew was that he had to leave here, he had to get away to someplace quiet where he could think. It was up to him, completely and solely, to find a way out of this mess. No Sword, no Way-Farer. No Way-Farer, no loyalty.

His head and chest aching as he fought himself back under control, he croaked out, "I must go now." He turned on his heel and left.

For long minutes, the Way-Farer stared after him and sadness shadowed his features. Then the old man sighed and shrugged. He looked at the Ko blossom he still held extended in offering. One by one, his fingers began to open, to let it fall to the ground.

Suddenly, he stopped, closed his fingers again and brought the flower close. He turned casually to his left to a young man who sat there calmly, with alert eyes and an air of barely restrained energy. "Edwyr," the Way-Farer spoke quietly, so that even those close had to strain to hear. "Edwyr, is the Ko blossom not lovely?"

Edwyr fixed his gaze on the blossom in the Way-Farer's grasp. It was lovely. He nodded.

"But that loveliness, is it not mere appearance? Does it not exist only in the mind? What if I tell you, this is *not* a Ko blossom, but in truth it is a Death Sting. What do you say to that?"

The young man smiled. He reached out and took the blossom from the old man's fingers. Then he breathed in the perfume. "Truly," he whispered, "it is lovely."

The Way-Farer smiled back. Slowly, he leaned forward until his mouth was next to the ear of the young man. Those seated nearby could see his lips move, but were unable to hear a word.

The effect upon Edwyr was remarkable, however. The young man stiffened as if struck a blow. His eyes went wide with surprise. Then just as suddenly, he burst out weeping, his body tossed by gigantic sobs, the tears gushing down his face. Yet his features positively glowed with joy at the same time. It was startling and everyone who saw it never forgot the strange contradiction of a joyous man weeping.

Just as quickly, Edwyr was calm again, smiling quietly at the old Master as the latter leaned back into his place. Carefully pushing the stem through a hole in his worn robe, Edwyr placed the flower over his heart.

Looking at those around him, the Way-Farer nodded. He straightened his robe. Then, in a soft voice that carried even to the farthest corner of the busy courtyard, he said, "I think it is time for me to die now."

Complete silence was instantaneous. All eyes turned to the old man. Calmly, with a ghost of a smile lingering on his lips, he folded his hands in his lap and closed his eyes. Gradually, his breathing became shallower. Finally, his chest stopped moving at all.

For several moments, everyone just watched the still form with total fascination. From the Ko tree another flower fell, and in its journey to the earth it lightly struck the old man's shoulder. Slowly, ever so slowly at first, but gathering momentum, the body keeled over. Edwyr quickly bent to the sprawled form and lifted an eyelid. He held his cheek against the Way-Farer's mouth. Taking the slender wrist, he felt for a pulse. Putting the limp hand back on the ground, he looked up at the circle of faces flickering in the torchlight. Then he spoke.

"The Way-Farer is dead."

III

Father Andretti leaned wearily against the window frame, gazing into the courtyard. The first rays of dawn were tumbling over the Brotherhood's walls and splashing to the ground where last night everyone had milled about in confusion. A lone Novice was carefully raking the area to remove all signs of the disturbance.

The Way-Farer's body had already been bathed and laid out in the shrine. Today people from all around would pass by the bier and bid a final goodbye to the beloved old man. Tomorrow, Johnston would be buried.

Exhausted by so much emotional strain and so little sleep, Andretti slumped down onto the window sill. For several moments, he stared dully at the growing light. Then, gathering energy from somewhere deep inside his large frame, he spoke without turning to the little man who stood across the room by the door. "If Mitsuyama did steal the Sword, why haven't you uncovered any information, or even rumors? I thought you had reliable agents among the Plains Lords."

Burke, looking as tired and worried as Andretti, shook his head, even though the other man wasn't watching. "I've been trying to tell you for the last half hour," he whined, "I'm as surprised as you are. Gods! Something this big, you'd think somebody would've let something slip. I just don't understand it. News of the secret army, that leaked. And stealing the Sword . . . that's bigger. A lot bigger! How the hell did Mitsuyama keep it quiet? Every stinking tree lizard should be singing about it! I don't know how . . ."

"You're supposed to know, though," interrupted
Andretti flatly, "You're a spy. Spies should know
things like that. Or they aren't worth anything."

The little man winced. Best just shut up, he
thought. Best just let him get it out of his system. Let
him beat on poor Burke. But by the Gods, I'm going
to do some beating of my own! My people must have
heard something and just didn't pass it on! Damn the
fools all to hell!

Abandoning the morning to its own devices, Andretti turned back to the dim room. "The situation's
too touchy to move without evidence. Until we have
proof, we can't even voice our suspicions. That's your
job, Burke. Find proof that Mitsuyama stole the
Sword of Nakamura. And find it immediately." For a
few seconds he paused, considering the small figure
in the shadows by the door. "And Burke, while you're
at it, remember that even though we can't make any
official accusations, a few little unofficial rumors
planted here and there wouldn't hurt. Do you understand?" The spy nodded.

"Now tell me," Andretti continued more gently,
"how do you think he did it? And when?"

Burke looked relieved by the change of topic. This
was something he could handle. He shrugged, confi-
dence returning. " 'How' is easy: the PlainsLords
have agents coming in and out of the Home Valley all
the time; Dembo alone gets four or five messengers a
week. Any one of 'em could have been trained for the
job, come in carrying a message, pulled it off, and left
the next day without the slightest suspicion.

"The actual job's not hard, either. The gates of the
Brotherhood are closed at night, but the walls aren't
high. So getting in or out's no problem. And the
shrine isn't closely guarded. Only some young
Brothers who pull honor duty. Hell, they're always

dozing off. No, stealing the Sword wouldn't be all that difficult.

"When?" he mused. "Who knows? Nobody ever checks on the Sword. It's not on display or anything. Only person who ever touched it was the Way-Farer and he never wore it, even on special occasions. But I'd bet it wasn't too long ago or some word would've leaked by now. How can they've kept it so secret?"

"All right, Burke," Andretti waved his hand in dismissal. "That's all. Get back to the Plain and see what you can find out. And tell Carston to come and see me." Not even waiting to see if the spy obeyed, Andretti turned back to gaze abstractedly out the window once more. So tired, he thought, so tired. Well, he comforted himself grimly, at least my exhaustion serves one purpose: I'm completely calm. Or maybe I'm just numb. Gods! I'm so dead on my feet I don't even know anymore!

In a few moments, a light knock sounded at the door. Father Andretti called out, "Come in," and a tall, dark, well-built man of middle age entered.

"Ah, Carston," Andretti greeted him. "Bring a cushion over and sit down. I'm too tired to move. What have you learned?"

"Well, sir," Carston began as he settled on his cushion, "there isn't much to go on. I've questioned everyone and searched everywhere, twice. Even ransacked the quarters of the representatives from the Plain. Figured it couldn't hurt, even though they're outside the walls.

"Oh, by the way, much protest there. Dembo's waiting to see you to register his complaint about being searched. Angry. Very."

"But you've found nothing at all, then? Not even a single clue?"

"Well, there was one rather strange story.

Amagansarni, that sixth frame Brother from the Long Hill Brotherhood out on the Plain, said something odd happened to him one night while standing duty at the shrine. Sounded like a typical prank to me. He thought so."

"Prank, on someone standing guard duty at the shrine?" Father Andretti's eyebrows raised in inquiry.

"Yessir. Not unusual, really. These young Brothers from the Plain are a feisty lot. No harm. Just high spirits. Anyway, seems the boy dozed off. Claims it was only a few minutes at most. But when he woke up, his sword was stuck in the ground about three paces away and a Ko blossom was in his scabbard."

Father Andretti suppressed a smile. "A most adept prankster. Who?"

Carston frowned. "That's the strange point. Nobody admitted to it."

"Even under questioning?"

The dark man shook his head.

"Hmmmmmm," responded the older man thoughtfully. "A thief would hardly risk waking the guard that way. How long ago did it happen?"

"Three days ago. That checks with the duty roster. The boy was on the graveyard shift that night. Triple moon night, plenty of light. Not a likely night for a robbery."

"Agreed. Sounds like a dead end. Let's drop it. You said Dembo was angry?"

Carston smiled one of his rare smiles. "Did I say angry? Not strong enough. He's frothing at the mouth. Got him out of bed myself just after the third-hour watch bell sounded. Tore his room apart."

Andretti grinned back. "Never did like that man. Sneaklizard if I ever saw one—but all of Mitsuyama's men are like that. Wouldn't trust a one of them."

"That was old Mitsuyama's motto: 'Never trust anyone.' "

"Too bad he didn't take his own advice." The two men traded a meaningful glance.

For a moment, Carston paused. "You don't think it really happened, do you? That Mitsuyama poisoned his father? I know he's ruthless, but his own father?"

Andretti shrugged. "All I know is what rumor says. And rumor says they disagreed. The old man saw himself and his clan as nothing more than *primus inter pares* among the PlainsLords. His son had higher ambitions. They quarreled, violently, and two days later the old man died. Whatever the truth of the story, Mitsuyama certainly acted swiftly to consolidate his power once his father was gone. Killed his uncle, three cousins, and several of his uncle's retainers. And then the Winston clan, his only real rivals, were wiped out by a 'Ronin' band that was never run down. He wouldn't stick at his father."

"Or at stealing the Sword."

Andretti nodded. "It's just the kind of bold move that would appeal to him. With one deft stroke he's managed to legitimate his refusal to support the policies of the Free Council. No Sword, no Way-Farer. No Way-Farer, no leader. No leader, no loyalty. And he doesn't even have to deny or oppose Jerome or the Great Way. Damn! What with this and his new army, a lot of the waverers will rally to his side."

A silence settled between the two men. From the corner of his eye, Carston studied the other man's face. *He looks so much older than he did yesterday*, he thought. *The lines across his forehead, between his eyes, and at the corners of his mouth are deeper, more pronounced. Last night took a heavy toll. But the determination and strength are still there, etched*

more firmly in place by the same events. He's the
hope of the Free Council and the Great Way. He's the
only one smart enough and tough enough to stand up
to Mitsuyama and get us out of this mess.

Father Andretti's sigh broke into Carston's reverie.
"Go see how many members of the Free Council you
can round up. Tell them we'll meet in the Council-
room in an hour to discuss the situation. Also, give me
about fifteen minutes to change my robe and then
have Dembo sent in. I have to listen to the man rage; I
might as well get it done with."

But Dembo wasn't raging when he arrived. He
knocked quietly and entered calmly when he heard
Andretti's muffled response. With a few quick flicks,
his eyes took in the room. It was moderate in size,
about ten by twelve feet. On the side opposite the
door were two windows, tall and narrow. On the left
wall was a door that undoubtedly led to the sleeping
chamber.

The room was sparsely furnished, as were all the
rooms in the Brotherhood. But the quality of the
furnishings clearly indicated this was the room of a
senior Father. For example, the mats on which
Dembo stood were finely woven with the best, thin-
nest reeds. And the scroll hanging on the wall between the windows was a work of art. The flower
arrangement on the floor in front of it was exquisite in
its simplicity and suggestiveness. The low table behind which Andretti sat, busily writing without looking up, was of the very smoothest glasswood, beauti-
fully grained and polished so that it glowed with dark
light. The cushions scattered about were plump and
covered with a tightly woven fabric that would be cool
and pleasant to the touch.

The whole room breathed of serene good taste, a
perfect example of the pseudo-Japanese style the

Brotherhood copied from the Home World. The affectation amused Dembo. Andretti, he could see, was anything but serene.

Mitsuyama's man sat quietly on a cushion across the table from the President of the Free Council. Andretti looked up briefly, muttered a quick excuse and returned to his writing. Dembo smiled internally. So transparent, Tomas, so transparent. He chuckled to himself. I can read you like a book. You're exhausted, unsure of what I'm going to say, but certain it won't be pleasant. You despise me, yet you fear my master and a bit of that fear rubs off on me. You're very surprised I'm so quiet. I made enough noise earlier and you expected me to come raging in here like a wounded ken-wolf. Now you're stalling for time, trying to reassess the situation.

Dembo allowed his eyes to wander over Andretti's person. So, he thought, a Council meeting, eh? Why else so fine a robe, one of such soft, delicate fabric, unfaded by the sun? And Andretti was wearing the Medallion! It hung from his neck in plain sight!

Although he had never seen the Medallion before, Dembo knew what it was. It was only worn on very special occasions, like important Council meetings or Audiences with the Way-Farer, events Dembo was not usually privy to. Strange, he thought, that something so small and plain should be so important. Next to the Sword of Nakamura, it was probably the most important thing on the face of Kensho. Jerome had worn the Medallion originally. It had been passed from father to son within his family for seven generations after the disaster at First Touch.

The Medallion had proven crucial in Jerome's search. It had given him access to a shuttle that had carried him up to the Flagship still hanging in geosync orbit over the site of Base Camp. Then, later, the

Keepers had used it in their journey to obtain information from the ship's computer. When the Keepers had been suppressed, the Medallion had been confiscated.

Now Andretti wore it, the symbol of his office, the Presidency of the Free Council. And, Dembo knew, the symbol and reality of the Council's sole control of access to the knowledge stored in the data banks of the Flagship.

Gradually, Andretti became aware of Dembo's gaze. Looking up briefly, he was somewhat startled by the nakedly avaricious look on the man's face. Realizing the gaze was fastened on the Medallion, he self-consciously tucked it away beneath his robe. Then, embarassed by his own action, and by the slight smile that flitted across Dembo's features in response, he cleared his throat and nodded curtly at the other man.

This man is the Enemy, he had to remind himself once more. For Dembo's looks were in direct contradiction to his character. He was of middling height, soft and round, with a moon-like, cherubic face surrounded by a fringe of unruly blond hair and beard. His eyes were big and misty with a trusting air about them. The mouth was full and friendly, always ready with a smile. Overall, the impression was one of a jolly fellow much given to laughter and back-slapping camaraderie.

Nothing could be further from the truth, as Andretti knew only too well. The man's mind was like a well-honed blade and he wielded it with deadly effect. Loyal to his Master, Dembo would stoop to any viciousness to serve Mitsuyama. 'Ruthless' was too good a word for the man.

Well, thought Andretti, might as well begin this.

Then it'll be over that much sooner. Settling back on his cushion he said, "Well, Dembo, you wanted to see me?"

The man from the Plain smiled sadly. "Ah, Father Andretti," he said mournfully, "you're bearing up so well, so well. But what a blow. What a blow!"

For a brief moment, Andretti missed the man's meaning. Then he understood. "You mean the Way-Farer?"

"What else?"

"Of course." Andretti replied. "His tragic death blots everything else from our minds."

"Just so, just so! I'm sure my Lord will be distraught when he hears the news. I'll be leaving posthaste after this interview to inform him."

"Naturally, and give him my kind regards and support in his grief."

"Thank you." Dembo bowed his head in reply. "So kind of you. But what a terrible plight this places you in, good friend!"

"Me?" echoed Andretti, once again missing Dembo's meaning.

"Yes. Why, from what I've heard, the Way-Farer gave several indications he meant to name you as his successor. And now . . . without the Sword . . . Ah, but it's too terrible to contemplate."

Andretti frowned. "You have good sources, Dembo. But no one was named as Way-Farer to succeed Father Johnston. We aren't trying to hide that from anyone. And the Sword, as you well know, is missing."

"As I well know? Why, what can you mean, Father? I only just heard of it as that rude man of yours burst into my room and literally dismantled everything in it. It's a terrible shock, to be sure. I mean, no Sword, no Way-Farer. We are leaderless!"

"The Free Council still exists," replied Father Andretti stiffly.

"To be sure! To be sure it does. And all thanks to the Gods for that. But the Free Council is not the Way-Farer. And to be frank with you, there are some misguided souls out on the Plain who don't think of the Free Council as the equal of the Way-Farer. Regretfully, to them, if there is no Way-Farer, there is no legitimate leader on Kensho." Ever so slightly, Dembo stressed the word "legitimate."

"The Council has already been convened to deal with the problem. You can be sure we will consider every angle of it. There are members from the Plain, you know."

"Yes, but of course there are. And all of them trained by the Brother and Sisterhoods right here in the Home Valley. There are some who might wonder at where their allegiances lay, but we more sophisticated souls know better than to doubt their loyalty to the Great Way . . . as they see it."

"Who is more likely to be loyal?"

"Why none, none at all! But," he sighed hugely, "there is the matter of interest, after all."

"Interest?" bristled Andretti. "What interest? Say what you have to say, Dembo."

"I mean to say simply that some would benefit, some in the Free Council, if there were no Way-Farer."

Andretti's eyes narrowed dangerously. His words hissed out with a harsh sibilance. "What are you implying?"

Dembo's suave manner changed and he glared back at the older man, his face twisted with loathing and contempt. "Just that no one has been fooled by your little charade! The Sword of Nakamura missing and the Way-Farer dead . . . what a perfect scenario for the Council to step in and declare their favorite for the job! Then you'd be able to give your hatred of us full rein and use all the prestige and power of the Way-Farership and the sanctions of the Great Way in your insane campaign to destroy us! But it won't work, my friend. Oh, no! I see through your scheme and so will everyone else!"

Andretti's face blanched a deathly white, his jaw falling open in utter astonishment. Then the rage came, rising from his neck, mottling the white with blood-red blotches. He struggled to force words out of a throat constricted by emotion. Finally they came, in a husky growl that rose to a crescendo as he spoke. "You . . . filthy . . . vermin! To even suggest . . .! You rotten, crawling, slimy . . .!"

Suddenly, as though a door had been slammed shut, Father Andretti's face became cold and hard as stone. Only his eyes blazed out his feelings. He took several deep breaths and then spoke again in a voice under tight control. "Crawl back to your Master, Sneaklizard. Tell him the Free Council is not afraid of him or his lies. We know who stole the Sword of Nakamura, and when we have proof, we'll show it to the whole world. Not all his schemes and slimy little agents will stop us from leading Kensho on the Great Way. We'll follow the dream of Nakamura and Jerome through the Madness itself. If he gets in our way, we'll smash him the way we smashed the Ronin!"

Dembo rose and stalked to the door. Once there, he spun about and thrust his finger menacingly toward Andretti. His voice lashed out. "You walk near the edge, Mr. President. Tread with care, for a slight crumbling of the path or a push from behind could plummet you into disaster such as you've never dreamed of!" He turned and yanked the door open.

Andretti laughed harshly.

A slam was the only reply.

BOOK II

LORD MITSUYAMA

IV

There were rolling, forested foothills on the other side of the Mountains. Before long, though, the Plain began in earnest. The hills flattened out and then disappeared, except for low, isolated groups that occasionally rose up, only to slump quickly back into the endless anonymity around them. The trees scattered until they became rare vertical interruptions in the horizontal monotony. Here and there, a lonely line of them marked the abrupt slash of a river or dry wash. In every direction, a thick, coarse, grass-like growth covered the ground. On windy days it heaved and surged like the wave-swept surface of a blue-green sea. And even when the breeze was the merest whisper—it never ceased entirely—the land rippled restlessly.

The Plain wasn't the harshest environment man had ever lived in. Nor was it the softest. It made its demands on body and mind and spirit. Those found wanting, perished. The strong, the smart, the determined, and the just plain lucky, survived.

The first settlers who came over the Mountains from the Home Valley clustered in the foothills. They felt at home there and built farmsteads identical to the ones their ancestors had lived on for the last ten generations. But as more people arrived, and as the lure of vast spaces began to work its magic on the adventurous, men began to trickle out onto the immensity that always promised more just beyond the horizon.

Most of those moving out onto the Plain clung to the patterns of the past and farmed the land. But a few rejected the ways of the Home Valley. They began to herd the docile, native ken-cows that grazed in thousands on the coarse growth of the Plain. Within two generations, these herdsmen had developed a new way of life. Tough, proud, semi-nomadic, they began to call themselves "PlainsLords."

For many years, the PlainsLords lived peacefully, side by side, with the farmers. If the 'steads around them became too numerous and interfered with the grazing of their herds, they simply moved further out toward the horizon. Eventually, though, the strongest among them began to consolidate their control. Soon there were several powerful clans, each with its own herds, grazing lands, and groups of retainers and allies. Territories became fixed, boundaries rigid, and the encroachment of new 'steads on their lands was met with growing resentment and hostility.

At first, with the dynamic Coran as Way-Farer, no one had perceived the PlainsLords as a threat. In fact, given the almost ridiculously proud and independent airs they had given themselves, everyone had found them mildly amusing. Under Johnston, the fourth Way-Farer, things changed.

The old man was loved and revered by everyone. Even the PlainsLords would gladly have let him mediate their quarrels and would have willingly embraced his decisions. Any rules or regulations he had laid down would have been followed to the letter.

But Johnston was not like Coran. He would not mediate, or solve other people's problems, or lay down the law. He was more than willing to walk and talk with his friends, but he would not lead them. He wanted companions with whom to travel the Way, not followers.

There were others who were quite willing to pick up the reins he refused to hold. The Mitsuyama clan,

one of the oldest and strongest on the Plain, soon rose
to such a position of power that it dominated and
controlled all the others. The head of the clan, William Mitsuyama, took the title of Supreme Lord of the
Plains. Those who opposed him, died.

Mitsuyama was no more than half-way through his
thirties. His unruly mop of shaggy black hair was
untouched by gray. The lines that gathered at the
corners of his eyes had been etched there by an
outdoor life beneath the harsh Kensho sun, rather
than by age. The eyes themselves, a startling blue in
contrast to his darkened skin, held a cool, calculating,
even cruel glint. The thin, tight line of his mouth,
overhung by a severe, aquiline nose, confirmed the
character foretold in his glance. He was tall and slender, this Supreme Lord, and moved with a lithe
arrogance that radiated a sense of tightly controlled
energy. His gestures were graceful, but somehow
carried an ominous undertone of barely restrained
violence.

One would expect such a man to have a harsh voice,
one made for bellowing orders in battle. But here
again, Mitsuyama was a man of contradictions. His
voice was soft, velvety, gentle; listeners had to strain
to catch every word, since he tended to drop his
volume at the end of each sentence. Despite the first
impression of effeminateness, the more one listened,
the more it became apparent that there was an under-
current as cold and hard as the man's eyes. Those who
spoke with him often compared his voice with the
delicate, slender daggers carried by many of the
Plainswomen: four inches of steel that could spill life
as quickly and more quietly than any man's sword.

The simplicity and severity of the Lord's dress
underlined the aura of stark power that surrounded
him. An unadorned robe, similar to that worn by the

Brotherhood, but in jet black, was all he wore. Soft, black, slipper-like boots covered his feet and legs to just below his knees. He carried no sword, but a plain, iron-hilted dagger was thrust through his waist sash on the right side.

As severe as himself was the Council Room in which he met with the other PlainsLords. Seated on cushions, they all faced him as he sat, legs crossed in full lotus, on a slightly raised dais. Aside from a few water jugs, there were no other furnishings to be seen. The walls were stark, except for a sword which hung just behind his head.

There may have been a few who loved Lord Mitsuyama. No matter: everyone respected him, and most men feared him. This pleased the Lord. It seemed right. And it matched his method of leadership like a glove to a hand.

"So, Dembo," Mitsuyama said, "first the Sword of Nakamura is mysteriously missing. Then the Way-Farer dies, somewhat unexpectedly, I gather. This is followed by the revelation that he named no successor, so for the first time since Jerome, Kensho is without a leader. Interesting, is it not? So many things happen at the same time.

"And now this new information. The Free Council, headed by that most estimable gentleman, Father Andretti, meets and decides to name their own President as Way-Farer on a temporary basis. Temporary, that is, until the choice can be ratified or rejected by a special Council to be composed of representatives from all the Brotherhoods and Sisterhoods, the Faithful, the Seekers of the Way of the Sword, various prominent 'steaders and settlers from the Plain, and delegates from the Council of the PlainsLords. Do I have the details correctly, Dembo?"

"Yes, my Lord. Most exactly. The Council is to

meet in three months time." Dembo was visibly uncomfortable under the unwavering stare of his master.

The young Lord turned to several older men who
sat about the room. He singled out one particularly
ponderous individual who sprawled more than sat:
"Lord D'Alams, what do you make of it?"

The fat man shrugged. "It seems not over-strange
to me. It's obvious what that lizard-loving Andretti is
up to. We know how the man hates us. Humph. He
stole the Sword. He poisoned the Way-Farer. He had
the Council appoint him. Once he's confirmed as
Way-Farer, he thinks he'll be able to do as he likes
with us. Nothing strange."

A very old man to the left of D'Alams laughed
harshly. Mitsuyama turned a baleful glare in his direction, but the old one returned it without flinching.
"Rubbish," he said in a voice as metallic and deadly as
Mitsuyama's own. "Utter rubbish. D'Alams never
could distinguish between truth and the party line.

"Andretti is neither that subtle nor that stupid. If
he had wanted to get rid of the old man and take his
place, he could have arranged the whole thing in
private. Announce the Way-Farer was sick, too sick to
see anyone. Have himself called to the dying man's
bedside, alone. Then, far from the sight of any living
soul, take the Sword from the dying man's grasp and
come forth into the light as the legitimate heir of
Jerome.

"But to have the Sword stolen? To have the Way-
Farer die in public? To allow it to be known by
everyone that no one was named as heir? Then to
have the Council declare him Way-Farer? And ask for
a general referendum on the appointment? Ha! That's
the plan of either a genius or an idiot! Andretti is
neither. My guess is he knew nothing of the Sword's

disappearance before it was discovered. Since then, the man's been frantically trying to make the best of a bad situation."

The Supreme Lord nodded thoughtfully. "Interesting, Lord Kondori, interesting."

"But if Andretti did arrange for the Sword to be stolen," Dembo posited carefully, "it would provide him a perfect opportunity to blame you, my Lord, for the disappearance. One could easily argue you had a great deal to gain from no Way-Farer being named to follow Johnston."

"Just so, just so. But there is one aspect none of you have mentioned. Why bother with the referendum? And why the wait of three months for the meeting of the special Council? What does the man hope to gain by such a long hiatus between his appointment and its confirmation? It would seem that the sooner he moves the better. The longer he waits, the more time we have to marshall opposition."

"Not only us, my Lord," added Dembo. "There are those among the Free Council itself who are not happy with Andretti's appointment. The final vote was unanimous, to be sure, but my sources indicate that debate over the matter took three days and was at times quite heated. Also, there is the whole question of the Seekers of the Way of the Sword. The group that were companions to the Way-Farer have said nothing, not one word, about their attitude toward Andretti."

Mitsuyama turned to another man who lounged over by the wall to the far right of the Lords. Sitting off by himself, he was surrounded by an air of aloof disdain. Although he seemed to be at ease, there was a tense readiness about his body that belied his calm. Looking at him, one had the feeling that he was like a coiled spring, capable of instantly exploding into action.

"Jimson," Mitsuyama addressed the man. "You walked the Way of the Sword for some time. You know the minds of those who travel it. What is your opinion?"

Lazily, contempt in eyes, Jimson surveyed the room. "Lord," he began, "those who walk the Way will have nothing to do with Andretti. Not because they dislike the man or disagree with his policies, but only because they don't care. He has nothing to offer them, nothing that will aid them in achieving their goal. He cannot make the flowers of the Ko more beautiful, nor the rain fall more gently."

"Would they be allies of ours, then?" interrupted Dembo.

Looking as though he had tasted something bad, the ex-Seeker looked at Mitsuyama. "Unless my Lord can make a ken-cow sing and a tree lizard give cheese, they will join neither side. Father Johnston was enlightened. They would have followed him into the Madness, for they knew that wherever the man went, he was walking the Great Way. Andretti merely stumbles in the Great Swamp. They will not follow him. Or you."

"Neutrality, then?" questioned Mitsuyama with raised eyebrows.

Jimson nodded. "Of sorts."

For several moments, a thoughtful pause settled over the room. Lord Mitsuyama stared abstractedly into the air just over everyone's heads. Occasionally he made little considering noises in his throat that made him sound vaguely feline.

Suddenly his eyes came back into focus and pounced to catch the glance of a little man who sat at the very back of the room, as near the door and as far from the dais as possible. "And now we must hear from Carlson," he said softly. "Yes, now Carlson must tell us how he thinks the Keepers and Artisans will react to all this."

Carlson blushed, half in fear, half in embarrassment. Unable to meet the Lord's stare for more than a fraction of a second, he looked downward and mumbled a reply.

"What's that, Carlson?" came Mitsuyama's question. "Speak up so that all the Lords may hear you. Come, show us your education, your intelligence. Let us all see how valuable a Keeper-upbringing can be."

Small, slender, awkward, Carlson swept a quick glance around the room, carefully avoiding anyone's eye while still taking it all in. He cleared his throat, then looked up, up just above Lord Mitsuyama's head, focusing his gaze on the sword that hung on the wall.

"The Keepers have no love for Andretti, or for the Brotherhood, for that matter," he began, his voice uncertain at first, but gaining in firmness as he spoke. "Jerome allowed us to go to the Flagship and gather information from the computer. Useful information. The ship prepared books, on special paper that will last for thousands of years, and we brought it all back. Then we set about studying it all, organizing, correlating, analyzing, deciding what was applicable to Kensho and what not. So much information. A lifetime or two at least. So much knowledge." He shook his head in wonder.

"But no weapons technology?" asked Mitsuyama quietly.

"What? Oh," the little man started, his voice unsure again, "no, no weapons. None. I've told you that

before. No. None. We didn't ask and the computer
didn't offer. But it was all cut short when the Message
came." He nodded, almost to himself, "Yes, when the
Message came it all ended."

"Enough history, Keeper. I need your opinion. Do
you think the Keepers will oppose Andretti?"

"Oh, well, I ask your pardon, yes, my opinion."
The little man blinked owlishly, then swallowed several times, trying to wet a mouth and throat suddenly
gone dry. He was of indeterminate age, neither
young nor old, with pale blond hair and watery blue
eyes.

"Well, we have no love for Andretti. He wears the
Medallion. He refuses us access to the ship. He has
confiscated all our books and spread us across the face
of Kensho so that no two of us live near each other.
Coran was no friend, either. But he just made us stop
gathering, stop going to the Flagship. That was because of the Message. But we didn't cause the Message. No. It just came while we were there. Andretti
has no right to take away our work. No. The Keepers
will not support him. Nor will the Artisans, if there
are any left. No."

The little Keeper subsided into incoherent mumbling, refusing to look up at Mitsuyama. The Lord
stared at him in disgust. This, he thought in anger, is
the only Keeper I have been able to draw to my side.
This miserable creature. I must have more. I need the
information I know they possess. Why won't they
support me? My desire to bring technology, the
technology of the Home World, to Kensho is the same
as theirs. I would allow them to study the knowledge
they brought from the Flagship. I would give them
access to the books, perhaps even to the computer
again. They would have to serve me and Mankind,
but that needn't interfere with their work.

Yet none come to join me. I've searched and searched to find some. They hide. Wherever they are, they hide from me as from the Brotherhood. But they're out there. Every now and then something new appears, some new idea for improving a 'steader's plow or for making better cabins. They're out there, slowly, carefully, bit by bit, trying to bring technology appropriate to the resources available back into the world again. I must find some more of them! He made a mental note to himself to put Dembo on the job. Find some more Keepers. Then either persuade them to join or force them. The future of Mankind on Kensho required it. Especially if he was right about the Message!

His reverie was interrupted by a young servant who entered the room quietly and came swiftly to his side. The lad held a folded square of paper and a lit candle in a lantern that shielded it against the breeze of his rapid pace. Mitsuyama opened the paper and glanced at it briefly. No emotion showed on his face, though Jimson knew the contents must be of utmost importance else the young messenger had never dared to interrupt. Mitsuyama carefully held the paper in the open flame. Thoughtfully, he watched it burn closer and closer to his fingers. He moved not a single muscle until the flames died out against his skin. He seemed not to mind the pain. Then he crumbled the paper ash and rose suddenly.

"Lords," he said, "I will leave you. Some interesting information has arrived which may be important to our deliberations." Dembo began to rise also. "Dembo, stay and amuse my Lords with your sparkling wit," he halted the man's movement with a gesture. Looking over at Jimson he said, "Come renegade. I have need of your knowledge."

Jimson followed Mitsuyama as he swept from the room without a further word. I was right! Jimson crowed to himself. Very important! So important he's willing to walk out of a full Council meeting!

V

The two men strode silently down a short corridor that ended in a barred door. As they approached, a guard, who had been watching from a hidden alcove, stepped out and saluted. At a gesture from Mitsuyama, he unbarred the door and swung it outward. Two more men were on duty outside.

Mitsuyama and Jimson passed through the door and turned left into a covered walk that ran completely around the square courtyard that was the center of the PlainsLord's fortress. Perhaps two hundred feet across, it was the scene of bustling activity. In one corner a group of youngsters was engaged in a mock battle using wooden practice swords. Not far off, another group was drilling on the techniques of combat with the bladed staff invented by Jerome. In the middle of the yard several peddlars had set up their wares and had been joined by local people who made specialty items to sell. Around them a small but lively market had formed.

Unlike the Brother and Sisterhoods, which were always composed of a group of buildings surrounded by a defensive wall, Mitsuyama's fortress was one large building. Made of packed and pounded soil, it was shaped like a huge, hollow square. The outer wall of the building itself served as the defensive palisade. It was windowless and higher than roof level so that men could stand behind it, protected, to repel anyone seeking to scale it. There were only two entrances to the building, one that pierced through to the courtyard on the east and another similar one on the west. Sturdy gates could be swung shut to close either.

It was toward the eastern gate that Jimson was now following his Lord, keeping beneath the cover of the shaded walkway. It was a slightly longer way to go, but one avoided the busy sprawl of the courtyard. Every so often, alert, tough-looking guards stood, trying to be inconspicuous and appear casual while keeping a close eye on everything. Jimson knew them all by name. He had trained each in the use of the sword.

In a few moments, they arrived at the gate. Four men were on sentry duty there, two inside, two without. Jimson knew two more were on lookout above on the wall. Even though their post was no more than fifteen feet from the ground, the land was so flat that they could see several miles in every direction.

Next to the gate, on the right hand side, was a small door, closed and guarded by another man. He opened the door as they walked up, slightly bowing his head in salute.

The two entered a dark little room. After the dazzling light of the courtyard, they could barely make out a vague figure, dressed in a black robe and hooded so its face was invisible. It sat huddled over against the far wall, as deeply in shadow as possible. The door shut, and the figure disappeared entirely in the sudden gloom.

As his eyes adjusted to the low light level, Jimson noticed that the hooded form was slightly turned away from them. Its long, drooping sleeves fluttered as if in agitation. "You've brought someone else," came a muffled complaint. "Our bargain was I report to you alone!" So, Jimson thought, it's a man.

Mitsuyama waved his hand negligently. "A technicality. I need Brother Jimson's special expertise in judging the news you bring."

A stifled grumble of protest was the only answer.

"Well," said the young Lord once he was seated on a cushion. "What did you find out?"

"The three month wait was demanded by several of the Council. They resented the hasty way in which everything was being done. At one point, Mother Adeline actually walked out. Said no Way-Farer was needed. Especially not one appointed by the Council. Claimed the PlainsLords were being used by Andretti as a boogey-monster just to frighten them all into ill-considered action. She even suggested the Great Way itself wasn't all that important."

"Fine, fine. But I'm not interested in a recap of the debate. Proceed."

"Aye. The telling argument was from Father Dubrick of Waters Meeting. He wanted the three month delay so as to mount a search for the Sword."

Mitsuyama leaned forward. "Then they don't know where it is?"

The dark man chuckled. "Andretti claims total innocence. Says you took it. Others aren't so sure. Father Dubrick, for example, says that's silly. Father Olson, though . . ."

"Continue, spy."

"Ummm, aye, my Lord. Well, the Free Council wants to see if the Sword can be found. That's the long and short of it and the main reason the special Council won't be held for three months. By the way, you'll be getting your invitation soon. It'll be held at First Pass."

"A search, eh? And who will conduct this search?"

"Ahhh. That's the one touch of genius in this whole thing. Dubrick's idea again. The companions of the late Way-Farer, the twenty young Seekers of the Way of the Sword, are to make the search."

Turning to Jimson, Mitsuyama asked, "Does that make sense? Will they do it?"

For a moment Jimson considered. "Yes. It fits. Jerome sought the Sword of No Sword after leaving the Mountain. He eventually found the Sword of Nakamura on the Flagship and it was the key that opened Satori. That's when he conceived the Great Way. So the Sword of Nakamura could be conceived of as No Sword. Seeking it would be seeking the Sword of No Sword which is the goal of the Way of the Sword. But finding it wouldn't be as important as seeking."

Impatient, Mitsuyama interrupted. "Yes, yes, enough of this mystical cant. Would they search diligently for the Sword? If they found it, would they return it? A brief answer, please."

"Yes and yes."

Nodding, the young Lord turned again to the shrouded spy. "Good, good. Now the three months makes sense. But can twenty men cover all of Kensho in three months?"

A surprised silence dropped into the room. The spy was the first to break it, mumbling "I never thought of that. Doesn't make sense."

"Well, renegade, what about it? Could they do it?"

The ex-Seeker frowned as he considered. "Yes and no. Of course they couldn't cover every square inch of even the Great Valley in that time. Nor could they examine every 'stead or settler's cabin. But they could cover a lot of ground, Lord. They wouldn't walk, you know. They're trained to trot and at their speed, they could easily manage 35 to 40 miles a day."

"They aren't going to go everywhere," interrupted the spy. "Edwyr set up a very precise plan of search."

"Edwyr?" queried Mitsuyama. "Who is Edwyr?"

"One of the companions of the Way-Farer. He's about 25 and he's been following the Sword for a good ten years now," came the answer.

Mitsuyama turned a questioning look toward Jimson, "Do you know him?"

"I know of him. He has quite a reputation for one so young. Some say he's the finest swordsman since Jerome. Also the most enlightened. I've never met him, though."

Again the Supreme Lord of the Plains nodded, considering. "Hmmmmmm, yes, interesting. And what makes this one companion among twenty so important that he decides on the search pattern? And will the others follow his orders?"

The spy nodded. "Aye. He was sort of the leader . . . no, that's not the right word . . . the *first* of the group that the Way-Farer gathered. I guess the others recognized his superiority and just let him speak for them to outsiders. When they speak at all!"

"So this Edwyr organized the others into a search plan. What was it?"

"Well, eight of the twenty are to search the Brother and Sisterhoods of the Home Valley for sign of the Sword. The feeling is that if the Sword of Nakamura is anywhere in the Home Valley, it'll be in a 'hood, and one of those with Mushin, at that. They figure that only there would people have the control necessary to keep such a thing around without cracking and giving the Mushin an opening.

"The other twelve are coming out into the Plains. They're to search at random, looking for leads, rumors, anything that might show them the way to the Sword."

"Where is Edwyr heading?"

"Why, I believe he's checking the zone closest to you here," exclaimed the spy. "Yes, I'm sure of it. He took the hardest, longest journey for himself."

For several moments, Mitsuyama sat wrapped in thought. Finally he stirred and turned to Jimson.

"This Edwyr interests me. I have a feeling about him. Call it a hunch." The Lord spun back to face the dark figure over against the wall. "Is there anything else about Edwyr, anything unusual, you can think of?"

"Ummmmmmm," mused the spy. "Aye, now that I think on it there is. Something most strange, too. Brother Edwyr was the last man the Way-Farer spoke to before he died. Yes, I remember it now quite clearly! The Way-Farer gave the lad a flower, then whispered something in his ear. Ha! That's right! Edwyr burst out crying at what the old man said, smiling all the while! Weird that was!"

Mitsuyama glanced sideways at Jimson. The renegade was sitting forward on his cushion, tense, his eyes wide with interest in what the spy was saying. "What did he say?" came the hissing question from Jimson's lips.

The shrouded figure shrugged. "I don't know. Nobody heard it but Edwyr. I understand Andretti tried to find out, but got no answer at all. Just a silent stare. They're like that, those Seekers of the Way of the Sword."

Jimson's mind was working furiously. Could it be? The description sounded right! The whispered words, the tears, the smile, it all sounded right! Had the old man triggered Satori in Edwyr? And if so, what did it mean? Johnston didn't just do things at random. If he had done it, he had done it for a very good reason. What reason? Did it have anything to do with the fact that he knew he was dying?

His thoughts changed direction slightly. What sort of Satori had Edwyr had, if any at all? It couldn't have been like mine, he realized grimly, or the lad wouldn't have been smiling.

Sudden despair filled his being. My Satori, he remembered. My personal Hell. Oh, yes, he thought, I followed the Way of the Sword. And one day I fell through the hole in reality and caught a glimpse of what really lies just beneath. I stood at the edge of the Chasm of Nothingness and looked full into its endless depths. I understood that all we can depend on, all that we truly know, is what our senses tell us. And all our senses say is that the world is fleeting, ephemeral, disconnected. What I see now, touch now, taste now, smell now, hear now is gone in the next instant and replaced by something new that I must sense all over again. And when I close my eyes the Universe disappears. When I walk away, what I was touching vanishes from existence.

All that we know, really know, is turmoil passing swiftly by into oblivion. Everything else, the existence of an external world, the public trees and mountains and Ko blossoms, even the very concept of a Self, is based on a supposition, an idea that always goes beyond immediate experience and constructs a continuity from a series of raw sense impressions. It's so easy to fall into such an assumption. Everyone does. But once you truly see the world with complete sensual clarity, stripped of all its pre-conceived notions and structures, the Emptiness appears, the Nothingness opens before you.

Some, he knew, were capable of accepting it. They launched themselves into the abyss and became one with it. Somehow they came out again, endowed with a new view of Reality, a view that managed to transcend and incorporate Nothingness in Thingness, a vision that achieved meaning and unity in the midst of the Great Vacuum.

He could not. He had stood at the Edge and his soul had shriveled at the horror of it. To fall eternally! To dissolve, scatter, shred into a billion tiny, unrelated, sense impressions! He had quailed at the very thought and the fear had come. With it had come the Mushin and the terror of the Madness. In panic, he had slammed the opening door in his mind and had stepped back.

He had stepped back. Forever. It was all lost to him now and only returned in vicious dreams and at odd moments like this. He shuddered and focused his attention outward once more. Mitsuyama was speaking, his voice full of annoyance.

"Jimson, do you hear me? I asked you what you make of it?"

The hurt, vulnerable look faded from Jimson's eyes and they took on their usual hard, brittle luster. He shook his head. "I don't know. It could be nothing. It could be crucial. But I'd like very much to find out."

Gazing at his man with open curiosity, Mitsuyama nodded. "Yes. And since the young Seeker seems to be coming to our very doorstep, perhaps you'll have a chance to ask him in person," he replied smoothly. Then he turned back to the spy.

"You've done very well, this time, spy. I'll double the usual reward. Go back now and learn all you can of Father Andretti's plans. I want a detailed report on who his opposition is within the Free Council. Find out if they might be receptive to our position. Also, see how united the 'hoods are. We may have more allies there than we know. And most important, check the solidarity of the Faithful. That's one of Andretti's strongholds, but unless I miss my guess, there will be more than a few who are disgruntled by his newest escapade. Check on the weak links we already know about and discover any new waverers. Go."

The dark form rose from its cushion and left the room through a previously unnoticed curtained exit opposite the door.

Mitsuyama stood and motioned to Jimson. "Come.

We'll walk outside on the Plain where there are no walls and no ears. Things are moving faster than I'd expected and I must have your report now, rather than this evening as planned. It doesn't have to be written; in fact, don't write down anything from now on. The game is getting dangerous—one slip could mean disaster!"

VI

They left the little room, turned right and passed through the gate and strode out of the fortress as the four guards saluted. Mitsuyama waved off two of them who started to follow as an escort. They walked for several moments in an easternly direction, until they came to the top of a slight swell. There Mitsuyama halted and carefully searched the horizon in all directions. He turned at last to Jimson.

"So. How are my Avengers?"

"Lord," Jimson began, "the training goes well, very well. Man for man, they're the equal of any group of the Faithful, and not a few of them would do against some of the Seekers of the Way of the Sword."

"Good, good. But will they follow orders? You know my tactics. I'm depending on their mass shock value. They must fight my way or they're no use to me. The last drills we did were not good, renegade."

"I executed three of the worst offenders. They'll obey now. I guarantee it."

"You always have been the guarantee, Jimson. Failure and death have much in common for those who serve me."

Jimson bowed his acknowledgement, mockingly, to show his lack of fear.

Mitsuyama noticed and overlooked the arrogance of his subordinate. It would serve no function to discipline the man right now, he thought. He does his job well. So far. If that should ever change, though . . .

"And the striders? How is that project coming?"

"Slowly. They aren't as easy to break as we'd hoped. And even once they're broken, they tend to go

57

wild at the smell of blood. Carnivores aren't the best mounts, my Lord. If we feed them too much before battle, they're sluggish. If we starve them, or even leave them hungry, they're likely to pounce on the dead and ignore the urgings of their riders. And besides, they're plain stupid. Perhaps we could achieve the same results of speed and mobility if our Avengers just rode the striders to battle and then dismounted to fight on foot."

"Hmmmmmm," mused Mitsuyama, "perhaps. But the shock value of foot soldiers being charged by men mounted on bipedal, carnivorous lizards—dragons, really—more than makes up for the expenditure of effort. No one else had ever thought of using the beasts. But once they're used, everyone will be doing it. I want to get the greatest possible effectiveness out of them by being the first. Keep at it, Jimson, keep at it. Time is getting short and we may have need of every trick in our bag before this is finished."

Again, Jimson bowed his acceptance of his Lord's commands. When he raised his eyes, he asked softly, "And when does my Lord see us going into action? Before the Council meeting in three months, or after?"

"Ahhhh, yes, timing. Crucial, as always. I think after, Jimson. We need all the time we can get to prepare. I have a growing feeling that the Sword of Nakamura will not be found. If so, Andretti's position is seriously weakened. At best, he will obtain half-hearted support from certain groups. We must let this brew simmer and mature. We must give all the others time to mistrust each other."

"The very motto of your father, my Lord," commented Jimson slyly.

Mitsuyama looked at the renegade Seeker coldly. For a moment his eyes rested heavily on the other

man's. Then, quietly, he said, "You walk near the
edge, Jimson. Very near. Don't try my temper. And
don't depend on your usefulness to preserve you if I
come to find you too distasteful. There may come a
time when—best to store up good will against that
moment."

Jimson looked away, not because he couldn't meet
the PlainsLord's gaze, but rather to hide the gleam he
knew must show in his eyes. Lose my usefulness? he
thought. Ha! It's only begun, my fine Lord! As has
your usefulness to me.

The game, he reminded himself, is not over once
Andretti and the Free Council are crushed. Indeed,
that is its true beginning. For Lord Mitsuyama, Jimson realized, despite all his devious intelligence,
didn't really understand that the true key to power on
Kensho lay not with the Free Council, but with the
'hoods. Obviously, never having experienced them,
the PlainsLord underestimated the danger the
Mushin represented to human existence on Kensho.
The 'hoods, following the Great Way laid down by
Jerome, controlled the invisible mind leeches, keeping them bottled up tight in the Home Valley so that
Mankind might expand and settle the Plain. It was
because of the 'hoods that the Mushin did not bring
the Madness to the farmers scattered across the
grassy expanse and did not visit raving lunacy and
death on those who herded the ken-cows.

But just because they were not active on the Plain,
did not mean that the monsters had vanished. Oh, no.
Jimson knew otherwise. Training as a Seeker of the
Way of the Sword in the Home Valley, he had directly
experienced them. It had been part of his mental
conditioning. A toughening-up exercise for mind control.

The Mushin were still there, still hungry. And

there would always have to be some method of controlling them if Mankind was to survive on Kensho. With no Way-Farer, no Andretti, and no Free Council, someone would still have to maintain the Great Way and keep the lid on the mind leeches. Mitsuyama was not that someone.

But I, Jimson thought, the triumphant feeling returning, I *am* that someone! I have studied and mastered the mind control techniques taught to those who walk the Way of the Sword. I can lead the 'hoods, keep them in control with my own picked men and replace the Way-Farer in all but name.

And then it will be me, and not Mitsuyama, who is supreme on Kensho! He will cut the path to the top. But I will occupy it!

Controlling his sense of exaltation, he bowed his head. "Yes, my Lord."

Mitsuyama waved his hand in dismissal. "Leave me."

As the other walked away, the PlainsLord thoughtfully watched him go. That one is potentially more dangerous than Andretti, he realized. He has too much power, is too close to my army and too privy to my plans. Plus there is a certain indefinable something in his manner, a certain sense of waiting and lurking, that is disturbing. I must be rid of him at the first propitious moment. But not just yet.

Reminded by Jimson's last remarks, his thoughts turned to his father. How he had loved the harsh, distant, clever old man! I would have won him over to my way of thinking eventually he told himself. I know I would have, if only there'd been a little more time. But Death . . .

Yes, he mused, they all think I poisoned him. I wonder who really did it? So many feared and hated him. Mother? Possible. But she was dead herself now and could not answer. Uncle Marcus? Even more possible, though if so, the man would never tell. Mitsuyama had had him killed within fifteen minutes of his father's death. Too powerful, too powerful by far. Andretti? He suddenly wondered. Far-fetched idea! The Father was not capable of such skullduggery. Or was he?

Thinking about Andretti brought him back to the current situation. How I hate all that man stands for. The Free Council! 'Free!' Ha! They rule with an iron hand, monopolizing education, trade, manufacture, religion, everything! The Council makes all the rules, leaving nothing for the settlers to do but obey.

And what did the Council's rules demand? Patience. Slow, careful, orderly growth, following the Great Way to the letter. So cautious, indeed, was the pace the Council set, that it resembled stagnation more than growth.

This was not the idea behind the Pilgrimage! he told himself. We should have spread beyond the Western Hills by now, to the Sea he had heard rumors of. The whole planet is destined to be ours!

But the Council plodded dully along, stressing control of the Mushin and mindless adherence to the Great Way to the exclusion of everything else. The 'hoods must follow men wherever they went, the teaching of the Way must always continue. That was their excuse. What they really meant was that they didn't want the people to get out from under their cursed control! So they choked off men's desire to explode across the face of the planet. Choked it off with the fear of the Mushin and the Madness.

Mitsuyama shook his head. Of course, he admitted, the Mushin had been crucial in the early days. They had virtually wiped the Pilgrims out at First Touch. And then had ruled them for seven generations through the Grandfathers and the 'hoods. But now the tables were turned, thanks to Jerome, and the 'hoods controlled the Mushin.

And anyway, who was to say that the Mushin were still such a threat? Who was to say that men weren't immune to the mind leeches and the Madness by now? Andretti? The Free Council? How could anyone trust them? Wasn't it in their interest to pretend the contrary?

And what about the Message? Weren't the Council's actions with respect to the Message and the Keepers proof that their only concern was the maintenance of their own power?

Inevitably, drawn by its mystery and importance, his thoughts turned to the Message. Ever since he had been a child, the Message had been hovering darkly just beneath the surface of everyone's thoughts.

What did the Message mean? Oh, in the strict sense he knew what it meant, or at least what it said. Some of the words were unintelligible, but most of it made sense. Earth was calling her colony. The colony had never reported in on its progress. What was wrong? Please reply. That was it. Just a simple query.

Simple? The Keepers who were on the Flagship when the Message came had brought it back with them. They hadn't answered for fear of saying the wrong thing. But what was the right thing? Should they tell the truth, describe the horror of First Touch, the virtual destruction of the colony by the invisible Mushin? Should they tell of the Madness that blew humanity apart and scattered the bloody remnants into near extinction? Or describe the Grandfathers and how humanity had been duped by the Mushin for seven generations until Jerome had found the key and unravelled Nakamura's Koan to free the race?

If they told it all, how would the Mother World react? With loathing? Would they come with a fleet to wipe the menace of the Mushin from the face of the galaxy, incidently destroying Kensho in the process? Earth was capable of it, they all knew that much.

Or would they come and take over the planet, bringing in hordes of new colonists, swallowing up the original Pilgrims and all they had struggled and died to create?

Even if they did neither, even if they just came, accepted things as they found them and opened up intercourse with the Home World and its advanced civilization, would Kensho's feeble, primitive culture survive the shock?

Or were there even darker motives behind Earth's call? Did Kensho have something the Mother Planet wanted? Some resource so precious it would pay to come all those light years to exploit? Would they strip Kensho as they had their own world?

Mitsuyama shook his head silently. The answer was so obvious. Both to the Message and to the future of Kensho. It was hanging right up there in orbit, right above First Touch. The Flagship, with its vast computer and almost limitless store of knowledge. There, access controlled by the Free Council, lay the technology Mankind needed to conquer and develop the planet. And once the world was developed, they would have the power to resist the Home World.

Technology. That was the key. We have all the knowledge Earth had at the time of the Pilgrimage he thought, and a virgin planet on which to use it. We know the mistakes they made and can avoid them. In three to five generations we can develop a strong, viable economy and culture, equal to, and perhaps surpassing the tired Mother World. Then let them

come and we will meet them as brothers rather than
as backward children.

But no. The Free Council said no. They suppressed
the Keepers, took away their books, confiscated the
Medallion, rejected technology, and doomed Kensho
to a slow, grinding, gradual climb out of a primitive
agricultural economy, with change put off indefinite-
ly. All in the name of fear of the Mushin and respect
for the Great Way.

Ha! he snorted. Mushin, the Great Way, indeed!
Whatever they might claim, whatever pap they might
feed the people, he saw their real reason. They
wanted to maintain their control, were afraid that if
things changed too rapidly and too greatly, they and
the Way would become as obsolete as religion had on
Earth. It wasn't fear of the Mushin that was holding
Kensho back. It was the fear of Andretti and his
cohorts on the Free Council that they would lose their
power!

His mind turned once more to the current situation. It offered so many possibilities! The Sword of
Nakamura is the key, he thought. If it were suddenly
found . . .

The companions of the Way-Farer, the twenty
young Seekers of the Way of the Sword, were out
searching for the Sword. So. If anybody could find it,
they could. That much he was sure of.

Would they find it? Perhaps. And if they did, it
would drastically alter the situation. The Sword was
the symbol of legitimacy on Kensho. With it in his
hands, Andretti would have strengthened his position
immeasurably. Foolish to put so much stock in a
sword, but that was the way of things. Andretti would
no more be a true heir of Jerome with Nakamura's
Sword than without it. But most of the settlers and

'steaders, and especially the Faithful would think he would.

This Edwyr, now, he interests me, Mitsuyama considered. It might be worthwhile to have a little talk with the young man. There were several questions the Seeker might have the answer to, including what the Way-Farer had whispered to him. In addition, he was curious to know if Edwyr was really as skillful and dangerous as Jimson seemed to think. Should I send out a group of my Avengers to bring him here directly?

No, he decided. According to the spy, Edwyr was heading in this direction anyway. A better idea would be to send a single man to test him. Challenge him, provoke him to a fight. Discover just how good he really is. If he turns out to be as tough as feared, I'll be forewarned at the minimal cost of one man, he reasoned. If he isn't, I'll be rid of a nuisance and save myself a lot of unnecessary worrying. Better yet, I'll send a second man to hang back out of sight and watch the first. That way I'll be sure to get an accurate report whatever the outcome. Yes, he concluded, that's what I'll do. Then later, if necessary, I can have him brought to me.

His plotting completed, Mitsuyama gazed out over the endless sweep of the Plains. This is our birthright, he mused. This is what the Pilgrimage is all about, why we came here from the Home System. Nothing can be allowed to interfere with our destiny. Not the Mushin, not the Free Council, not the Way-Farer, not even the Great Way itself.

I will act, he declared to the sky and the earth. I will free us from the restrictions just as Jerome freed us from the Mushin. On my life!

With a small smile of self-irony, he turned and

walked back toward his fortress. There was still much
to do. His face set in a look of grim determination, he
entered the gate and headed for the room where
Dembo and the other Lords waited to resume their
Council meeting.

BOOK III

EDWYR THE SEEKER

VII

The twelve sat in a silent circle. Around them, the night-darkened wilderness of the high mountains tumbled off in all directions. Over their heads arched the star-sprinkled coldness that preceded the rising of the moons. The only sound was the gentle, lost moan of the wind softly wandering through the dark.

Stillness enfolded them so profoundly that they seemed like dead things made of stone. Unlike the motionless sprawl of death, however, their quietude was but a means to a deeper level of awareness. It allowed them to pierce the veil that common sense spread across the face of Reality and plunge directly into the Nothingness—the fragmented, here-now flux of pure, unthinking sense perception—that lay just beneath. Then they dove deeper yet, finally merging with the Ultimate Reality, flowing and moving with the dynamic, unified surge that was the true Universe.

Eventually, the moons rose, one, two, three, and the silvery moons-light bathed the twelve unmoving figures, giving shape and definition to their vague, dark bulks. All looked much the same: young, slender, and dressed in worn, brown robes of coarse material. All sat cross-legged, in full lotus posture, with swords laid, hilt to right, about six inches beyond their knees toward the center of the circle. The eyes of each were open, gazing abstractedly down at a 45 degree angle.

Only one bore any mark that distinguished him from the rest. Over his heart, he wore a Ko blossom, the stem thrust through a hole in his robe. Carefully slipping his voice into the night without breaking its fragile peace, this one spoke.

"What is this that always is and never is becoming?" he chanted.

Immediately a figure directly across from him responded with the same soft rhythm. "What is this that is always becoming and never is?"

Another form continued. "It is not This, it is not That."

The response hissed into the night from across the circle. "It is not Not-This, it is not Not-That."

Moving constantly one to the left of the originator, then directly across for the response, the chant went on and on. Finally, it returned to the one with the Ko blossom who intoned, "What is this thing that is No-Thing?"

With one voice the group answered, "It is the Way."

For several moments, total silence again ruled the night. Then the one with the flower spoke once more. "I asked a man of the Way, and he told me."

The silver-lit shape to his left responded. "Neither of you knows it." A pause followed, then the same individual said, "The wind is moving my hair. My hair is moving the wind."

"Your mind should be still" came out of the dark from his left.

The words circled, moving clockwise, back to their origin. When the Ko Flower had been reached again, he stated "I walk the Way."

"Tell us," came the quiet demand from the rest.

"I eat when I am hungry."

"I walk the Way," said the next.

"Tell us," was the response.

"How lovely the moons-light."

"I walk the Way."

"Tell us."

"The smell of the Ko."

Each repeated the sequence, answering the same demand with a different proof. As the last concluded, a new stillness settled over the group. One by one, the three moons that had risen sank behind the mountains to the West. The fourth would not come tonight; its faint orb hung high in the daytime sky.

The dark settled thickly about them until a faint touch of light crept in from the east, announcing the return of the sun. As the dawn began to spill sideways over the edge of the mountains, the twelve moved as one, reaching out and grasping their swords. In unison they stood, bowing to the center of the circle, then thrust the weapons through the sashes that wound about their waists. With great precision, each tied the cords attached to the scabbard to hold the sword firmly in its place.

Finished, they looked at each other calmly. One suddenly said. "The sword in the scabbard is a treasure beyond compare." Another spoke out, "One draw, one life."

"Better not to use the sword. Instead use the Sword."

"And better than the Sword, is No-Sword."

"Only the Sword of No-Sword is sharp enough to cut Nothing."

"Only Nothing is worth cutting."

They all nodded and murmured agreement.

The one with the Ko blossom spoke. "In three months, then."

Murmured agreement.

"Search without looking. Seek without wanting," he continued. "The Sword is not to be found, because it was never missing. Those who see it, are not looking. Those who are looking, do not see it."

Smiles and murmurs of "Good, good" floated in the growing dawn.

"Complete your missions and return with your strength to take the burden of the Other from our Brothers. Each must carry the Other that all may feel no burden. Thus will we wield the Sword of No Sword," he concluded.

"Thus will we cut Nothing," came the united cry from the rest.

"Jerome be with you."

As one, they all turned and began moving away down First Pass and out onto the Plain. No further glances or words were spent by any. It was as if each had instantly entered an empty world of his own.

VIII

The sun burned down, creating in the distance a wavering uncertainty and turning the area immediately around the lone runner into something to be endured rather than enjoyed. Only the barest breath of air stirred the tall grass of the Plain.

Since sunup, the lone runner had been trotting across the flatness that extended westward beyond the forested foothills that flanked the Mountains. At first, the huts of the settlers had been common. He had even run past the walls of a Sisterhood. Now, however, the population was thinning; the homes were farther apart. They weren't sparse yet, for he hadn't reached the grazing grounds of the PlainsLords, and wouldn't for several days. But they were far enough between to give him a pleasant sense of solitude.

It wasn't that he didn't like people. It was simply that he had a great deal of mulling over to do and other humans talking, calling, even waving or standing silently as he ran by, disturbed his concentration.

Now, though, he was into his rhythm, his legs beating out the basic structure and his breath providing the counterpoint. In his present state, he could run for hours and hours. And since his body was virtually on automatic, he could detach his mind to deal with the problems that faced him.

He considered his situation. His mission was to enter Mitsuyama's territory, contact one person, and then return in time for the special Council. In a detached way, he estimated his chance. Good, but not very good. There were simply too many variables.

He could see several possible scenarios. A few resulted in success. But most ended in failure. Defeat could take a great number of forms. He might be killed before he could contact his man. He might be unable to achieve Identification. He might be struck down in the very act of attempting it. Or he might accomplish all this and still die before he could make use of the information himself or pass it on for others to use. Victory had only one form: contact, Identification, return. There were no alternatives, a fact which made his task much harder. But his success was critical to the success of the Plan. If any of them failed, the Plan was jeopardized. If he failed, it was doomed. Well, he shrugged mentally, it can't be helped. It can only be attempted.

For a while, he let his mind worry freely around the edges of the problem. Thinking was, after all, a natural activity of the mind, continuing even when not under conscious control. It helped the mind organize the chaotic mass of perceptions that flooded into it through the senses, transforming them into coherent patterns. Then it structured these patterns to create the everyday, commonsense world in which one lived and acted and survived.

But the world the mind created went far beyond the mere ordering of sense perceptions. It had to. After all, the senses were limited. They didn't cover the entire range of possibly perceivable phenomena, nor even the whole range within those actually experienced. The runner, for instance, had no sense organ that could see or feel or hear or smell or taste the magnetic lines of force which constantly sliced through his body. And even though he had eyes and could see part of the electromagnetic spectrum, the portion he perceived was only a small segment of the whole. Out of almost limitless possiblities, natural selection and development had restricted his senses to those necessary to his survival.

These limitations created a problem. There were many aspects of commonsense reality which simply couldn't be explained in terms of direct perceptions, even after they had been shaped into an understandable whole. So it became necessary to invent new explanatory structures that went beyond the commonsense one in the same way that it went beyond pure perception. These new systems were often highly abstract, consisting of unsensed or even unsensible entities. But as long as they were ultimately correlatable back to the commonsense world, they had predictive value in everyday terms and were eminently useful.

Thus thinking, even in abstract terms, had a positive value. Indeed, all language was a conceptual structure of this type. It was also part of the scientific method, the value of which was proven by the very fact that he, a son of Earth, was running through the coarse grass on the Plain of Kensho. The technique worked, and from at least one point of view, that was enough.

But he also realized there was a danger lurking here. It lay in letting abstraction get the upper hand, in losing connection with the original ground of experience. When words and symbols lost their reference points in reality, they ceased communicating and became barriers standing between mind and meaning.

The runner was constantly aware of the problem and actively sought to resolve it. As long as words were seen as the tracks of reality, he knew, thinking at any level of abstraction was safe. For then the tracks eventually led to the reality itself. But as soon as you became more concerned with the tracks than with the quarry, the mind became a trap with thinking as the bait.

It was an ancient, endless struggle, he realized. It had begun when the first spark of consciousness had been struck in the human mind. The only way to fight the battle was to keep the mind open to all the levels of reality at the same time. Then one could plunge from the plane of highest abstraction to the original ground of experience, to the very source of all meaning, with complete freedom.

Someday, he told himself, it'll all be as natural to us as breathing. Someday we'll be totally aware of our minds and how they interact with reality, simultaneously creating and reflecting it. Jerome had understood that. He had seen how the Mushin would shape the race in that direction. And he had given Mankind the Way so they could begin the development and guide it themselves.

Kensho, he thought, is the place where this can be accomplished. It's here where we have a chance to break out of the cocoon of our nature and spread the wings of power that lie latent within us. It's here, among the Mushin, where we can follow the Way and create a new Humanity.

This is a good world, he realized. It gives us everything we need to become what we should be. Now all we have to do is see that we're wise enough and strong enough to accept what we're given.

His body told him he was thirsty. Since he was only a little way from a settler's sod hut, he decided to stop and ask for a drink. Turning from his path, he trotted off to the right at an angle, making for the barely visible roof of the dwelling.

The little girl spotted him first. "Mommy, Daddy!" she cried in delight, "Here comes a man!" Then she ran to hide behind the corner of the hut. The woman came to the door, shading her eyes against the bright sunlight, to see the approaching runner. Her husband and older son came around from behind the hut where they had been working on the garden. " Looks to be a Brother of some kind," he muttered. His wife nodded and went back in again. "Thirsty, like as not," she threw over her shoulder. The man nodded and turned to his son. "Fetch fresh water, Yarra."

The settler stood watching the runner come up to the hut. He saw a young man, perhaps 25, with jet-black hair, sun-tanned skin, and rich brown eyes, slightly flecked with yellow. The face was plain, with high cheek bones and a straight, thin nose. It was a strong face, but held no hint of harshness. Dress was simple; a worn brown robe, caught up around the waist by its sash to make running easier. The only strange thing was the wilted Ko blossom thrust through a hole over the young man's heart.

The runner stopped about two yards away and calmly received the settler's scrutiny. When the man had finished, he spoke quietly. "I am without Desire and free of Mushin."

"There are no Mushin here. If you come without Desire, you will find Calm," responded the older man in the traditional manner. "For that matter," he smiled, "I was born on this Plain and never seen nor felt a Mushin in my life. For which I'm much obliged to the 'hoods."

"I'm not from a 'hood," replied the young man, moving his sword around from his back where he slung it while running. "I'm a Seeker of the Way of the Sword."

The man's eyes widened slightly. "Then all the more welcome."

His daughter, peeping around the corner of the hut took this as official assurance that the stranger could be approached and walked hesitantly up to the young Seeker. "I'm Andy, that's short for Andrea Lynn and what's your name."

He bowed. "Edwyr. Simply Edwyr. Nothing so grand as Andrea Lynn." He smiled at the child, then looked up at the father. "You were born on the Plain, but the child's mother was from the Home Valley, wasn't she?"

Startled, the settler nodded.

Squatting next to the child, Edwyr took the Ko blossom from his robe and held it out to her. "It was prettier hours ago."

"Pretty now," the child replied, sniffing the remnant of perfume that clung to the flower. "Are you thirsty?" she asked, looking at him owlishly. "You think thirsty."

"Hungry, too?" he asked.

"No. Only thirst. Hungry later."

He nodded. "Hungry later."

"Drink now," she stated. The child looked at the flower. "Gone. Gone now, come back later."

The young man stood and looked at the father. Solemnly, he crossed to him and placed both hands on the man's shoulders. "Cherish the future. See the child follows the Great Way. And let her marry whom she will. She will only be drawn to the right ones. Let her decide, no matter how unlikely it seems to you." He paused for a moment, searching the man's eyes with his own. "Cherish the future," he repeated. "Only thus will it come to pass."

At that moment, the older brother came up with a clay pot, brimming with water. The mother also appeared from out of the hut with something wrapped in a cloth. Without a word, the boy handed the water to Edwyr. The father began to say, "It isn't cold or . . ." but the woman cut his words short with a gesture.

Edwyr drank deeply. When he had finished he handed the pot back to the young lad.

"My thirst is satisfied. Beyond that I have no desire," he told the man. Then he turned to the woman and bowed. "You bring the future to the Plain. All honor, Mother."

She thrust out the cloth-wrapped package. "For later, when hunger comes." Then she turned and went back into the hut. Placing the package, which by the feel of it contained some biscuits and a piece of Ken-cow cheese, in the pocket of his robe, Edwyr smiled at the man.

"Thanks for your welcome, my friend. What lies ahead?"

For a moment the man thought. "Oh, let's see. About ten miles further west, you'll be comin' to the First River. Big, broad, can't walk across no place. Need a boat, 'cause though its wide, it's got quite a current. If you go sort of northwest, you'll come across a track that leads right to a ferry run by a man name of Robards. He'll take a Brother across free, though he charges most everyone else a little something."

Edwyr bowed. "Again, my thanks. And remember: cherish the future. You are creating it yourself."

With that, Edwyr turned and trotted off to the northwest.

The man and his son went back to work, but the little girl stood there and watched the Seeker of the Way of the Sword leaving until he disappeared among the waving heads of the grass. Then she looked down at the Ko blossom. "Pretty gone?" she asked herself. "No." she decided. "Not gone, just resting." Carefully she scraped a hole in the ground, dropped the flower in, and patted the soil smooth again.

IX

The ferryman, didn't like the looks of the man with the sword. The fellow had been hanging around the area on the east bank of the First River for several days now. No good reason for an able-bodied man to be loafing like that, the old man thought.

He scowled over in the direction of where the swordsman lazily sprawled beneath some ironwood trees that grew in a clump next to the road. Why's he carry a sword? Robards wondered. Not a Brother, that one. Not even one of the Faithful. In the Old Days, he would have been Ronin, the boatman decided grimly. Arrogant, lazy, and armed. Rotten combination.

A few other people were also sitting around. Two itinerant peddlers over next to the water, talking animatedly, their huge packs on the ground; a man with a push cart, taking ken-cow cheese to the Brotherhood on the other side of the River to trade for something; three gray-haired Fathers also on their way to the 'hood; a family of five, heading Gods only knew where. A good load, he estimated, but if I wait a little longer, it might be better. He leaned back against the hull of his boat and closed his eyes, relaxing.

It was the eldest son of the family who saw the approaching figure first. When Robards stood and looked to the east, it was still a good way off, but coming fast at a trot. Huh, he thought, only know of one type can run like that. A Seeker. No pay for rowing that one across.

Out of the corner of his eye, he noticed something strange. The swordsman was no longer sprawling beneath his tree. Instead the man was standing alertly, intently watching the runner. No business of mine, the old man shrugged to himself.

As the runner arrived and everyone saw he was a Seeker, the entire group of those waiting turned back to what they had been doing. All except for the swordsman by the trees.

For a moment, Edwyr stood in the sun, quickly surveying the situation as he dropped the skirt of his robe back down to his ankles and tied his sword into place at his waist. Finishing, he walked calmly over to the shade of the ironwood trees. The swordsman stood there, trying hard to look casual. The two peddlers, having moved out of the sun by the river bank, squatted and continued their voluble discussion. The family was slowly drifting in the same direction, perhaps drawn by a mild curiosity in the newcomer, perhaps driven by the sun.

"Jerome be with you," Edwyr greeted them all. "And with you," responded the peddlers in chorus. The swordsman merely grumbled something inaudible.

Silence settled on the little group, broken only briefly as the family reached the sanctuary of the shade and each was greeted in turn. Finally, the swordsman cleared his throat and spoke to Edwyr. "Huumph. A Seeker are you? Pretty good with the blade?"

Edwyr nodded amiably. "Fair."

Turning to stare arrogantly at him, the man with the sword said loudly, "What? Only fair? What sort of Master do you study with that he lets you run around loose if you're only 'fair?'"

The young Seeker smiled. "A good Master. He laughs a lot."

"Laughs?" snorted the older man contemptuously.

"What in the name of the Gods has that to do with swordsmanship?"

"Nothing, but it has a great deal to do with how good a Master he is."

"Nonsense! I study with a Master who's never smiled in his life! What do you think of that, young one?"

"I pity him."

"Pity? You dare to pity a Master? How can you pity my Master? He knows the best techniques in all Kensho! His draw is so swift the eye can't follow it. Is your Master that swift?"

Edwyr shook his head.

"And my Master's upper block is so powerful, it's been known to shatter swords. Can your Master equal that?"

Again the young man shook his head.

"And my Master has developed his cut so perfectly that he can split a wand of wood in half without making it fall over."

The Seeker of the Way of the Sword sighed. "My Master can do none of those things, at least, I've never seen him do them."

"What in the name of the Gods can he do then?"

"Well," considered Edwyr carefully, "let me think. I've seen him laugh when he's happy . . . and cry when he's sad. I know he eats when he's hungry, drinks when he's thirsty, and sleeps when he's tired. Other than that, I can't really say. You'd have to ask him yourself, I guess."

The swordsman exploded. "Eats, drinks, sleeps, cries, laughs! What the devil are you saying, fool? Everyone does those things!"

"True. But not everyone knows why he does them."

"Rubbish! Mystical cant! I'll wager you can't even use that silly sneaklizard-sticker you carry!"

"Perhaps not."

At that moment, the boatman called out. "Crossing time. All as is crossing, come up and make payment."

Edwyr smiled at the swordsman. "Perhaps you could use the things your Master has taught you as payment." He immediately turned away and walked into the sun and over to the old man standing in the boat.

"Ah, Seeker, no charge for you. It's my policy."

Edwyr bowed and said, "But it's my policy to do something for you in exchange. I'll man a sweep and help with the work to earn my passage." He looked out across the broad waters of First River. "It's a long trip and you could use the help."

"I could," nodded the old man. "Indeed I could and much thanks to you. Accepted. Help me push off when the others are on."

Each paying something, the rest climbed aboard the small craft. The boat was about eighteen feet long, with a broad beam of nearly ten feet amidships. The stern was squared off and the prow was blunt. The ferry was of shallow draft, for shifting sand bars in the river made a boat that drew much water dangerous. This made propelling the ferry harder work, since it gave the current more surface to act against; but the additional safety outweighed the additional labor.

The boat was powered by sweep oars at the stern, the rowers standing on a slightly raised platform with three oarlocks and room enough for two men—though usually the boatman was the only motive force available. In the bow, the old man stationed the eldest son of the family with a pole to fend off floating logs and to push away from snags and sand bars. The

passengers sat, facing each other, on two long
benches that ran the length of the boat just below the
gunwales. Baggage was piled in the middle.

After helping push the ferry off, Edwyr took up his
position on the port, or downstream, sweep oar as
directed by the boatman. The sullen swordsman was
sitting right in front of him. The first few moments of
the trip elapsed in anxious silence. Then, becoming
rapidly used to the ride, everyone began their normal
conversations again.

The swordsman looked up at Edwyr in a calculating
manner. "I think that oar becomes you better than the
sword, youngster. Why not become a boatman?" he
sneered.

Edwyr didn't bother to answer, concentrating instead on rowing. The boatman looked annoyed, but
only muttered, "A bit more to starboard, lad."

But the swordsman wasn't about to let up. A vicious
glint showed in his eye. Inconspicuously, he rear-
ranged his robe and scabbard so his sword could be
quickly drawn. "If your so-called Master didn't teach
you a swift draw, a strong block, or a clean cut, what
did he teach you, puppy?"

The young man looked calmly down. "He taught
me that the fastest draw is when the sword never
leaves the scabbard, that the strongest way to block is
never to provoke a blow, and that the cleanest cut is
the one withheld."

The other stared at him for a moment, blinking in
astonishment. Finally he gritted out, "You mock me,
you little sneaklizard!" His hand went to his sword
hilt.

Before he could draw, however, the old ferryman
had his long oar out of the water and raised threateningly over the man's head. "Not on my boat you don't,
Ronin! And not with someone as is rowing, either! Put

that damn sticker away or I'll bash in your brains! We're coming to the bloody island and the bars and I'll be needing help, not fighting. Besides, you fools wouldn't just kill each other. So damn stupid you'd probably split half the innocent folks aboard. Pick your fights elsewhere, Ronin!" Grumbling, his eyes narrowed, but afraid of the power of the raised oar, the swordsman complied.

"You young puppy," he addressed Edwyr. "I'll wager you're a fraud! You don't even know how to use that sword. It's likely some rusty old blade you've strapped on to make yourself look big and get free rides and food from stupid settlers. I challenge you, faker! I challenge you to fight me when we get to the other side!"

Edwyr took his eyes off the water ahead long enough to meet the man's glare. He nodded briefly. "Very well," he answered. "If you insist. On the other side. But please be quiet now. We have to concentrate or we'll never get to the other side."

"Big log to the right up ahead!" sang out the boy in the bows.

"Damn!" muttered the old man. "Sand bars to the port by the island. We'll have to try and squeeze through. Head for that area just off the starboard bow. And pull like hell!"

X

The trip to the other shore was difficult and filled
with alarms. Robards was glad to have the young
Seeker of the Way of the Sword manning the other
oar. He could have managed it all alone, of course. He
usually did. But the current was unusually strong
today and he probably would have ended up a good
half-mile south of his regular landing place.

The lad seemed to be a decent sort and the ferryman was a little worried about the outcome of the
duel. At the same time, he knew there was nothing he
could or should do about it. As long as they didn't
bother him, he figured it was none of his business.

As they approached the shallows, Edwyr shipped
his oar and moved into the bow. As they touched
bottom, he jumped off and grabbed the bow line,
pulling the craft firmly aground with a mighty heave.
He offered a steadying hand to each passenger as they
left the boat. The swordsman sneered at his assistance
and leaped lightly ashore.

Although he pretended to be busy helping Robards
unload and secure the ferry, Edwyr watched the
swordsman closely. As the man looked around, automatically checking the lay of the land and the
crowd, Edwyr noticed his gaze halted slightly in
well-concealed surprise as it passed over one figure.
Covertly, the young Brother turned his attention to
this individual. There was, he observed, a great deal
of similarity between the swordsman and this man he
had obviously recognized. Not so much in their
looks or clothes as in the way they both stood and
moved. They've both been trained in the use of the
sword, Edwyr concluded, and by the same master.

So, he thought as he helped the ferryman pull the empty boat higher on the shore, two of them! Yet the first was surprised to see the second, so they weren't here together. Which meant they haven't planned some kind of combined attack or ambush. Still, it would be prudent to avoid getting caught between the two of them. Best to stand so he could keep his eye on both.

The passengers from the boat had immediately whispered to those waiting on shore about the challenge and Edwyr's acceptance. Now they all stood, expectantly, waiting to see if the duel would actually take place. As Edwyr turned from securing the ferry, the Swordsman stepped up to confront him.

"Well, puppy," he snarled, "are you still brave enough to accept my challenge?"

Edwyr looked around at the crowd. No hostility there. Just ordinary faces filled with a mixture of curiosity, expectation and a touch of fear. He smiled. Several smiled back, tentatively. He turned back to the older man. "Yes. Certainly. But may I make a suggestion?"

"As long as you don't try to wiggle out of it."

Edwyr nodded. "It seems to me this is the wrong place to hold a fight." He indicated the crowd with a sweep of his arm. "All these people would be endangered. Some innocent bystander might be wounded or even killed." He saw the fear leap up in their eyes. His words were having the effect he'd hoped for and he heard a dim murmur of agreement from several in the group.

"What are you suggesting?" asked the swordsman warily.

"Simply that we hold the duel someplace where we won't hurt anyone by mistake." He pointed out into the river to a sand bar that lay about fifty yards off shore. "I suggest we fight out there. Everyone can see us from here, so no one will miss the show. And no one is endangered but you and I."

The other man followed his pointing finger. The sand bar was clear of all vegetation except for a few clumps of harsh grass. The ground looked good and firm, well above the water level. The tiny island was no more than fifteen yards wide by some thirty or forty long. There would be no place to hide and nowhere to run.

His eyes flicked back to the young man and then quickly to the man who stood at the back of the crowd watching him. Curse that damn Mitsuyama! He's sent someone to watch me, he raged silently. Someone to report on how I handle this. Someone, he thought grimly, to relate what happens in case I die. Perhaps, he mused, this lad is tougher than I was told.

He decided and nodded. "Fine. I can kill you there as easily as here. Who'll row us out?"

Edwyr bowed his head slightly. "I will. Provided the ferryman will lend us the small boat I saw beached a little downstream.

Robards grumbled forwards, annoyed at being involved, but pleased by the way the young Seeker was handling things. Better to have them fight out in the river than here. Never know what damage the two idiots might do. "Aye. I guess I can. But listen, you two fools. I want my boat back! I fish in it every day. If the lad wins, I know he can row it back. Can you?" he glared at the swordsman.

The man drew himself up haughtily and glared back coldly. "Don't worry, old man. You'll get your boat back."

"Aye, to be sure," he grumbled again, "and probably two miles downstream! Provided, of course, the two of you don't kill each other!"

Still mumbling under his breath, Robards led the two men down the beach to the little boat. It was built on the same design as the ferryboat, though only big enough for three passengers at most. There was a platform at the stern and room for one sweep oar. The ferryman pushed the craft into the river and held it as the swordsman climbed in and moved to the bow seat. He settled himself, his sword arranged for a quick draw, facing aft. Edwyr stepped onto the rowing platform and shoved off with the long oar.

For a few moments there was silence between them, filled with the gurgle and whisper of the river. Then the young Brother spoke. "When we get to the island, I'll beach the boat. You jump out and move to the middle of the island. It's the best place to fight and I can get off the boat without having to fear that you will try to cut me down while I'm wading ashore."

The older man replied with an arrogant sneer. "I don't need tricks with a puppy like you! But your plan makes sense. I agree." He turned his head slightly to get a glimpse of the approaching island while still keeping Edwyr in view out of the corner of his eye.

When they arrived at the sand bar, Edwyr nosed the boat smoothly onto the sand. "Now jump off and go inland," he instructed.

The man stood, turned, and looked swiftly back over his shoulder at Edwyr. "Don't try anything. I'm ready for you." His hand remained firmly on his sword hilt as he leaped into the ankle-deep shallows.

Taking no chances, he quickly splashed a few feet to reach firm, dry ground. Then he spun around, ready.

What he saw left him speechless. Edwyr had pushed the boat away from the island and now was standing about fifteen feet offshore, grinning delightedly.

He found his voice. "What is this?" he roared.

Edwyr laughed. "I've just won the duel."

"Won?" the swordsman sputtered. "Won! What the hell do you mean?"

Still smiling, the young man thrust the oar deeply into the sandy bottom to hold the boat steady against the current. It was still near the shore, tantalizingly near, but too far for the man on the island to reach quickly enough to do anything.

"Those who walk the Way of the Sword have a koan given us by Jerome," Edwyr explained. " 'The sword in the scabbard is a treasure beyond compare.' What it means is simply that once the sword is drawn, blood must flow and someone must die. We prefer to avoid that. We serve the Sword of Life, the Sword that rights wrongs and helps others, not the Sword of Death which destroys for ego satisfaction and personal gain. So, whenever we're challenged, we try to avoid fighting or attempt to bring the issue to a bloodless conclusion. We consider that a true victory."

The man ripped his sword from its sheath and waved it furiously at Edwyr. "Damn you, come ashore! I want your blood! You haven't beaten me, you fool! You've just run away, you rotten little coward!"

"Oh," Edwyr replied calmly, "but I have beaten you. Yes, very completely. And if you don't have the sense to realize how true that is, I'll even be the indirect cause of your death."

That brought the swordsman up short for a moment. He regained his control and looked carefully at the young man. He isn't afraid, he noted. Not in the least. He never was. He's no coward. But what in the hell does he mean, he's beaten me?

The man's confusion showed on his face and Edwyr laughed again. Then he sobered. He leaned against the upright oar and quickly calculated how much he dared tell the swordsman. *It has to be enough to make him act the way I want him to, but just in case he doesn't do what I think he will, I don't want him knowing enough to jeopardize my mission. Especially if he's what I believe he is.*

Edwyr had realized from the very first that the swordsman wasn't acting on his own initiative. The whole incident was clearly a set-up. The man had been sent by someone else for the specific purpose of challenging him to a duel. But who? And why?

The young man had played for time, hoping the swordsman would let something slip. The clue he needed came when they landed on the other shore and Edwyr noticed the second man.

To Edwyr's knowledgable eye, it was evident both men had been trained by the same master. But where had they gotten their training? It wasn't at one of the Brotherhoods, or even among the Faithful. Both trained their members, but neither one taught the sword. And it was precisely that weapon these two had studied. That left the Way of the Sword as the only other official source of instruction. But it was easy to see neither of the swordsmen had ever walked the Way.

Which meant they had been trained unofficially, perhaps even surreptitiously, by someone with both the resources and the motivation to undertake such a difficult project. Out here on the Plain, only one man fit that description—Mitsuyama. And as Edwyr had thought about it, he recalled the rumor that the PlainsLord was training a secret army with the help of a renegade Seeker. It all fit together nicely.

But why? Why would the Supreme Lord of the Plains be interested in a mere Seeker of the Way of the Sword? And one that hadn't even entered his

domains yet? It occured to Edwyr that the Lord undoubtedly had spies in the Home Valley, perhaps
even close to the Free Council itself. If so, he would
have heard that the Seekers were coming out onto the
Plain to search for Nakamura's Sword. Since he probably knew relatively little about the Seekers, it would
make sense for him to send his men to feel out the
searchers. Perhaps even to stop them. After all, it was
to Mitsuyama's advantage if the Sword was never
found.

So Edwyr had deduced that the swordsman was
one of Mitsuyama's new army, trained by the renegade, and sent by the PlainsLord to kill him.

The problem was how to best use the man to
further his own ends. The young Seeker had instantly
seen he could cut the older man to ribbons if it ever
came to a fight. But if Mitsuyama was unsure enough
about the Seekers to send out spies, why let him know
even so simple a fact as that? The best strategy was
plainly to keep him confused and guessing. Edwyr's
path had been clear from the moment he had reached
that conclusion. Now if only he could get the
swordsman on the island to cooperate, and the one on
the other shore to do his part . . . .

The swordsman was tired of waiting for the young
man to explain himself. "All right, puppy," he
snarled, "go ahead and run away pretending you've
beaten me. But it won't take me long to get off this
island. And when I do, I'll be after you and I'll chase
you until—"

"Mitsuyama sent you," Edwyr interrupted calmly.
He felt gratified by the look of surprise which flashed
across the other man's face. "But don't forget, he sent
a second man, too. Someone to watch you, see how
well you did, and report back. Most likely, he has
orders not to get involved, just observe. And as soon

as he realizes what's happened, he'll head back for Mitsuyama's fortress to report." Involuntarily, the swordsman's eyes twitched shoreward as if trying to see whether the other man was doing what Edwyr had suggested.

"In any case," Edwyr continued with a sigh, "you'd better face it. You've failed. And you know what that means for one who serves the Supreme Lord of the Plain."

The man's mouth dropped open and he turned pale as the implications of what Edwyr had said sank in. *He's right,* he thought in anguish. *If I return to Mitsuyama, I'm a dead man!*

"My advice to you," the young man suggested gently, "is to stay as far away from your former master as possible. I wouldn't even land on that shore again. In fact, since I've heard Mitsuyama's reach is as long as his memory, a little visit to the Home Valley, perhaps even a pilgrimage to First Touch, might be a very healthy trip to undertake at this point."

A look of sadness settled over Edwyr's features. "I'm really sorry you have to suffer this way, friend. But you can see I have no choice. And I think you'll agree this is a much better outcome for you than the duel would have been. Because, you see, I would have killed you very quickly. You're not very good with that sword, you know. If you were, Mitsuyama wouldn't have sacrificed you so readily."

Thunderstruck, the swordsman just stared at the young man in the boat. *Everything he says is true,* the older man realized. Suddenly he knew for certain that the Seeker of the Way of the Sword would have killed him easily. His knees felt weak and watery, his throat dry. His hands trembling slightly, he sheathed his sword.

For several moments he simply looked down at his

empty hands. Then he lifted eyes filled with uncertainty and fear and looked quickly at Edwyr. He couldn't meet the Seeker's calm gaze for more than an instant. "Yes," he mumbled. "Yes. I think I will visit the Home Valley." With that he turned and shuffled off down the island toward its middle.

His face still sad, Edwyr watched him go. Finally, he pulled the oar out of the river bed and began to row thoughtfully back toward the shore.

One obstacle surmounted, he thought. One small one. He chuckled. The PlainsLord would not be happy over the outcome of this little incident. He'll send others, Edwyr was sure, to amend the situation and seek revenge. He looked toward the shore and noticed a single figure heading rapidly westward. Ah, he thought, there goes the second one now. I was right.

So. Now it really begins! He smiled. At least it won't be a boring journey! With a laugh, he gave the oar a mighty shove and swept shoreward.

BOOK IV

YOLAN THE KEEPER

XI

"I won't stop!" the young woman shouted angrily.

Mother Elena sat quietly, watching her. Only the older woman's raised eyebrows indicated her surprise at the other's outburst. When she spoke, her voice was calm. "This isn't the way we've trained you, Yolan. Control yourself. Repeat the Litany a few times to regain your composure."

"Damn the Litany! Damn composure! We're not in the Home Valley and there aren't any Mushin around! I'll be damned if I'll be calm and double damned if I'll stop!"

"Yolan, Yolan, it's for your own good," crooned the older woman.

Yolan laughed harshly. "For my own good! Ha! It's for the good of the Sisterhood, for the good of the Free Council. But it's not for my good or the good of the settlers out there grubbing a living on the Plain. Oh, why won't you fools open your eyes and *see*!"

Mother Elena shook her head. "It's you who refuse to see, my Daughter. You who refuse to open your eyes to the Truth of the Way." she sighed. "Here on the Plain we never experience the Mushin, thank Jerome, so I can understand how hard it must be to understand.

"But I *have* felt them, my dear, felt the burning of their probing, itched with the gnawing fear they bring. And I've walked the ruins of First Touch, over the very ground where our ancestors murdered each other when the Mushin brought the Madness. I've lived in 'hoods where Grandfathers still sit in dark, silent cells and men pretend to do their bidding. I've joined with other Brothers and Sisters, Fathers and

97

Mothers in feeding the mind leeches to keep them
chained to the 'hoods as Jerome planned.

"I've seen these things, experienced them. I *know*
the Way is right. It's the only hope we have here on
Kensho."

"I don't doubt that, Mother," Yolan replied. Her
voice was calmer now, but still held a hard core of
undissolved anger. "But I don't see what all that has to
do with me, here on the Plain. What you ask is
impossible. I will not—cannot—stop."

A look of perplexity passed across the face of the
older woman. "But don't you see that the Free Council . . ."

"The Free Council!" Yolan said bitterly. "Why
should I have any love for the Free Council? They
ripped my parents away from their work, their home,
their friends and threw them out onto the Plain! The
trees, the mountains, the valleys they loved, the
'stead they had lived on for so long—all gone! If it
hadn't been for me, the Council probably wouldn't
even have left them *each other*. A lot of couples were
split up.

"And why? Why did they do such a horrible thing?
Because they were afraid! Afraid the Way might be
threatened in some obscure way! Gods, to destroy
people's lives for the sake of an idea? What kind of
sickness is that?

"So don't bother to play on my imaginary loyalty to
the Free Council or to that fat idiot Andretti." She
thrust her chin forward defiantly and sat glaring at
Mother Elena with cold hostility.

For several moments, the older woman gazed silently down at the hands that lay quietly in her lap,
wrinkled and covered with the brown spots that age
had brought. I have no answer for such bitterness, she
thought.

It was a pity. Yolan was a bright, charming girl. And very adept with the bladed staff. Very adept. She would make an excellent candidate for the Sisterhood. Yet she refused to accept the facts that shaped her life or learn to flow with them.

The facts of the young woman's life were unique and inescapable. She was the only daughter of a former Keeper and Artisan sent out from the Home Valley to live on the Plain when the Keepers had been disbanded some fifteen years ago. Yolan had been a child of eight or ten at the time.

The Council had had a hard time deciding what to do with the family. They represented a dangerous combination of talents. The wife, the Keeper of the two, had managed to gather and organize a prodigious amount of information from the computer on the Flagship. Rather than writing the material down as had most of the other Keepers, she and a group of close friends had carefully constructed a series of interconnected chants incorporating the data and then had committed them to memory in the traditional Keeper fashion.

The husband's abilities complemented the wife's. He was a skillful Artisan, a highly creative inventor capable of turning technical abstraction into functioning reality. With her knowledge and his skill, the two of them clearly represented a potential nucleus for the renaissance of an Earthlike technology, even with all the books confiscated.

The debate had been long and soul-searching. Finally, despite the danger, a spirit of compassion had prevailed. The Council had decided to send the family far out onto the Plain, isolated from their friends and other settlers, but together.

Swallowed up by the endless sea of grass, they were almost forgotten. But not quite. And when an im-

proved plowshare and hitching device slowly spread
from west to east across the Plain, someone on the
Council remembered.

Suspicious, they sent Mother Elena, who was the
head of a Sisterhood on the Plain, to investigate.
What she had found shocked her. The couple had not
given up their work. The Keeper had written down all
the chants and was organizing a network to distribute
them among the settlers in her area. The Artisan was
actively experimenting with a technology geared to
the resources and knowledge available to the settlers.

Even the child was contaminated. She had been
raised in the tradition of the Keepers, was learning
the chants, and was almost totally ignorant of the
Way!

The Free Council had acted. The woman's writings
and the man's workshop, including all his plans and
models, had been burned. The couple had been
moved to a different location to break the connections
they had made with the local settlers. And the girl had
been brought back and placed in Mother Elena's
Sisterhood so that she might learn the Way.

For the last four years, Mother Elena had done
everything she could to make Yolan understand. But
it was difficult. This was not some small child to be
easily molded. Yolan was already in her twenties and
had been formed by her mother and father. Plus she
was very, very stubborn! But the older woman had
kept at it, kindly, patiently, hoping to win this mind
back to the Way.

And now this!

She raised her eyes and looked at the young woman
once more. "Then you don't deny these?" she asked
motioning toward the papers that lay on the table
between them.

"Deny them? Why should I deny them? Who else

could have written them? Surely none of the ignorant little fools here could have done it. Yes, those are the chants my mother taught me. And if you knew enough to read and understand them, you'd realize how well she taught me!"

"And you don't deny that rather than meditating on your lessons, you mutter the chants to yourself?"

"I don't 'mutter' them. I chant them. Softly. They have a beauty you could never grasp."

"But you know such things are proscribed. They endanger the security of the Way. Jerome himself . . ."

"Jerome never said any such thing and you know it! Jerome was the one who suggested the Keepers go to the Flagship. He wasn't afraid of knowledge."

"How then, my Daughter, do you interpret his Koans?"

"I'm not your daughter," Yolan gritted out. "And I don't see what Jerome's Koans have to do with it."

"Precisely," answered Mother Elena quickly, "you don't see. But think a moment. 'The sword in the sheath is a treasure beyond compare.' The sword is clearly technology, the sword that cut Earth down and destroyed it. Jerome is saying that it must be kept in the sheath, that it must not be drawn here on Kensho, or else it will destroy us.

"And his second Koan reinforces this interpretation. 'As the Ronin strikes, oh, how beautiful the constant stars!' Obviously, he's trying to tell us that even in extreme emergencies, we must never forget the Way and its emphasis on the natural life. He doesn't call on technology to save him as the killer attacks. He looks at the stars, the Eternal Truth of the Way, as his only salvation."

Yolan snorted derisively. "Rubbish. I can give you ten different interpretations of what Jerome's Koans

mean. You just twist them to support your viewpoint.
The Keepers see them differently."

"But technology nearly destroyed the Home
World!"

"And technology is the only reason we're even here
on Kensho!"

"Ah, but once we got here and the Mushin attacked, it wasn't technology that saved the day.
Nakamura had all the resources of the computer at his
fingertips, all the scientific knowledge of Earth at his
beck and call. But he chose not to use them! Instead
he conceived the Way of Passivity, complete with the
Grandfathers and the 'hoods and tricked the Mushin
into adopting his plan. He did it knowing that sooner
or later someone would discover the Truth and find
the Great Way. Jerome did just that. Without science. Without technology."

"Also without knowing about the Message." Yolan
looked solemnly at the older woman. "I wonder how
he would have reacted to the Message. In any case, it
changes everything. If Earth does come and we're
still a backward bunch of farmers scratching a meager
living from the soil, we're wide open to whatever they
decide to do with us."

It was the older woman's turn to smile ironically.
"You almost sound like Mitsuyama."

"I don't like the man any more than you do. But
that doesn't automatically make him wrong on all
counts."

"Perhaps. But it does raise the issue of just how far
the Keepers would be willing to go in supporting him
for the purpose of achieving their own goals."

"You already know the answer to that. Not at all.
None of the Keepers has joined the PlainsLord."

"One has. We know that. He's not very important,
true. But there's nothing to stop others. And Mit-

suyama has launched a new attempt to find and convince Keepers to throw in with him.

"Besides, even if you aren't on his side, what's to stop him from taking advantage of the innovations you'd introduce? How would you keep him from using the things you create for his own purposes? That's the real issue, you know. How do you keep the fruits of science from being used by evil people for evil ends? Or what about the simple fact that you can't even foresee the unintended consequences of your own discoveries? Surely the people of Earth didn't set out purposely to ruin their world.

"No, Yolan. It's not the 'hoods and the Council who are blind. It's those who reject the Way and refuse to see and understand the lesson of the Home World."

"That's exactly the point! We *do* see the example of the Home World. We know where they went wrong. We don't have to repeat their mistakes!

"And we don't reject the Way. We see it as essential in guiding us, in providing the values we need to keep Kensho from repeating the disaster of Earth. The Way gives us . . ."

"Nonsense," Mother Elena interrupted. "The Way was not intended to serve as an ethical guideline for science or technology. It was created to help us survive here on Kensho among the Mushin.

"Besides, ethics never stopped the scientists of the 20th and 21st centuries on Earth from exploring and developing dangerous areas. They considered science to be ethically neutral. They only sought the truth. What others did with their findings was not their responsibility.

"And they were right. The science of their time was ethically free. It contained no moral prescriptions. And every attempt to impose them from outside was doomed to failure or ended in tyranny.

"It's not hard to understand why, either. Historically, philosophy and science had been united disciplines. In ancient Greece, Aristotle had developed a natural science and a philosophy, complete with ethics, based on the order he perceived in nature from actual observation. Saint Tomas Aquinas took Aristotle's hierarchical structure and blended it with Christian ideas to create a unified whole which related religion, ethics, science and social order in a way that dominated Europe for several hundred years.

"Then when Galileo and Newton broke the mold with their new views of the way the world worked, philosophy and ethics were restructured by men like Locke and Descartes. The new science, with its independent atoms of matter, interacting with each other in predictable patterns, perceived and comprehended by separate minds, gave rise to political systems like the English and American that stressed the separateness and independence of individual men.

"I'm generalizing, of course. Painting a picture in broad sweeps of the brush. But the point I'm trying to make is that philosophy and ethics always derived from the same source as science—from the way men perceived the world.

"And that's where things went wrong in the 20th century. A new view of the world gradually emerged with the ideas of Einsteinian Space-Time and Quantum Mechanics. But no corresponding philosophy was developed. Why? Because the philosophers had shut themselves away in their own little corner. And the religions had refused to face up to the changes that Newton had wrought, so they weren't about to be able to deal with Heisenberg. Instead of deriving ethical prescriptions from within the new world view, those in power tried to impose old forms from the outside. It was doomed to fail. And it did.

"The result was that science went its own way, unaffected by ethical considerations. And ruin came to all alike.

"Yolan, Yolan. We can't ignore the example of Earth in any way. It's just too final, too horrible. The Way was not meant to be imposed on science and technology in an attempt to force them to accept ethical presuppositions that are not part of their tradition. And since we cannot control them, we must reject them."

Yolan was silent for a few moments, looking down at the papers on the table between her and Mother Elena. When she raised her eyes to the older woman's, there was a sardonic glint in them. "So. The Free Council didn't destroy all the books. And it seems you've even gone so far as to study them yourselves!" She barked a sharp laugh. "There's no other way to account for the knowledge you've just displayed, the names, the history! Surely you didn't think up that little lecture on your own?"

Mother Elena nodded. "Yes, we have looked at the material. And we still have it, hidden. What we learned from our investigation just reinforces our determination to keep it hidden."

She looked at Yolan, her eyes seeking some sign of softening, some glimmer of understanding. There was none. The young woman's features remained as rigid with stubborn determination and righteousness as ever.

I've failed, she thought. I've never reached her, not once in all these years. There's a barrier between us, a gulf as great as that between Kensho and Earth. I can't change her. All I can try to do is control her.

"Well, my Daughter, you still refuse to stop? I thought so. Then I have no choice. Believe me, I wish I did. But I can't risk the danger you represent. You're free to move about the Sisterhood. The Sisters are strong enough to withstand your foolishness. But you may write nothing more and I can no longer allow you to pass through the gates. I can't allow your contamination to spread to the settlers." She rose from her cushion and turned her back to the shocked and stupefied look on the young woman's face. "Go now," she said with harsh finality. "Leave me."

XII

I just hope my act was convincing enough, Yolan thought as she turned and left Mother Elena. I've got to walk slowly, head down, as if stunned and defeated. Let them all see me that way as I go back to my cell. Then close the door and don't even come out for evening meal. That should do it.

Looking dejected, her face drawn and tired, she trudged back to her cell. As she passed the little knots of Sisters, she could hear their muted whispers. Finally she reached the rough door, opened it and stepped into the cool darkness of the tiny room built against the wall that surrounded the Sisterhood. She closed the door, barred it, and threw herself onto the narrow pallet that lay on a raised platform next to the far wall.

A sense of exaltation surged through her as she stretched out. Did the old fool really think I didn't know what she was going to do? she wondered. Confined to the 'hood! She snorted in derision. As if a herd of ken-cows couldn't escape from this place if they wanted to! The simpletons really believed that the two gates were the only ways in or out. If Mother Elena knew how many times I've left here without anyone knowing!

That thought gave her pause for a moment. Could the old woman know? No, she decided. I can read her like a book and there's no indication she's aware of anything more than the writing and the muttering. She has no idea of the scope of this thing.

But still, I've got to warn the College. This silly restriction will cut into my freedom during the day.

We should be more cautious for a while, meet only at night the way we used to.

I'll go tonight, she decided. They think I'm thunderstruck, shaken to my very core, unable to do anything. Fine. So I'll move immediately, not wait for them to have second thoughts and set someone to watching me.

Good. Tonight it is. We'll have to make some shifts in our organization, but nothing major. Best to do it right away so we'll run less risk. Also, I want to get them started on the next chant as soon as possible.

She settled back and folded her hands over her stomach, pleased with her decision. She closed her eyes, took several deep breaths, and began to quietly chant the text she would teach that night. Eventually, the murmur died away and she slept peacefully . . . .

Two moons spilled a dim light over the Plain. A bell sounded from the east gate watch and was echoed from the west gate. The twelfth hour, first of the new day. A shadow flitted briefly on the north wall of the Sisterhood and was gone. Heading north, an errant breeze caused the long grass to ripple slightly more than usual. Soon there was nothing to be seen or heard. Within the walls, everyone slumbered quietly. Even the guards at the gates dozed fitfully at their posts.

About a mile and a half north of the Sisterhood stood a settler's hut. Several more made low humps to the east and west. A dark form crept up to the door of the first and a hand came from beneath cloaking robes to knock three times, pause, then twice more, pause, then four final times. The door swung open, and the form flowed into the blackness within.

Yolan took off her cape and moved to the far end of the single room. No light was lit, but she knew her way by heart. After a few more moments, another knock was heard and another person entered. The room stayed dark.

A voice came out of the quiet to her right. "We are all gathered, Keeper."

"Is the College as one?" she chanted.

"We are as one," came several quiet voices from the darkness.

"Then know that we must Know."

"We must Know."

"To Know, we must Remember."

"We must Remember."

"To Remember, we must listen and Keep what we hear."

"We must listen. We must Keep."

"We must become Keepers of the Knowledge."

"We must become Keepers of the Knowledge."

Silence settled over them. No one stirred. Even breathing seemed to cease. Finally, Yolan clapped her hands softly, and a great sigh came from all sides.

"So," she said, "there are problems. Mother Elena has discovered the chants I was writing down to give to you for circulation among yourselves. You must learn to do without them. We'll have to go more slowly as a result, but Dark Learning is the best method in any case. Dependence on sight and reading is inferior. The only eye you need is that of Mind.

"Also, I have been temporarily confined to the Sisterhood. Which means we can't meet in the daytime any longer. Until the confinement's been lifted, we'll meet at night. Damion will work out a schedule and inform you all. One of you can leave it at the usual place for me." There were murmurs of agreement.

"Keeper," came a hesitant voice from her left. It was that of a young man, concerned about something. "Keeper," he repeated, "I have news. There are rumors I think you should know about."

Yolan muttered for him to continue.

"I heard only today that Mitsuyama is looking for more Keepers. He's scouring the areas near his territory to find some and make them join him. I . . . I know that's the area where your parents were sent and I wondered . . ." His voice trailed off in uncertainty.

"Thank you for your news." Yolan's voice was as calm as ever, but her mind was alive with speculation. Mitsuyama! Looking for Keepers! What if he discovered her parents? She didn't like the idea at all. Reluctantly, she filed it away for later consideration. There was work to be done now, Keeper's work.

"Keeper," another voice spoke up. "I have news. Mitsuyama sent the Free Council a message accepting their invitation to the special meeting at First Pass. He, all the Lords, and a group of selected retainers will attend."

Yolan grunted non-committally. She had heard whisperings to this effect in the 'hood. The only unexpected thing was the large number of men Mitsuyama intended to bring with him. The Free Council had only invited a few 'delegates' from the Council of the Lords. Why take along so many? This was another problem to be filed away now and thought on later.

"Keeper," came a third voice from the far end of the room. "I have news. There is a new story sweeping the Plain that it was the Keepers who stole Nakamura's Sword."

The young woman barely managed to suppress her curse of surprise. "Where did you hear this?" she demanded.

"A Father from the 'hood over by the Brown Hills was passing and stopped at our well for a drink. He told us. He was travelling from the east."

She nodded to herself in the dark. Andretti is up to his usual tricks: rumor and insinuation. First the stories that Mitsuyama had stolen the Sword had trickled across the Plain. But no proof had been produced, so they died out. Now this. It's typical of the tactics the President of the Free Council employs, she thought. When he doesn't know which of his enemies did something, he simply accuses them all, indirectly, using lies and innuendos. Rotten bastard! There isn't even any way we can fight back. We just don't have the communications network Andretti possesses with the 'hoods and the Faithful.

Would anyone believe such obviously idiotic tales? Possibly, she admitted. After all, very few people know very much about the Keepers, our ideals, methods, and goals. What little the general public does know is primarily the result of propaganda spread by the Free Council at the time of the Disbanding. And because the Keepers are required by circumstances to move slowly and secretly, we haven't had much opportunity to counteract the vicious lies told by our enemies.

Yes, this rumor could seriously hurt the relationship we've managed to establish with the settlers, she realized. It's still such a tentative thing, based largely on trust. Right now there's nothing to offer but long-range hopes and danger. If anything disrupts the tenuous faith they have in our good intentions . . . File it now. Consider it later.

"I thank you all for your news," she said. "Remember to collect everything you hear. Catalog each item in your mind, correlate it with the store of information you already possess. Look for links, connections, meanings that go beyond the surface. Thus is Knowledge born."

"Thus do we Know," they responded.

"Is the College ready?" Yolan asked, her voice assuming a ritual tone as she began the real business of the evening.

"We are ready."

"Tonight we'll start to work on the Newtonian conception of Time. We've already learned the chant on Newtonian Space, including the basic axioms of Euclidian geometry. Once we have Time firmly in mind, we'll tackle the concepts of Force, Matter, and Causation. Then we'll be ready to memorize and understand the chants on Newton's Mechanics."

There was a brief pause as she settled herself on her cushion, carefully arranging the folds of her gown. She cleared her throat, took several deep, calming breaths, and composed her mind. Then her voice began to roll out of the blackness, the phrases pouring through the night to wash over their minds. Every few sentences she would pause and they would repeat what she had just said.

"What is this world that we can know it?
And what are we that we can know?
There was a time when Time was twofold,
one within and one without.
Within was time that had no firmness,
each man beating out his own.
Without was time that all could share in,
absolute, unyielding guide.
Measured off in fine divisions,
hours, minutes, nanoseconds.
Flowing onward, ever forward,
constant current to the future.
Speed, location, all unheeded,
coursing sure and never varied . . ."

On and on it went for hours, the chant rising and falling, the united, murmuring replies echoing in the dark and ringing in the ears. There was a cadence, a hypnotic rhythm that insinuated itself into the mind and carried it along, impressing itself on the very fabric of the neurons. Synapses closed and opened, pathways formed and settled in. Memory was born and reinforced. And Keepers came into being . . . .

By the end of the session, Yolan was exhausted. She closed with the standard admonition to Remember and then sat silent and weary as the others slipped out, one by one, into what was left of the night. Eventually, with a brief word of thanks to the host settler, she herself crept off into the darkness.

The grass was tossing restlessly beneath a rising breeze as she walked slowly back toward the Sisterhood. A storm was coming. She looked to the west just in time to see the lone moon that still clung to the sky swallowed by a ragged line of inky clouds. It would probably break before she reached her destination. No matter. The rain would provide her better cover when she climbed the wall. Head down, picking up her pace just slightly, she ignored the approaching storm and concentrated on the thoughts that buzzed around in her mind.

They were the usual doubts that plagued her after every session with the College. Perhaps they were only the result of fatigue. Perhaps they were something more.

Is there really any hope? Or am I just one of a band of blind fanatics desperately trying to keep a dying thing alive? Is our task even possible, or are we only fooling ourselves?

After all, the science of the Home Planet had been more than a series of chants droned in dark rooms. It had been an evolving community of concepts and ideas, of problems and solutions, of men and women working toward understanding.

Here on Kensho all we have left is the language of

that community. The day-to-day reality, the experience of actually practicing science, is gone. We can't experiment or test the ideas to see if they really do explain the world as we perceive it. We can only sit idly by and intellectually appreciate the complex structure of abstract scientific theory developed by our ancestors.

But that was contrary to the very nature and purpose of the whole scientific endeavor. Abstract theory, in and of itself, simply wasn't enough to constitute a science. No formalized system, no matter how logically complete or coherent, gave any guarantee as to its own empirical applicability. Scientific theory wasn't an attempt to make 'true' or 'false' statements about the empirical world. At best, it only referred to such things obliquely and indirectly. One couldn't identify a word with an object, even an immediately sensed one, in a one-to-one relationship. Things weren't 'this' or 'that.' They were only 'suchlike.'

The real meaning of science wasn't to be found either in its own immediate logical or empirical truth. It wasn't a series of eternally 'true' or 'false' statements. Instead it was a collection of conditionally 'adequate' or 'inadequate' explanations. Scientific theory occupied the crux point between the abstract and the empirical. Its true meaning and value lay precisely in its explanatory power, in its ability to order and make sense of the world around us. Even Newtonian mechanics didn't really assert anything about the 'true nature' of the world. It simply provided a unified form for our description of the world, a form which changed again and again as better explanatory systems were developed. And a form whose value lay, at all times, in its usefulness.

But what happened when science was cut off from

the world it was meant to explain, when it was never applied to reality? Eventually, no matter how carefully tended, it would sicken and die, degenerating into a simplistic empiricism or floating off into utter abstraction and other-worldliness. She could see no alternatives. Without a chance to practice it openly, all the Knowledge gathered by the Keepers would dissipate in a stagnant, tradition-bound technology or metamorphize into mystical mumbo-jumbo, void of meaning or value.

She sighed. I can already sense it happening. These new ones, they don't really understand. They memorize, but the real meaning of what they learn is hidden from them.

Damn Andretti! And damn anyone else who suppressed knowledge for their own political or ideological advantage! It was almost enough to make you want to support Mitsuyama. But she realized that those who *supported* knowledge for their own political or ideological advantage were just as dangerous as those who *suppressed* it. In either case, knowledge came out second best, subjugated and controlled by lesser ends and personal expediencies. Was there an answer?

Close to the walls of the Sisterhood now, she focused her attention outward once more. The storm was almost on her and flashes of lightning ripped the sky with increasing frequency. The grass was whipping in the wind, hissing viciously. Bending low and hurrying along in an awkward, hunched-over position, she took what advantage she could of the swishing growth. The north wall she was approaching was blind, since the guard platforms were at the east and west gates and the wall itself wasn't patrolled. Still, she used all possible caution. It wouldn't do to be seen outlined in a lightning flash.

The rope she had left hanging was still in place. She waited as several glares lit the sky. Then, with the world dark, and the after-image partly blinding her and anyone who chanced to be watching, she swarmed up the rope and over the wall. She landed lightly in the shadow at the base of the wall. Carefully she untied the rope and coiled it. Moving swiftly from shadow to shadow, waiting for lightning to blind any watcher, she passed through the 'hood toward her cell, stopping only long enough to replace the rope in the shed she had taken it from.

With a sudden downpour, the rain arrived. In a last dash, she bolted across an open space and came to her door. She opened it quickly and ducked in, just as a huge glare lit the heavens with blue-white fire. The light flooded into her room before she could slam the door shut.

She closed it and stood leaning weakly against it, her cheek pressed to the coarse wood. Rigid with fear, she could barely breathe. For in that last flash, as she had swung the door shut, the light had bathed her room in a dim glow. And over against the wall, sitting on her bed, had been a dark shape.

XIII

A suddenly unshuttered lantern poured its yellow light into the tiny room, driving the shadows into the corners. The stern features of Mother Elena gazed angrily at the young woman leaning against the door. A small, glistening puddle of water spread over the hard-packed floor as the rain dripped from her wet cloak.

"Where have you been?" demanded the older woman harshly.

"Out."

"What were you doing?"

She did not reply.

The two glared at each other with unconcealed hostility. "I cannot tolerate disobedience of my orders," Mother Elena said.

"I cannot tolerate your orders," snapped Yolan. She had quickly recovered from her surprise at seeing the woman in her cell and now stood erect, folding her arms defiantly across her chest. Her heart was still beating wildly, but her mind was clear and cool.

"You were confined to the Sisterhood. Where have you been?"

"Out for a walk in the night air. It's healthy."

"Do you deny you left the Sisterhood?"

"Can you prove I did? The whole place is still asleep. You obviously didn't mount any search for me inside the walls. How do you know I wasn't walking over in one of the practice yards?"

"You're sopping wet."

Yolan laughed. "Step outside for a moment. Even a great Mother like you will find it hard to stay dry right now! The rain doesn't respect rank!"

Annoyed as much by the young woman's cleverness as by her insolence, Mother Elena kept her rising anger in check. "I know you left the Sisterhood. I can't prove it, no. But I know it just the same. And I suspect the reason why." Her eyes narrowed. "You are your mother's child! Infected with the evil of the Keepers! You worship the devil of Science, the Destroyer that maimed the Home World and forced the Pilgrimage! Deaf and blind to the Truth of the Way, you pollute Kensho with your vile teachings!"

She stood, her features distorted and hardened by the light of the lantern. Pointing her finger in accusation, her eyes blazing with righteous indignation, she spat the words at Yolan. "You are a blight, an infection here on the Plain! Spreading your lies and filth among the settlers! Seeking to reenact the horror of Earth on Kensho!"

In two steps, she was across the tiny room, her arm raised to strike Yolan. The young woman spun away quickly and the blow landed on the air. The Keeper laughed and sneered. "Try again, old woman! Only next time, be prepared to defend yourself!" She flung off her damp cloak and stood in the Ready Stance of the Way of the Fist.

But the older woman already had the door open. With a harsh, victorious laugh, she stepped outside and pulled the door shut, ramming home the bolt on the outside with a crash.

"This time you'll stay here until I let you out, Keeper!" yelled Mother Elena. "And that won't be until I decide what to do with you! Perhaps I'll send you on a nice, long, guarded trip back to visit Father Andretti! He'll know how to deal with scum like you!" The woman laughed triumphantly again. "I'll have a guard at this door in five minutes, so you might as well give up. You can't escape this time!"

Silent, Yolan stood at the door, her ear pressed against the wood, listening for the sounds of Mother Elena's departure. Finally, almost drowned by the noise of the downpour, she heard the squelching footsteps moving away.

Swiftly she stepped back across the room. There wasn't much time! The guards would be in no hurry to come and stand outside her door on a night like this, but they would be there, nonetheless, in no more than fifteen minutes. She opened the trunk that stood at the foot of her bed and took out a travel pack. Working with practiced speed, she emptied her clothes from the chest. Then she pried up a false bottom and revealed a long blade and three sections of rounded shaft. Laying these on the bed, she next took three wrapped packages from the hidden compartment. Dried strips of Ken-cow meat and carefully sealed packets of cheese from the same animal. From the pile of clothes she had dumped on the floor, she retrieved an undershift, an extra robe, and several pairs of socks. She stuffed them into the sack. Two pairs of sandals followed, then the packages of food. Last, a piece of greased paper folded over the top to help keep the load dry. The blade and disassembled shaft were strapped on after the sack's flap was secured.

With a jerk, she pulled the mattress from her sleeping platform. Then, straining with effort, she tugged the platform itself away from the wall. Behind it, a hole leading down and under the wall was revealed.

Looking around one last time, she moved to the door and barred it. Then she moved back to the hole and blew out the lamp. In the pitch dark, she stooped down and crawled into the hole headfirst, pushing the travel-sack ahead of her. With a sudden curse, she pulled herself back out of the hole and groped about until her hands found her cloak. She turned back again and soon wriggled out of sight.

It wasn't a long crawl. The wall wasn't more than four feet thick at its base. The escape tunnel had taken months to build, carefully dug, the dirt smuggled out of her room bit by bit. At times she had almost given up. But her mother had trained her well and one of the prime tenets of the Keepers was to always have a way of escape. Now she fervently blessed that teaching.

Reaching the end of the tunnel, she pushed hard against the planks holding the soil that concealed the exit. At first they refused to budge, but suddenly, with a mighty shove, she was sitting in the hole, covered with dirt and washed by the pouring rain. She stood, shrugged into her cloak, put the pack on her shoulders, and began to jog through the storm-whipped grass. Thank the Gods for the rain, she thought. It's almost dawn, but the clouds and the downpour make things dark as night.

For almost an hour, she ran steadily north, putting as much space between herself and the 'hood as possible. With any luck, it would be hours before they discovered she wasn't in her cell. Exaltation filled her.

As she traveled in the steady rain, however, the excitement of the escape began to wane and her spirits to sag. All her efforts with the settlers would go for nothing now. They hadn't gotten past the very first chants. With no one to lead them, they'd soon forget what they knew. But perhaps they'd at least remember her fondly and maintain a positive attitude toward the Keepers.

Finally she stopped beneath the shelter of a few scrawny trees that stood in grand isolation in the midst of the Plain. Exhausted, she slumped to the ground.

I'm away, she thought. But now what? Do I go someplace new and try to start again? For long minutes, she pondered her next move. Unable to reach a decision, she finally fell into a fitful slumber.

She woke with a start to find the sun fighting its way free of the last, high-flung, tattered remnants of the storm. Carefully and slowly she stood, hugging close to the tree she had rested against, and cautiously surveyed the Plain. The only motion was that of the waving grass.

Satisfied no one was nearby, she stretched and moved her body to work out the stiffness and soreness in her muscles. Then she squatted next to her sack and took out one of the packets of ken-cow cheese. Unwrapping it, she picked out a large chunk of the firm, brownish stuff and sat back, chewing and swallowing it with great appreciation. Nothing like a long run through a stormy night, followed by sleeping on the damp ground hunched up against a sopping, dripping tree to whet the old appetite, she thought. From a small cavity formed between the trunk of one of the trees and a large branch, she sipped a little fresh rainwater to complete her breakfast.

After repacking the food into her sack, she once again surveyed the Plain carefully in all directions. Far off to the northwest was a thin line of smoke that undoubtedly came from a settler's hut hidden just below the horizon. Best avoid that, she advised herself. No sense in letting anyone see me for a couple of days. This is still too close to the Sisterhood.

The only real question was still where to go. Reluctantly, she admitted that her options were rather limited. Running them over in her mind, she sud-

denly remembered the news one of the members of
the College had given last night. Mitsuyama was
hunting for Keepers in the area where her parents
had been sent. Her concern over what would happen
should the PlainsLord find them flared up again.

She made a decision. Perhaps not the best one, but
certainly the most human. She would go and warn her
parents. They were isolated, on purpose, and might
not have heard the news. They were in danger and
must be made aware of it. Besides, they might have
some idea as to what she should do next.

Her destination chosen, she immediately picked
up her travel-sack, shrugged into it, and began to
walk across the Plain, heading directly away from the
morning sun. After she had passed the settler's hut off
in the distance to her right, she turned northwest and
broke into a gentle trot. It was a journey of several
days and she wasn't completely sure of their exact
location. She estimated a trip of some five days to a
week, barring unforseen problems.

The unforseen problem arose on the morning of the
second day. She was moving along at her usual pace
when suddenly she felt an overwhelming premonition of danger. Stopping, she scanned the Plain in all
directions, right out to the horizon. Nothing.

Shaking her head, she moved on again, but at a fast
walk instead of a trot, and with all her senses fully
alive.

Nevertheless, she almost stumbled over the body
before she saw it. It was a man, a settler from his
dress, hacked nearly in two. In his hands he clutched
the broken shaft of a bladed staff. Then, ahead, she
noticed a slight depression in the grass. Warily, she
approached, poised for instant flight.

It was further than she thought, and when she got

there, the depression turned out to be a clearing. In the middle was a partly built hut, not even waist high yet. In it, were a woman and a child, both dead.

Controlling her nausea, she checked the bodies carefully. Cold, but not completely stiff. They had died no more than ten hours ago. Possibly the previous evening.

Finished with the two bodies in the hut, she began to circle the area, looking for more. She finally found one, not too far north and west of the settler. It was the corpse of a man, unshaven and filthy, the blade of a bladed staff protruding from his chest, his face twisted in a hideous rictus of death. A Ronin.

A shadow crossed her and she looked up with a start. A lone carrion lizard was circling in the sky. Others would soon join it, she knew. Best leave before their presence brought someone to investigate.

What had happened was obvious. The family had been building a new farm in a less settled area of the Plain. But they had not built swiftly enough. Ronin had found them.

She shuddered at the very name. Ronin. The insane killers who actually sought out the Madness the Mushin brought to heighten the ghastly thrill they felt while slaying. Once they had dominated the Home Vally, murdering as they chose. The Mushin had used them to control the human population and to provide orgies of emotion at the expense of the dying. The Mushin fed on emotive energy, and madness and death were two of their favorite sources.

Jerome had ended all that. He had invented the bladed staff, organized the Faithful, and crushed the Ronin in their camps at the Passes that led out of the Home Valley. At one stroke, he freed the Home Valley from the dreaded killers and opened the way to expand onto the Plain.

But not all of the Ronin died. A few escaped out
onto the Plain itself. They took their Mushin with
them and thus some of the mind leeches managed to
avoid the virtual captivity Jerome engineered for the
rest with the establishment of the Great Way in the
Home Valley. The Ronin and their Mushin now
roamed the Plain, far fewer in number than before,
but still quite fatal to the isolated settlers they surprised. Going back to the settler's body, she looked
down at him with great sadness. At least he got one of
them, she thought. But she couldn't hold back a few
tears as she remembered the child.

Roughly, repressing her emotions, she grabbed the
corpse by the heels and began to drag it slowly back to
the clearing and the partly finished hut. Panting with
exertion, she pulled the man into position next to his
wife and child.

Unable to contain herself, and not really caring any
longer, her tears flowed freely as she gently
straightened their clothing and arranged each body in
as restful a pose as possible. Finally she tumbled the
half-walls in over the family, making a burial mound
to cover them. The dirt mingled with her tears, and
her face was a streaked, muddy mess by the time she
was done.

She stepped back, surveyed her work, and then
carefully took in the whole horizon again. By now
there were several carrion lizards floating in the sky.
Feed on the Ronin, she thought at them. He's your
kind.

With one last look, she began to walk away. I
haven't the slightest idea which direction the Ronin
took, she realized, so I might as well keep going the
way I planned. The odds are pretty good I won't run
into them.

The odds changed early that afternoon.

For several hours a low range of stark, eroded hills had been humping up on the horizon. They were several miles long and lay directly across her path. To go around them would be a waste of time and energy, so she decided to go through.

As she approached the hills, a sense of unease began to grow in her mind. It was nothing sharp and distinct, just a vague sense that something was wrong. She slowed her pace and scanned the bare hillsides ahead. Nothing. Cautiously she proceeded, her head constantly moving, noting and evaluating every tiny motion with her eyes, every whisper of sound with her ears.

The grass between the hills was shorter, stunted and lighter in color. The wind died down, cut off by the masses surrounding her. For the first time in many days, she walked in relative silence, empty of the hiss of the swaying grass and the constant breeze. Rather than being relaxing, this increased her tension.

The hills rose higher and steeper, gullied and blasted into harsh forms by the weather. Feeling naked and exposed in open places, she chose narrow ways, pressing as close as possible to the reassuring bulk of blank walls.

She entered a narrow defile, literally tiptoeing. As she moved down it, it twisted at a sharp angle to the right. For a moment, she paused before making the turn, her head cocked, listening and trying to foresee what lay around the bend. Finally, angry at herself for her hesitation, she stepped boldly out and around the corner.

The man who was coming quietly in the opposite direction almost crashed into her, his eyes wide with startlement, his mouth a round O of surprise. One glance told her she had found the Ronin. Without even pausing for thought, she lashed out with her foot, smashing the man in the groin. A quick step brought her close enough to jab her rigid hand into his throat. As he crumpled, she brought both hands down in a great arc on the back of his neck. The snap she heard as he hit the ground was immensely satisfying.

A blood-curdling scream brought her head up in a jerk. Some hundred feet further down, the defile twisted again, this time to the left. Another Ronin had just stepped around the corner. The man clawed for his sword and began to run at her.

Instantly, she spun on her heel and fled. Her heart was pounding massively in her chest but her mind stayed cool.

Find a place to make a stand, she told herself. There's no escaping. Run just far enough to find a place to fight on your own terms. And then kill as many as you can before they kill you.

BOOK V

CONTRARIA SUNT
COMPLEMENTA

XIV

Father Andretti stood at the window watching the purple light of late afternoon slide through the Brotherhood. The complex shadowings of the Ko tree were splashed haphazardly across the central courtyard and were beginning to creep up the walls of the buildings that stood on its eastern edge.

There was a soft knock on the door behind him. As he turned back toward the cool shadows of the room, his eyes fell on several sheets of paper covered with a crabbed scrawl. Graceless, he thought, crude and hurried, filled with vicious slashes and savage points instead of flowing lines and full circles. It wasn't bold, merely cruel . . . and sloppy. A mirror of the man's soul, a reflection of his true character.

The knock sounded again. Andretti folded himself down into a sitting position on his cushion and picked the report from the table. "Come in, Burke," he called quietly. The door opened a crack. The spy's sharp face peered uncertainly into the room. A quick sweep of suspicious eyes and the crack widened and disappeared as the man stepped into the room.

He bobbed his head nervously toward the seated President of the Free Council. "You wanted me, Father?" His eyes were fastened on the papers held in Andretti's hand as if fascinated by their existence.

"Sit, Burke." Burke sat. "This report of yours bothers me. There's too much said about some things and nowhere near enough about others. Like this," he continued, looking down at the page. "You say, 'Mitsuyama intends to bring the Lords and a retinue of servants as well.' Interesting, but hardly sufficient. How many Lords? Which ones? Are they all securely his? And the servants. How large is the retinue? Are they really servants, or some of his Avengers dressed up as servants?

"And why bring so many? If I remember correctly, only a few delegates from the Council of the Plains-Lords were invited. What's behind his move?"

He slapped the papers down on the table top. "What good is a spy who tells me nothing I haven't already heard? Mitusyama himself told us he was bringing Lords and a retinue. I don't need you to repeat what's obvious! Now I hope you've got something significant to report orally."

Burke nodded. Oh, yes, he thought, I've something more important to report orally. I always save the best so you'll never forget how useful Burke is. Yes, my fine President of the Free Council, I know you and how to play you as I play all the others. They think Burke is just a stupid spy, a little man who counts for nothing, a mere Group Leader in the Faithful.

He looked slyly up at Andretti. "Aye, I've more to tell. No sense in putting things like this on paper; the wrong parties might read 'em. No sense at all.

"What Mitsuyama's bringing to First Pass is nothing less than his army. Oh, not all of it. But as much as he can stuff in his retinue and that of the other Lords. Plus, I've heard tell he's bringing more to follow behind and on the flanks. They'll be a reserve, so to speak, ready for use as required."

"How many?" asked Andretti, his eyes narrowed.

"A good hundred Avengers all told. Maybe a hundred and fifty."

"All armed?"

"All armed, though the swords'll be hidden in baggage and beneath robes."

Andretti stood and began to pace the floor. "Then

he means to contest the appointment if the special Council ratifies it."

"Aye, with cold steel."

"Curse that man! He'll push us into a bloody war!" For several moments he paced about, muttering softly to himself. Finally he stopped and stood over Burke, a determined look on his face.

"The Faithful. Can we count on them?"

"Sorry to say, but they're a mixed bag, Father. Some of 'em we can count on. Some we can't. If we could only find the Sword and prove the Plains Lords took it . . ."

Andretti waved his hand in dismissal. "That doesn't seem very likely. Of course there's always a chance the Seekers will turn up something, but so far they haven't done any better than you did. I find it hard to believe that Mitsuyama would just leave the Sword laying around somewhere for some young Seeker to stumble over.

"No, we have to plan for the worst. We've got to be sure we have a sufficient number of men at the special meeting to neutralize anything Mitsuyama might do. And that means loyal men."

"Loyal and armed?"

The older man nodded.

Burke felt a sense of excitement rising. Control your feelings, he cautioned himself. Don't let on how good it's all working out. He cleared his throat. "Aye, loyal and armed it is. That means the Faithful."

"The Faithful, backed by a selected group from the 'hoods. And perhaps some of the Seekers. But the Faithful will have to be the bulk of our support, Burke. Can you see to it that only those totally loyal to the Free Council are picked as delegates? And that they come armed, with their bladed staffs hidden somehow?"

The spy's eyes darted up to look at Andretti's face,
then down again at his own hands, twisting together
nervously. "Aye, I can do that. I'll pick the men
myself, Father. I know those to trust, those who can
take orders and aren't afraid of standing up to the
Avengers. I'll pick 'em and lead 'em myself. I'll take
care of the whole thing. Leave it all to me."

"Good. Do it. Give me all the details when you've
worked out a plan. We'll coordinate your group with
Brothers and Fathers I organize." He rubbed his
hands together. "Lord William Mitsuyama may be in
for a surprise. A very nasty surprise."

Aye, thought Burke. And he may not be the only
one! With a jerky bow, he stood and left the room.

Mitsuyama strode angrily back and forth. Jimson
stood with his arms crossed over his chest, a grim
smile resting lightly on his lips. The soldier who had
been giving the report was still kneeling in the middle
of the room. Every time the PlainsLord came near
him he cringed.

The room itself was small and plain, a windowless
antechamber to Mitsuyama's more extensive quarters
that he used primarily as an office for transacting
business when the Council wasn't in session.

"Damn!" his voice crackled with suppressed rage.
He stopped next to the soldier, towering above him,
glaring down at the man. The soldier hung his head,
unable to meet his Lord's fury.

"So, the young Seeker tricked Villaverde. And we
still don't know a damn thing about his abilities."

"We know he's clever," commented Jimson drily.

Mitsuyama snorted, his anger slowly cooling down.
"But how good a swordsman is he?

"What did that stupid bastard Villaverde do? Did
he just stay on the island? Or did he follow Edwyr?"

"I . . . I . . . don't know. You said to come back and report as soon as the fight was over. When . . . I saw the Seeker coming back . . . alone . . . in the boat, I . . . I just came back. Lord, I—"

"Did Villaverde see you?" interrupted Jimson.

"Yes, sir. When the ferry landed he—"

"Then he won't have followed the Seeker!" The renegade laughed harshly. "By now he's probably half way to First Touch and gaining speed!"

"If he isn't, he'll wish he was!" growled Mitsuyama. He looked down at the quivering soldier. "All right, Durpee, get the hell out of here. You're a lousy spy, but you did your job within the narrow limits of your mediocre intelligence. Because you succeeded in bringing back some information you get double pay this week. But because you failed to get all you could have you'll draw double duty next week. Get out."

When the man had left, bowing and murmuring obsequiously, the PlainsLord returned to his cushion and sat. He glanced at Jimson and motioned him to sit as well. "Well, what's your analysis, renegade?"

Jimson gazed at the floor for a moment before answering. "I think the Seeker's harmless. He won't find the Sword, even if he comes right here to the fortress. I don't think we should waste any more men testing him. Let him come to us. Once here, he'll be at our mercy."

"But what about the Avengers? What if he should find out about them and report back to Andretti?"

"We've got enough men on patrol to make that unlikely. I doubt he'll slip through the net, especially since he doesn't know it's there. No, let him come. Once he's here, we can question him, see if he knows anything of interest, and then dispose of him as you see fit, Lord."

"Question him, Jimson? And if he doesn't want to

talk? I've heard the Seekers are very quiet types when not around their own."

"Then torture him, Lord. Let me handle it. I know the Seekers. I can make him talk. He could be a goldmine of information. After all, the spy said he was the leader of the Seekers. He might know a good deal about Andretti's plans."

Mitsuyama nodded, his eyes looking abstractedly off into space, his expression one of vague musing. "Yes," he replied softly. "I'll think about it. Perhaps you're right, renegade.

"Now, are the men ready? Have they learned their roles? The Meeting is less than two months off."

The ex-Seeker shifted his weight uncomfortably. "Well, they're coming along. We've worked out the drill on getting to the weapons concealed in the baggage. But there are problems with those concealed beneath the robes. The best place to hide swords is across the back. But they're hard to get at unless one takes off his robe. It's awkward."

"Then have the men fight without their robes! Fix the robes so they split easily along the back seam or something. Then they can rip them off each other quickly.

"Look, renegade, I don't care how you manage it. Just do it and make it work. I want those men to respond instantly. One minute they're to be unarmed retainers, scattered haphazardly about. The next, they must be armed Avengers, in battle formation and ready to attack. There must be no delay.

"Now, the reserves. Have they learned the marching orders I gave you?"

"Yes, Lord. Unit One under Flamma will be on right flank. When we come within two hours of First Pass, they'll stop and wait, then advance at first light, single file, to enter the pass and hug the right side.

Unit Two under Drummond will do the same on the left flank. Choi's Unit Three will stay in reserve at the western mouth of the pass. We can fall back through them, if necessary."

"But they'll be mounted on Striders if I need them to break any defense Andretti might set up?"

"They'll be ready, Lord. Ready and eager."

"Good, good. Jimson, we'll do a dry run in one week. Anyone who fails in his part will be immediately executed in front of the Avengers. Anyone. Let them all know how serious I am."

"Yes, Lord."

"Now leave."

Jimson stood, bowed low, then turned and swiftly left the room.

Andretti stood looking at the door for several minutes after Burke had left. There was something about the little man's behavior that disturbed him. He couldn't quite put his finger on it so he pushed it out of his mind, promising himself to return to it at a more opportune moment. Right now he had something more important to consider.

What were Mitsuyama's actual intentions? The man was so devious, nothing he did could be taken at face value. All the possible combinations and permutations had to be thought out. The PlainsLord delighted in intricate schemes filled with false leads, diversions, feints, and ploys. No action ever had a simple, straight-forward purpose. There were always wheels within wheels.

Yet, twist his information as he might, Andretti could only come up with one plausible answer: Mitsuyama intended a real showdown. He can't accept my appointment by the Council as Way-Farer. He's run out of maneuvering space; he has to act. He'll do everything he can to stop ratification at the meeting, but when that fails, he'll resort to the sword. Monstrous! The man's willing to plunge Kensho into a war to force his will on the Free Council!

A sharp sense of sadness and loss almost overwhelmed him. How tragic to think that a mere three generations after Jerome had revealed the Way and freed men from the Mushin, we're already at each other's throats, ready to kill. Even now, after so much hard work, suffering, and death, it would take so little to undo all the progress we've made in realizing Nakamura's dream.

All the more reason I must not fail, he told himself with fervent determination. I must not, *will not*, yield to Mitsuyama! For the sake of the entire human race, I must be victorious!

Strange, he mused, that it should be me, here, at this exact moment in history. I've dedicated my entire life to the Great Way, hoping that someday I might make a contribution to it, no matter how insignificant. Because I *believe* in the Way, *believe* that it's the most important thing on Kensho, both for mankind's present and for our future. Any interference with it, or with the institutions that guard and perpetuate it, is tantamount to treason to the human race!

Nevertheless, Andretti realized that despite his belief and his untiring efforts, he had always been a failure at the one thing which counted most. He had never experienced Satori. Without it, he knew he could never repeat Jerome's direct, intuitive understanding of the meaning of the Great Way. Knowledge, according to Jerome, had to be firmly rooted in the personal experience of Satori. Of course, once this subjective realization had been achieved, it had to be recaptured in the light of reason so that an objectively confirmed understanding could be attained. But the first step, the crucial one, had to be taken in Satori. Abstract, intellectual understanding was not enough. Yet that was all the President of the Free Council seemed to be capable of.

For a long while he had despaired of ever accomplishing anything meaningful for the Way. How could he hope to extend or improve it if he didn't even understand it? Ashamed and disturbed by his inability in this respect, yet never flagging in his faith and determination, he had worked all the harder to excel in other ways. Sensing his eagerness to take on tasks considered onerous by most, the Way-Farer and the other Fathers had added to his responsibilities until Andretti had had to abandon his futile attempts at enlightenment for lack of time. In this manner he had slowly but surely risen up through the institutional hierarchy of the Great Way until now he stood at its top.

And now he was suddenly the right man in the right place at the right time. At long last, he was in a position to do something significant for the Way. Something no one else was capable of doing. Even Johnston, for all his enlightenment, had never grasped the danger represented by Mitsuyama. Only he, Father Andretti, had seen it clearly and known what must be done. If he succeeded in his efforts, he would go down in history second only to Jerome himself. Jerome had been the founder of the Great Way. Andretti would be its preserver.

What was this Great Way he was dedicated to saving? Its teachings had been repeated to him so often that every word was as much a part of him as his own name. His knowledge of it, even though it might be intellectual instead of intuitive, was nevertheless quite extensive.

The Great Way was Jerome's solution to the problem of the Mushin. It was the answer he had found after spending many years searching for the way to freedom hinted at in Nakamura's Koan. This cryptic message, handed down from the original leader of the Pilgrimage to Kensho, said that a man could be free of the mind leeches if he followed the way that led to "the place where he dwelt before he was born."

The core of the Great Way was Jerome's discovery that human susceptibility to the Mushin was caused by the view individuals held of their relationship with the world around them. Most men perceived the world as being filled with solid, enduring, independent, material bodies. Consciousness of this world and of the things in it was the result of an interaction between the senses and mind of the individual and the objects of which the world was composed. From the very start, then, a person's worldview was the result of his "Being-in-the-world."

Since the world was a very real place, the individual's success, even his survival, depended on the accuracy and usefulness of the image his consciousness formed of it. His continued "Being-in-the-world" was determined by his ability to discriminate between Self and Other and to distinguish which forms of Other were beneficial to Self and which harmful. The natural end-result of this process was the creation of a separate, persistent, egocentric 'I.' The rest of the world became mere 'equipment' to be used to support this 'I.'

'Equipment,' however, often resisted being used. It regularly refused to cooperate or sacrifice itself to satisfy the 'I.' This quickly led to the universe being perceived as a hostile place, full of conflict and opposed to the wishes and wants of the Self. When consciousness saw the world in this way, it inevitably and necessarily limited perception to a narrow focus, concentrating on those things, or aspects of things, relevant to successful "Being-in-the-world." Everything else tended to be ignored. Men clung frantically and blindly to those things which fulfilled their needs, whether object, person, or idea. They eagerly killed each other over a worthless bauble, entire races were wiped out to prove a point.

It was precisely this kind of involvement with the objects of the world that gave the Mushin their opening. Desire for the 'equipment' necessary to satisfy the Self was endless and could never be permanently fulfilled. Inevitably, it led to frustration. Frustration, in turn, was attended by a whole gamut of emotions which constantly simmered within the mind and made it a perfect source of emotive energy for the invisible mind leeches to feed on. The creatures took the emotions they found, intensified them by cycling them back through the mind in a spiraling feedback loop, and then feasted when the over-burdened mind exploded in a frenzy of Madness.

The history of the Home World was filled with examples of religious, philosophical, social, and political systems that had attempted to overcome or resolve this conflict between the 'I' and the world. Most of them had failed, even without the presence of the Mushin to aggravate the situation. A few had been more successful. Unaware of their teaching, or even of their existences, Jerome's search had nevertheless paralleled several of these systems. Eventually, experiencing what the ancients had called 'Enlightenment' or 'Satori,' he found the answer he was looking for.

In Satori, the whole ego-centric perceptual structure of the 'I' was suspended. Sensing became immediate and direct. Things were known in and of themselves. The Thing-in-itself emerged and was experienced totally as-it-is at the instant of perception. In its immediacy, it was necessarily complete and self-contained, without connection, continuity, or meaning beyond the moment of its sensed existence. It was in, of, and for itself alone.

In Satori, the world could no longer be viewed as 'equipment', for the Thing-in-itself, being utterly in itself, could not be perceived in terms of any relationship with the 'I.' Even opposites disappeared from the universe, since opposition implied connectedness.

Without 'equipment' or opposition, there was nothing for the 'I' to define itself against. It dissolved. And consciousness, source and servant of the 'I,' vanished along with it.

The pure perception of Satori failed utterly to discover anything, including the sensing Self, that transcended the moment and was enduring. The 'equipment' of ordinary perception was reduced to the Thing-in-itself of direct sensing. Consciousness, and the 'I' that had developed in response to the needs of Being-in-the-world, disappeared as the universe of opposition it had created melted away in disconnectedness. All that remained was the perception and the perceived, joined and inseparable.

But the disintegration of everyday reality did not stop there. The deeper Jerome went into Satori, the more profound it became. The pure perception of Satori was a momentary, fleeting thing, existing only at the Here-Now instant of sensing. It implied nothing beyond itself. The same disconnectedness it discovered between the Thing-in-itself and the rest of the world, applied equally to the moment by moment perception of the Thing-in-itself. For example, the fact that a thing was sensed as red, round, and firm at this instant in no way necessitated or even implied that it would be red, round, and firm at the next instant. Such a conclusion simply went beyond the competency of pure perception. And if the sensed object was somehow removed for the moment, so that it was no longer perceived, it no longer existed in any manner that could be determined by the senses alone.

Furthermore, the senses were, by their very nature, fragmentary, partial, and limited. They were incapable of perceiving a thing in its entirety. Ordinarily, consciousness, functioning as Being-in-the-world, organized the disjointed pieces into a picture of the whole. Over time, with repeated sensings, this picture could be corrected, added to, and improved upon until a workable semblance of the actual object had been constructed. But there was no consciousness, nor any "over time," in Satori. So the fragments remained isolated and no whole could be discerned.

The result was that without consciousness to construct a coherent, enduring perceptual framework, reality utterly collapsed. Even the Thing-in-itself fell apart into what could only be called No-thing. And the universe was transformed into a place of flowing and motion, of restless becoming and ceaseless change, where permanence was a mere deception, a trick played by a prankster who no longer existed.

In the face of this experience, the absurdity and futility of clinging to the things of the world was clearly revealed. Jerome realized that he had found the place of freedom hinted at in Nakamura's Koan. The "place where he dwelt before he was born" simply meant that a man had to put his mind back in its original condition. Before he was born, before his mind experienced Being-in-the-world, before his consciousness created the 'I,' there were no preconceived perceptual frameworks. No world of opposition existed and there were no entanglements with 'equipment.' A mind in this condition was No-mind. It left no opening for the Mushin since it clung to nothing and never experienced frustration. Here, at last, men could find refuge from their enemies and the Madness they brought.

Yet Jerome recognized that there was great danger here as well. The very message which freed men from the Mushin could, if carried to its logical conclusion, set them adrift in a meaningless void of despair. For if the world view derived from the experience of Being-in-the-world was nothing but a delusion, if there was no true persistence in everyday reality, if even the Self was merely a trick played by consciousness—where then was Purpose in the Universe? How could one act in such a world? And why? What possible value could there be in struggle, even against the Mushin, if everything was ultimately Nothing, if Entropy and Meaning were one?

When the answer came, it brought Jerome full circle back to his starting point in the everyday world.

He noticed that the transient, differentiated sense data he experienced in Satori appeared to be embedded in some sort of background. They rose from, and fell back into, an undifferentiated continuum which couldn't be seen by the eye, heard by the ear, felt by the hand, tasted by the tongue, or smelled by the nose.

This continuum was unsensed and unsensible. It could never be defined or described in terms of what-it-is, because it could only be approached in terms of what-it-isn't. Empty, it was full of creative potential, brimming with an endless variety of possibilities that were realized, sustained, and then reabsorbed. It was the undifferentiated source of all differentiations, the Unity that gave birth to all opposites and finally resolved them once more in Unity. Through it, all things were related to all things, each having the same source as the other, and all being determined by their mutual relationship and involvement. In it, everything was reduced to the same level, no one thing more fundamental than the next, since all had the identical origin. Even the continuum itself was not fundamental. It was simply all possible things, simultaneously existing in both their differentiated and undifferentiated states. Jerome called it the Ultimate Void.

Yet this Ultimate Void was not mere random fecundity. No matter how chaotic it might appear at first knowing, certain forms undoubtedly repeated themselves with relative frequency. Otherwise, the mind would simply be unable to create a useful perceptual framework and it would be literally impossible to put one foot down in front of the other with any certainty of being able to walk. But the fact was that Being-in-the-world was possible; consciousness could construct a livable, relatively coherent world to live in.

Even acknowledging the limitations of the senses through which the mind received the information it used to create its world view didn't make any real difference. It only meant that the patterns discerned were limited and subject to change, a qualification which was completely understandable given the infinite character of the Void.

Nor was there any suggestion here that the world was merely Mind-stuff or illusion. However fallible, limited, subject to delusion and downright inaccuracy the objects created by the perceptual structures of consciousness might be, they were nonetheless real. The sword cut, and that was that. In no way total, in no sense determinate of any "truth," the word-view of Being-in-the-world could only be judged on the ground of whether its approximations were adequate or inadequate as a basis for successful action. The final, acid test always lay in experience.

When Jerome had begun his journey to understanding, mountains had been mountains, trees had been trees, and streams had been streams. Then, as he had passed beyond the everyday world and gazed upon the No-thingness Satori revealed, everything had lost its shape. Mountains were no longer mountains, the trees no longer trees, and the streams something other than streams. Finally, by way of the Ultimate Void, he returned to the beginning. The mountains were once again mountains, trees were trees, and streams were streams. Everything was the same, but utterly different.

This was the final meaning of Nakamura's Koan. At last Jerome had truly found the place where he had dwelt before he was born. Aware of both the reality and the nothingness of the world around him, immersed and one with the Void even while separate, he was as unfettered by the delusions and attachments of everyday life as he had been before his eyes opened for the first time. He could once again act in the everyday world without hesitation and without fear of the Mushin.

And through his actions, Purpose re-entered the Universe as a human value rather than a transcendent one. Struggle, especially to free the mind from the Mushin, gained meaning because it was the mind that created meaning. Human awareness, no matter how partial or imperfect, reflected, contained, and involved every other possibility in the Ultimate Void. In turn, it was equally reflected, contained, and involved in them. Without consciousness, the Void itself could not exist. It was infinite and must contain every potentiality, including consciousness before it could be itself. Meaning and Entropy were not one, though both came from the One and eventually returned there. Mankind, for all its fallibility, was an anti-entropic element in the Universe, and the creation of Purpose and Meaning were at least part of its function.

Developing a mind capable of action-without-attachment in the day-to-day world was the central purpose of the Great Way. Jerome's hope, corroborated by the computer on the Flagship, was that eventually, through the pressures of natural selection caused by the Mushin, the mental attitude developed by the Way would become natural and hereditary among the human population on Kensho. But the computer had also estimated that it would take at least ten to twelve generations, some three to four hundred years, before such a transformation would be widespread!

Jerome was unwilling to accept the death and suffering such a prospect entailed. He decided to short-circuit the process by introducing the Great Way. Teaching as many as could learn, he had turned the 'hoods from places where the Mushin kept men and women in docile captivity as emotional cattle, into traps which tied the invisible creatures to their food source. This freed the rest of humanity to expand beyond the limits of the Home Valley, to grow and live their lives without fear of the Mushin and the Madness.

This is what I'm defending against Mitsuyama, Andretti told himself. Nothing less than the happiness, sanity, life, and future of every man, woman, and child on Kensho!

And yet . . . and yet . . . the doubt echoed through

his mind. I do not, can not, share in it fully. Jerome had often said, when people had asked him to tell them of the Way, that he could only ask them to walk it with him. He told them there was nothing he could say, no words that could equal the experience. Unless they actually walked it themselves, they were like would-be travellers who, instead of making the trip, stay at home and read guidebooks.

I stay at home. I stay and hold the gate against the barbarian that others may travel. That is my destiny.

But someday, he vowed, I will lay aside my burden and sit until I achieve Satori and stand where Jerome stood, firmly and completely on the Way. Someday, he repeated the pledge. Perhaps when Mitsuyama has been crushed and the Way is forever free from danger.

Let it be soon, a tiny voice cried from the depths of his soul. Let it be soon. For I am old and weary and sense the approach of night.

Mitsuyama waited a few moments after the door closed behind Jimson, then turned halfway on his cushion toward the inner door that led to his rooms. "What do you think?" he asked softly.

A woman entered with a fluid movement and knelt in front of him. Her hair was loose, long, and blue-black. There was great strength in her face and the curve of her jaw. Her full lips were set in a firm line which made them seem decisive rather than sensuous. Her eyes were large and liquid brown, but a hardness glinted in their depths that matched the rest of her demeanor. Dressed in a robe as plain as her Lord's, Miriam Mitsuyama, wife of the Supreme Lord of the Plains, was not a woman to be underestimated. She wore a dagger in plain sight at her waist.

"Where will Jimson be at the Pass, Lord?"

"Commanding the Bodyguard, as usual."

"I would advise you to see he meets with an accident before then, William. I wouldn't trust a man like that behind me at the moment of victory."

"But he's still useful."

"Then use him up quickly."

"Hmmmmmm. Perhaps something could be arranged on the march itself."

She bowed. "Shall I see to it? Perhaps something in his food?"

He nodded. "Yes. If I don't find a better way before then. I have a feeling he may find his own end, though. I sense his fate approaching across the Plain."

"The Seeker?"

"Somehow the two are joined. The Renegade and the Faithful. Perhaps they were meant to cancel each other out. It makes a neat equation."

"Sureness is better than neatness."

"We have time for both."

They were silent for a moment. Then Miriam spoke. "This Seeker is an unknown. I don't like it. Jimson is too casual about him."

"The lad is clever, no doubt about it. His trick with Villaverde was perfect. He foiled our attempt to feel him out with an ease that makes one pause. I couldn't have done better myself. I admit I'm curious about him. It would be interesting to do as Jimson suggests and let the lad come here."

"No. I think he must die. As soon as possible. He makes me very uneasy, William."

"Feminine intuition?" he laughed softly.

"Call it what you will," she replied with stony calm, "but I'm seldom wrong, Lord."

"What do you suggest?"

"No more half-measures. Send out some men. With orders to kill on sight."

"Isn't that rather extreme?"

Suddenly she smiled and her whole face was transformed with a sensual beauty that took the breath away with its very unexpectedness. "William, give me this one thing. I only want it for your sake."

Fascinated as always by her rapid changes of character, he nodded and stood. "Yes. You'll have what you want. And now I'll have what I want."

"What we both want," she whispered as she moved to him.

Physically shaking himself out of his black mood, Andretti forced his mind back to practical matters. It's time, he decided, to tally and order my forces for the confrontation at First Pass. I can count on support from the 'hoods. But I must see to it that those chosen as delegates to the meeting are Masters of one of the Ways, men and women capable of holding their own against Mitsuyama's Avengers. Masters of the Way of the Staff might be best because they can carry their weapon with them without arousing suspicion. And the staff can be a formidable weapon, even against the sword.

He estimated it would be impractical to arm and organize the settlers or 'steaders. Many knew how to handle the bladed staff, but there was no way to set up a central command system to train them to work as a unit. He was making sure that as many as possible were sympathetic to the Free Council's position by having the delegate selection take place in the 'hoods. Well, he concluded, they won't do as soldiers, but at least they'll count in terms of numbers on our side.

What about the Seekers? he asked himself. They were swordsmen to be reckoned with! He had no doubt that one of them was equal to ten of Mitsuyama's half-trained Avengers. There weren't very many of them, and the best of the lot were presently spread out all over the place looking for Nakamura's Sword. But they were all due to return at least a week or so before the meeting. They'd be a tremendous addition to his power.

But would they be willing to support him? A nagging doubt crept into his thoughts. Would they accept him as Way-Farer?

The Seekers had been completely loyal to Johnston. The old Way-Farer had once been a Seeker himself. He had walked the Way of the Sword, that dangerous, narrow path created by Jerome for those few able to follow it. Andretti had always felt it was somewhat superfluous and irrelevant and couldn't imagine why Jerome had developed it in addition to the Great Way.

In any case, Andretti admitted, I'm no Johnston. I've never studied the Sword. I can't hope to command the respect and devotion the Seekers showed the old man. It's foolish to expect them to accept *me* as competent to lead *them* in the Way. They'll probably view my appointment to the Way-Farership as a formal, political thing, even if it's ratified by the Special Council.

Well, if they won't be followers, he wondered, will they be allies? After all, they're as interested in the survival of the Way as I am. And they're already siding by searching for the Sword of Nakamura, so they must be somewhat favorably inclined to the Free Council. Or at least that was the case with the twenty ex-companions of the Way-Farer led by Edwyr.

A new idea struck him. Did the twenty represent the rest of the Seekers? Just who or what were those twenty young swordsmen, anyway?

He thought back to the time, some five years ago, just after Mitsuyama had succeeded his father, when he had first noticed them. They had simply begun showing up at the Brotherhood, one by one. The Way-Farer seemed to be expecting each, almost as if he had invited them. Soon, new ones stopped arriving. The group became a cohesive, isolated unit generally ignoring the rest of the 'hood. Johnston began to spend almost every waking hour with them.

Why? he asked himself for the first time. Why had the Way-Farer gathered this group together? What could they offer the old man that the regular Brothers and Fathers at the 'hood could not? They hadn't been a bodyguard. That was ridiculous. Nobody would have harmed Johnston. And besides, they went unarmed in his presence. No, they were more like students or disciples, sitting and listening to the old man talk for hours, or quietly meditating with him beneath the great Ko tree. But that was nothing different from what the ordinary Brothers and Fathers had done before the Seekers arrived.

Then what made the twenty trained warriors so important to the Way-Farer? Johnston might not have been my idea of an effective leader for the Great Way, he admitted, but the man was no fool. He must have had a reason for doing what he did. What could this group of swordsmen be for?

He shook his head with sudden weariness. There are still so many unknowns! Well, at least there's no harm in trying to get their support when they return. In the meanwhile, I can probe the other Seekers and Masters of the Sword who stayed behind at the various 'hoods in the Home Valley to see how they feel.

Andretti sat down on the cushion behind his table. His eyes fell on Burke's report and he was reminded of the man's strange behavior. Furtive, he thought. But then, he always seems furtive. It's his nature. He's a spy.

No, it was more than that. He was being furtive toward me! That's it! Burke had acted as though he was trying to hide something from me!

His mind raced back over the recent interview. Was he lying to me about Mitsuyama's plans? No, that wasn't when I noticed his strange manner. It was later.

Suddenly it hit him. Burke had done something totally out of character! The little man had actually volunteered to do something, something dangerous! He had offered to organize and lead the loyal group of the Faithful to fight Mitsuyama!

Thunderstruck, the President of the Free Council paused to consider the possible implications of Burke's action. The spy had promised to hand-pick and lead the most important part of Andretti's forces at the special meeting. Would they really be loyal to the Free Council? Or would they be traitors, favorable to the PlainsLord? Was the little man a double agent, the key to an elaborate double cross being planned by Mitsuyama?

Or perhaps, he thought with a sense of growing wonder, perhaps Burke plays an even deeper game. Could he just possibly be planning to let both sides destroy each other? And then with his loyal little army pick up the pieces himself? Could Burke's ambition be to make himself the leader of Kensho?

Staggered by the ramifications of his suspicions, Andretti struggled for several moments to regain his composure. How can I fight Mitsuyama, he wondered with anguish, when I have no one I can depend on? Even within the Free Council, I meet with resistance everywhere I turn. Father Olson and Mother Adeline fight me every inch of the way! Burke betrays me! I have to scheme and argue and persuade endlessly.

But Mitsuyama . . . ahhh, yes, the PlainsLord is not bothered by such problems. He can decide and act instantly. A trouble-maker like Olson would simply be eliminated! But I, the President of the Free Council, Way-Farer Elect of Kensho, must patiently endure infighting, bickering, and treason!

Yet, he reminded himself, that was the price one paid for freedom. And freedom was the essence and tradition of the 'hoods, the Free Council, and the Great Way. Jerome had begun it, Obie had developed it, Coran had institutionalized it, and Johnston had allowed it free rein. Freedom. Freedom from the Mushin. Freedom from the Madness. Freedom from the Grandfathers. Freedom to follow the Way. And even before that, freedom had been the driving force behind the Great Pilgrimage that had brought humanity to Kensho. Freedom from the horror that Earth had become. Freedom to live a decent, human life once more.

He shook his head. I understand it all, he told himself. Freedom is our heritage and our goal. But still, it's hard to reconcile freedom with the needs of the moment. We need to act, and act swiftly. If we don't, Mitsuyama may destroy us and freedom along with us. How much freedom can we sacrifice to save freedom?

Brooding, he began to plot.

William looked down at his dozing wife. In sleep, her face was relaxed. The hardness dissolved in gentle, sensual curves. She was beautiful.

Careful not to disturb her, he rose from the bed. Miriam sighed and turned slightly, but didn't awake. He dressed quickly, then returned to stand and gaze down at her once more.

What is it she wants? he wondered. Is it love,

power, wealth? A little of each? Or a lot? She's wife, advisor, and friend of the most powerful Lord on the Plain. And one of the most important men on Kensho. Yet that doesn't seem to be enough. She always reaches for more, more.

He shook his head. We're all like that. Take Jimson, for example. He obviously isn't content with being the mere leader of an army, the first army ever on Kensho. No, the ex-Seeker wants more. He wants to be Supreme Lord, to stand here in my very boots, in this room. Mitsuyama snorted. The fool thinks I can't tell, thinks I can't see the little wheels going round and round in his head. Miriam is right. The man can't be trusted at my back in the moment of victory.

But why? Why does the ex-Seeker court death so stupidly? Once the man walked the Way of the Sword, seeking Satori and true understanding. Then he stopped. Now he walks the way of self-destruction, seeking power without any understanding of what he's even risking. Fool! Fool? Yes, a fool, but one with ambition. Yet what gave fools as well as wise men ambition?

And then there's Father Andretti. No fool, that man. Clever, determined, dedicated, fanatic, capable of doing almost anything, sacrificing almost anyone to protect the Great Way. A believer, that one, and therefore twice as dangerous as someone who merely desires self-aggrandizement like Jimson.

Father Andretti truly believes in the Way. So he isn't interested in things like wealth or even power. No, loss of power wouldn't really bother the man. But even a hint of losing his purpose and the President of the Free Council would set the whole world ablaze with his fear and anger.

The Great Way is what gives Andretti's life its

meaning. He sees himself as its first line of defense, as its protector against the unbelieving hordes, as the bulwark holding up the whole system. As long as the Way exists, Andretti has a reason for existing. So he takes any threat to the Way as a direct threat to his own person.

And if I should defeat the Free Council, if I should prove stronger than the Way, then his whole life has been a silly dream, a mere exercise in futility. No man of any intelligence and sensitivity could stand that. No wonder Andretti would rather die defending his purpose and meaning in life than lose it. Even if the price is the future of his whole race. I can almost admire the man, he grudgingly admitted.

That's what's really at stake here, he knew. The future of the whole race. This isn't just a silly spat between brothers. This is a head-on collision between two opposing views of the road man should follow on Kensho. Andretti faithfully clings to Jerome's vision with austere, uncompromising purity. The Great Way, and only the Great Way, is to determine what men think, how they think, the way they act, the speed and direction of their development . . . everything. It alone is the Truth. Mere human reason, mere logic, are insufficient as guides for the future. There can be no deviation from the Way. Jerome's plan is final, unappealable, unchangable. Growth has to be gradual, restrained, and wholly within the predetermined patterns of the Great Way. Anything outside that pattern in anathema, blasphemy, treason.

Narrow, narrow, narrow! All Andretti understands is slavish devotion to the teachings of a man long dead, a man who lived and died in a very different world! There's so much more to existence than his philosophy allows for!

And that's what I seek. That "more" I sense in the

world. That "something" that always lies just beyond reach, just beyond my fingertips, just at the edge of my mind. Like the horizon here on the Plain.

I'm not alone in wanting more. That desire, that urge, that compulsion, is one of the main forces that drives the race onward to greatness, and to despair. It wasn't merely to escape the Home World that humanity launched the Pilgrimage. There were other solutions to the problems of Earth. No, the real reason mankind surged forth from the solar system in wave on wave of starships is because we wanted the stars, the galaxies, the Universe. The Beyond.

No philosophy, no religion, no Way that tries to hold men back can triumph for long. Eventually, it will be swept away. Even technology can't be suppressed forever. For technology is simply the practical application of man's eternal search for more. It provides the power and tools necessary to carry out the search. Its results might be destructive or even evil, but that is only because men themselves are destructive and evil. Technology itself is neutral and its bad effects must be tolerated for the good.

I am destined to sweep away the Great Way so that my people can move proudly and swiftly into our future here on Kensho. We must free ourselves from the dead hand of the past. We must develop science and industry. We must dominate the planet and everything on it, including the Mushin. Through technology, we will find a way to destroy the mind leeches. Just because Nakamura and the Flagship computer failed didn't mean such a thing is impossible. Only that the right techniques haven't been discovered yet. Free, we'll search for them and find them. And then Kensho will be completely ours.

Yes, he thought, we're all Seekers. Miriam, Jimson, Andretti, I, even this young Edwyr who comes looking for the Sword. We all seek our destinies, faithfully following them wherever they may lead us. Some will find victory. Others defeat.

Brooding, he began to plot.

BOOK VI

THE RONIN

XV

After the incident with the swordsman at First River, Edwyr spent several uneventful days traveling due west across the Plain. He was still a good two days from the territory claimed by the PlainsLords and at least three more from Mitsuyama's stronghold. Last night, at the Brotherhood where he stayed, it had been whispered that the Supreme Lord was bringing his secret army with him to First Pass for a showdown with the Free Council. Edwyr had nodded calmly on hearing the news. Things were progressing exactly as expected. Now, if only . . .

The area he had been passing through since dawn was becoming rougher and more rolling with every passing mile. He had already detoured slightly southward to avoid a range of low hills that humped off northwards. Now another, higher group bunched up dead ahead on the horizon. As he ran nearer, he decided it would be simpler to cross them than to turn left or right for another detour.

He had barely entered the hills when he heard the sudden howling chorus of Ronin in full pursuit of human prey. Surprise brought him to a dead stop. It was hard to tell exact direction, but the sounds seemed to be coming from off to his left, deeper into the hills. From the noise they were making he estimated there were four of the killers.

Without bothering to consider the odds, Edwyr began to sprint in the direction of the yells. As he ran, he unslung his sword from its position on his back, holding the scabbard with his left hand, his right on the hilt, ready for an instant draw. I just hope I'm in time, he thought.

Suddenly he heard a wild shriek of agony that ended in a stifled gurgle. Someone, he realized, has just died. And from the sound of it, it was one of the Ronin! Yes, I'm sure of it! I hear only three of the monsters bellowing now.

As he rounded the shoulder of a steep hill, he pulled up short. Before him, in a narrow gully that ended in a blind wall, he saw an incredible tableau. A young woman stood, her back to the wall, brandishing a bloody-bladed staff. About five feet in front of her lay the writhing body of a dying Ronin. The man's throat was so completely slashed that only his spinal column and a flap of skin held his head to his body. A few feet beyond the body, their backs to him, three more Ronin were milling about, waving their swords and working up their courage to attempt another charge. It was clear to Edwyr that the woman would probably kill at least one more when they attacked. She herself would die at the same time.

Quickly his glance took in her whole figure. She was so intent on her attackers that she hadn't even noticed his arrival. She seemed calm, unbothered by the Mushin which Edwyr could feel swarming around the area. The frenzied mind leeches were feeding on the last emotions of the dying man and hungrily preparing for the rest of the feast that undoubtedly awaited.

The wielder of the bladed staff was small and slender. Her long brown hair flowed down her shoulders. Her mouth was set in a grim, determined line, but it was easy to see it was capable of arching smiles as well. The nose was small and straight. Overall, she radiated a sense of self-confidence and gentle power. And the light, sure way she handled her weapon indicated she was no one to trifle with. Edwyr nodded approval to himself. This one was a fighter!

Suddenly the timeless moment ended, and with a wordless cry the young Seeker ripped his sword from its scabbard and charged the Ronin from behind. The three swirled in surprise to meet his attack. Edwyr struck at the nearest before the man could block and split him from his shoulder to his crotch in one blow. Already dead, the Ronin tumbled to the ground, his guts spewing before him.

The second stepped in and aimed a blow at Edwyr's head. As Edwyr blocked, the third killer, who had angled to the right to attack from there, suddenly stiffened, his eyes wide with astonishment. The Ronin crumpled and the young woman was revealed behind him, a fierce grin on her face.

The last Ronin realized he was alone against two opponents. He took one last swing at Edwyr, which the Seeker parried easily, and then turned and fled.

Rather than chasing the killer, Edwyr spun around to see how the wielder of the bladed staff was faring. Mushin still swarmed dangerously about in the little valley. He didn't know whether or not she had been wounded and might be open to their attack. What he discovered as he turned was the blade of the staff almost at his throat and the calm, grey eyes of the young woman burning into his. Oddly, the only thought that occured to him was that the blood which smeared the blade smelled vaguely metallic.

"Thanks for the help," she said quietly, "and I'm sorry about this," she nodded at the staff. "But I don't know who you are or what you intend."

The Seeker smiled slightly, keeping his eyes locked on hers. That way he knew he would gain a crucial split-second warning if she decided to thrust. It would probably be enough.

"I'm Edwyr. A humble Seeker of the Way of the Sword. Minding my own business. Killing a stray

Ronin. Taking a run for my health. And who, pray tell, am I addressing over the tip of this staff?"

"Yolan. Simply Yolan." Relaxing somewhat, she lowered the tip of the staff. "Guess you're no Ronin, at least." She looked at him quizzically. "I've heard of you Seekers, but I've never met one. Are there very many of you out here on the Plain?"

"Twelve, to be exact," he said as he walked over to retrieve his scabbard from where he had dropped it while attacking. Thrusting it through his obi belt, he returned and knelt next to one of the dead Ronin. "Though perhaps there should be more of us if there's vermin like this around." Carefully, he began to wipe his blade clean on the robe of the dead man.

Yolan shrugged and squatted down on the other side of the corpse. "Don't know. I think this bunch has been working the area. Found a settler family massacred off to the southeast this morning. Must have been this band that did it." Falling silent, she began to follow his example and wipe the bloody blade of her staff.

The silence lasted for several moments as each one concentrated on his task. Finished, Edwyr stood and sheathed his sword, firmly tying the cords on the scabbard to his obi to hold it in place. Yolan leaned on her staff, watching his precise movements. With studied nonchalance, she finally spoke. "What are you doing out here anyway? I thought you Seekers stayed pretty much in the Home Valley? And you mentioned a dozen. Where are the others?"

"Here and there. We aren't travelling together if that's what you mean. As to why I'm here, well, let's just say I'm seeking something. That seems like a logical thing for a Seeker to be doing, wouldn't you say?"

For the first time, the young woman smiled.

Edwyr looked at the corpses again. "You did pretty well. Two out of three."

"Three out of four. I killed one earlier when they first jumped me. It would have been four out of five if you hadn't let that last one go. Why'd you do that, anyway? You could have gotten him. Or at least held him so I could have speared him."

"Best to let him live. The Mushin will all return to him. If we'd killed all the Ronin, the Mushin would just have roamed around until they found some susceptible minds and then attacked. Might cause more havoc than one lone Ronin. He was the last one, wasn't he?"

She shrugged. "Guess so. Though I can't be sure. I'm sort of surprised there were five in one group. I always thought they only traveled in groups of two or three."

"That was true a long time ago, say during Jerome's day. But even Jerome noticed they were changing. They're calmer now, believe it or not. That bunch actually stopped and thought about how to attack you rather than just swarming at you mindlessly. That's quite a change from the old days."

"Ummmmmm. How long have you been a Seeker?"

"About ten years."

"So you were born, or at least raised, on the Plain, right?"

Edwyr laughed. "Right. And how did you deduce that little bit of information?"

Yolan shrugged. "It's obvious. For the last ten years you've been in the Home Valley studying the Sword. There aren't any Ronin left in the Home Valley, but you nevertheless know them and their habits pretty well. Since you couldn't have gotten that knowledge in the Home Valley, you must have picked it up before you went there. The most likely conclusion is that you got it by living on the Plain in an area where Ronin are found."

The Seeker grinned. "Wonderful! A perfect example of how you can draw the right conclusions from the wrong information!" His grin grew even broader as he saw a quick look of confusion flash across Yolan's face. "First of all, yes, I was born on the Plain, or at least in the foothills of the Mountains near the Plain. And to save you the trouble of asking, it was far to the north of here, near Last Pass, the one Obie finally cleared.

"Second, there were Ronin around while I was growing up. In fact, they're much more common in the foothills than on the Plain itself. They seem to prefer areas like those they were used to in the Home Valley, probably because they offer more opportunities for ambush and concealment. It's only been in the last generation that they've started moving out onto the Plain in any real numbers.

"The rest of your logic doesn't hold up so well, because it's based on some faulty premises. You seem to think that I've spent the last ten years stuffed away in some 'hood, meditating and mumbling rituals. That's not quite the way we follow the Sword. True, there's an initial period of very intense and rigorous mental and physical training that can last from two to five years. During that time we're completely cloistered.

"But it ends rather abruptly and completely. One day the Master decides you're ready, gives you a sword and a pack with about two day's worth of food, and kicks you out into the world with instructions to 'go and wield the Sword of Life.'

"I made the same decision most of us make at first and spent a couple of years protecting settlers and killing Ronin. A lot of us don't survive that period, but

I did and *that's* where I learned what I know about Ronin."

Yolan was silent for a moment as she absorbed this information. Edwyr allowed his eyes to roam around their immediate area, noticing the little things for the first time. Suddenly, his gaze focused on a bright patch of color and he gave a small cry of delight. "Look! A Bright Eye!" In a few quick steps he strode to the base of the hill and pushed aside the stunted grass to reveal a small white flower with a purplish splash at its center.

Yolan joined him, her eyes drawn to his face rather than to the blossom. She could hardly believe that this . . . this . . . excited child was the grim-faced warrior who had come slamming into the Ronin from behind just a few minutes ago. Not knowing how to act or what to say, she said the obvious. "It's a flower."

He glanced up, delight shining from his eyes. "Not just a flower! It's one from my childhood. An old favorite. We used to make chains from them. They're much commoner up north. Why, I haven't seen one for . . . maybe eight or nine years now. Isn't it beautiful?"

Realizing that the Seeker's joy at finding the flower was genuine, she decided to play it straight. She knelt down in the grass and looked carefully at the blossom. Five delicate, slightly ruffled white petals radiated outward from a black mound in the middle. The base of each petal was a deep, rich purple. If she closed her eyes just slightly, the flower indeed looked like a "Bright Eye." Edwyr had named it well. And it really was beautiful.

As he eagerly described the fields of his youth, literally covered with the tiny blossoms, his boyish enthusiasm began to infect Yolan. Caught up in Edwyr's excitement, she suddenly felt an overwhelming urge to say or do something that would increase his pleasure. The only thing she had to offer was knowledge. "Yes, it's beautiful. But even more than that, it's crucial."

"Crucial? How so?"

"Well, it's an angiosperm—that is, it's a plant whose seed is protected by a shell. If there weren't any angiosperms on Kensho, if the planet had only evolved to the gymnosperm stage, we couldn't survive here."

"Couldn't survive?"

She nodded, his interest warming her to her topic. "You see, angiosperms are very efficient energy sources, much better than gymnosperms. Until they come along, a planet can't support high energy-demand creatures like mammals. It takes a lot of fuel to maintain warm-bloodedness! Not to mention live birth."

"But then why isn't there any native warm-blooded life here?"

"Ah, there was! But the Mushin destroyed it all. In fact, the absence of mammal-like creatures combined with the presence of angiosperms should have alerted the original colonists that something was wrong. Instead, they just put it down to anomalous evolution and . . ."

Damn! she cursed herself silently. Stupid, stupid, stupid! To hide her confusion she stood and turned away. No ordinary Sister knows things like that! How could she have been so foolish, to rattle on, using scientific terms and ideas that only a Keeper could know? Had the Ronin attack and her unexpected deliverance shaken her so much that she wasn't thinking rationally? Or was it simply that her whole life was so centered around preserving and spreading knowledge that she found it difficult not to share it with someone who was plainly interested? No excuses! she told herself. Remember that you're a fugitive. Your whole mission in life is proscribed by the leaders of Kensho and you yourself are running, after recently being discovered. Everyone is a potential enemy. Even this Seeker. Start thinking that way or you'll never survive!

A sudden weariness settled on her soul. Must I carry this burden, alone, forever? a small voice within her cried. There was no answer, so she left the question softly echoing through her mind as she turned back and looked down at Edwyr. An amused and slightly taunting half-smile hung on his lips and around his eyes. She wondered briefly how much he guessed. This Seeker was no fool. Could this whole thing with the flower have been a trick to lure her into revealing herself? Carefully, move carefully, she cautioned herself.

She paused slightly before speaking, giving him a searching, considering look. "You, ah, came from the east, I guess?" He nodded. "Directly from the east? You didn't happen to be down to the southeast, did you?"

The Seeker cocked his head to one side, a mischievous glint in his eyes. "Yolan, I don't know who's looking for you or who you're running from. But it has nothing to do with me."

She flushed slightly. "Uh, ummmm, yeh, well, I guess I was kind of grilling you wasn't I? Sorry. Maybe it does sort of sound like I'm running or hiding. But I'm not. I'm just going to visit my folks. My Dad's sick, you see. So, I left the 'hood where I live now and I'm . . . ." her voice trailed off as Edwyr's grin grew wider.

"If you say so," he said, filling her embarrassed silence as he rose. "Not to change the subject, but that bladed staff of yours is pretty unusual. Can I see it?"

Without a word, Yolan handed him the weapon. Fascinated, he looked it over carefully. "Hmmmmm. Blade's smaller than usual. Edged on both sides. Cuts either way, huh? Nice balance. Does this thing come apart? Is that what these little rings are for?" He pointed to two metallic rings that circled the staff, one just beneath the blade, the other half-way down the shaft.

"Yeh. Like this." She took the weapon back, twisted the rings up and around. "Beneath the rings there's a joint, see? The rings twist to the right. But the shaft pieces twist to the left like this," she demonstrated, twisting the blade off the shaft, "so the whole thing breaks down into three pieces, each about two feet long. Makes it easy to carry."

Edwyr nodded admiringly. "Very nice. I've never seen one like that before. Did you make it?"

Instantly Yolan's eyes became hooded, her expression stiff with suspicion. "Yeh. Look, I think I'd better be going. I've still got a long trip ahead of me and I'd like to put as much distance as possible between myself and this place before dark. So thanks for the help." She twisted the rest of the staff apart and walked back to where her travel pack lay against the side of the hill. While Edwyr watched, she put the pieces into a special bag and placed the package into the sack.

When she had finished securing her weapon, she stood and turned to face him. Her jaw fell open as she looked over his shoulder and she said very softly, "Oh, damn."

Slowly, Edwyr turned to see what had surprised the young woman. Standing about thirty feet away, blocking the way out of the gully, were four Ronin.

Calmly, Edwyr rested his right hand on his sword hilt. "Good afternoon, gentlemen. Can I help you?" Casually, he began walking toward the silent killers.

The Ronin simply stood and stared at him as Edwyr approached. The Seeker recognized one of the four as the Ronin he had allowed to flee.

When he had come within ten feet of the four, one of the middle ones took two steps forward and held up his right hand, palm up, to show he bore no weapon. His left hand turned palm outwards to indicate it was likewise empty. Taking his hand from his sword, Edwyr copied the action.

"What is this one?" the Ronin questioned softly, as if speaking to himself. "This one is not like the others. Totality cannot find him. This one is not like a mirror or a fog. This one simply isn't there. Totality is confused."

"I am a Seeker of the Way of the Sword," Edwyr replied. He was astonished at the way the Ronin were acting. Aside from the three guardians at First Touch, who had talked to Jerome to frighten him away, Edwyr had never heard of a Ronin speaking to an ordinary human.

"Seeker? Seeker? Totality does not know this one. Are there more like this one? Is this a unity or a multiplicity?"

"There are more."

"A multiplicity, then." For a few moments, the Ronin was silent, his eyes unfocused. But his lips moved as if he were carrying on an internal conversation. Then his eyes brightened again and his gaze shifted past Edwyr to Yolan.

"This second one. It is different, too. Not invisible,

no. But not shiny or dark, either. Totality can sense this other one, but cannot find it. This one moves, slips away, cannot be contained or held. Totality is confused by it, too.

"Both are unusual. Totality cannot decide. Totality will observe further." With that, the Ronin spun on his heel. The other three parted to let him pass. Then they turned, too, and the group trotted off down the gully and out of sight.

Edwyr sensed Yolan as she moved up alongside him. "What was that?" she asked in an awed voice.

The Seeker looked over at her and nodded. "Never seen anything like that. That leader or whatever, seemed completely in control. There were Mushin all over the place, I could sense them. But they weren't swarming. They were, like . . . like . . ."

"In order!" Yolan said excitedly. "Yeh! They were in order!"

"I guess that's as good a description as any."

"And what do you suppose he meant that you were invisible? Or that I was 'slippery'?"

"He was referring to our minds. The only thing the Mushin can sense is a person's mind. When he said 'Totality' he was referring to the Mushin. That's how the Grandfathers in the 'hoods in the Home Valley always refer to them. Totality. Jerome thought that they must be some kind of an aggregate consciousness. Maybe whenever any group of them forms they call themselves 'Totality.' "

"I didn't like the implications of what he said after that."

"What? About being confused?"

"No. About observing further. That sounds like they intend to stay nearby and watch us."

"Hmmmmmm. I see what you mean. As long as

they hang around they're still a menace. They could attack again at any time."

"Yes. Which means one of us could have a big problem."

"How so?"

"Well, we aren't traveling together. Probably aren't even going in the same direction. So when we leave here, we'll be splitting up. Which means the Ronin'll have to make a decision. They'll either have to drop the whole thing, split up and follow each of us separately, or forget one and stay with the other.

"My bet is they'll pick the first alternative. Observing just doesn't seem in character for Ronin. I wouldn't be surprised if they've already forgotten the whole thing and gone off hunting for easier prey.

"If they take the second choice, fine. Two Ronin tailing me are no real problem. They couldn't ambush me out on the Plain and in a straight fight I'd win hands down. I'm sure they'd just give up after a day or so anyway.

"The third possibility is the one that worries me a little. Four of those killers are too many to have following you around. But to be brutally frank about it, I think if they're forced to choose one of us to shadow, it'll be you, not me."

Yolan looked at Edwyr, her face set in a grim, determined expression. "That's how I figure it. The odds are pretty good, and, in any case, I don't have much choice. I've got to find my folks, so I'll just have to take my chances." She shrugged her pack more comfortably into place.

She took one step to leave, hesitated, then turned back to Edwyr. "Thanks, Seeker. They'd have gotten me if you hadn't come along. I . . . I . . . well, thanks. See you." With a slight salute and a stiff smile, she turned and started to follow the direction taken by the four Ronin.

Edwyr stood quietly for several moments, considering. Then he untied his sword, slung the scabbard across his back, hitched his robe back up into running position and started down the gully.

Not knowing quite why he was doing it, the Seeker decided to follow Yolan. Given the twisting path she took between the hills, it wasn't hard to stay mostly out of her line of sight. Whenever he did come to an open space, he would hang back until she had crossed and then cross himself. Since she never looked back, he assumed he was unseen.

As he moved along, he kept all his senses fully extended. Not a blade of grass moved in the fitful breeze but he saw and evaluated it. The slightest sound was caught and analyzed to see if it held any hidden threat. And with his mind, he constantly probed about for sign of the Mushin, sign that would reveal the nearby presence of the Ronin.

He puzzled over the situation. Yolan was obviously running from someone or something. The story about looking for her parents was true, but the reason for the search was completely fabricated. And why would anyone have to "hunt" for their own home? Settlers seldom moved. It simply wasn't feasible. They put too much labor into their little farms to just pick up and start over. There was something very strange here.

In any case, the young woman didn't want anyone else around. She was traveling alone and liked it that way. But she was in great danger, whether she admitted it or not. Granted, she was good, very good, with her bladed staff. But against four Ronin? And out on the open Plain where there were no gully walls to guard her back or flanks? Edwyr knew *he* would try to avoid such a confrontation, even though he might well survive it. The young woman simply didn't stand a chance. If she continued on her way alone, she would probably die.

It really wasn't any of his business, he reminded himself. He was on a very important mission. The whole future of Kensho hung on his success. Nothing could be allowed to interfere. Yet . . . there was something about Yolan, her cool defiance, her strength, her readiness to fight regardless of the odds, that pulled at things deep inside him. Without bothering to reason it out, he knew he could not just walk off and leave the girl to die.

Deciding, he picked up his pace to catch up with her. She had just disappeared around the hip of a hill which stood near the edge of the range. Ahead, he could occasionally catch glimpses of the Plain.

As he rounded the hill, he found Yolan standing there waiting for him, hands on her hips, an annoyed expression on her face. His appearance brought a snort and a quick glare.

"Took you long enough to figure it out."

"I . . . figure what?"

"You've been making enough noise back there for an army. I knew you were there. So I knew you had to be feeling it, too. Even with all that racket, you have to have picked it up a long time ago. Gods, it's so thick you can almost cut it!"

"Pick what up? I don't know what you mean." He saw a flash of blank surprise flicker across her features. Then, abruptly, almost as if snapped back into place, the annoyance returned. But not before he caught a quick glimpse of the fear and worry that lay hidden just beneath it. He realized that Yolan was using a relatively innocuous emotion to mask more serious ones. Something had badly frightened the young woman!

"Can't you feel it?" Edwyr shrugged helplessly. A weary note entered her voice. "No, no, I guess not. Maybe I'm just imagining things. Maybe I'm crazy. But, damn it, I can sense something!

"It's . . . it's . . . vague," she groped for words. "Nothing definite. A sense of menace, an aura of danger." Her eyes became frightened and her voice dropped to a strained whisper. "But it's so strong! so strong!"

She took several deep breaths and rubbed her temples, eyes closed. When she opened them and turned to Edwyr again, they held their usual calm light. "They're out there, watching." She gestured vaguely at the surrounding hills. "But there's something wrong. My feeling's just too strong to be accounted for by four ordinary Ronin. Either there's more than four or they're different somehow.

"In any case, all previous bets are off. It's a whole new game. I think the odds are pretty poor for either one of us alone. They'd cut us to ribbons. Frankly, I'm scared. I don't want to die. Not that way."

She shivered, then flashed Edwyr a small smile. "So I guess we'll just have to put up with each other, like it or not. I can't believe they'll follow us too far. It's only a temporary inconvenience. You're heading more or less due west, right?"

Edwyr nodded. "You're sure about this?" The look she gave him required no words. "O.K. I trust this sense of yours, whatever it is. Can you tell where they are?"

"Some are back there, the way we came, following. And I think some are on our left flank, maybe even between us and the Plain. It isn't far now, but I think we should hurry anyway. It's just too damn easy for them to spring an ambush in these hills. Once we're out there on open ground, though, it'll be impossible to surprise us. We'll be able to see them a long way off. Let's go." Without waiting for a reply, Yolan turned and began to jog off to the west. Edwyr, wondering exactly what was happening, followed silently.

By the time they reached the Plain, the sun was getting low over the waving grass to the west. Its slanting, purplish light shone in their eyes and lit up the hills behind them in bright relief.

As he turned to look back over his shoulder and enjoy the beauty of the scene, Edwyr was stunned by what he saw. With quiet urgency he called to Yolan to stop. When she turned to look, she uttered an awed oath.

Standing on the crests of the hills nearest the Plain, front-lit in sharp detail against the sky, stood five . . . six . . . seven . . . eight figures. As the two on the Plain watched, the eight Ronin, moving as one, broke their stance and began to calmly trot down the slopes toward the flat ground.

With a wordless exchange of grim glances, Yolan and Edwyr turned westward again and, side by side, resumed their journey toward the setting sun.

XVI

It was light enough to see his face quite distinctly now, even though the dawn was still lingering behind the horizon. He was sleeping, calmly and peacefully, the barest smile turning up the corners of his mouth. It wasn't exactly a handsome face, she decided. But his looks were pleasant and the strength of his character was evident even in slumber.

Nervous, she stood and swept the area with her eyes. The only thing she could see in any direction was the long grass, waving and hissing beneath the constant wind. There was no sign of the Ronin. The fact didn't relieve her tension. I'd almost rather see them, she thought. At least then I'd know they aren't creeping up, swords drawn, ready to attack . . . now! She winced at her own imagination. Silly. Useless to think about it. There's nothing I can do. And since there are two of us, they won't be overly eager to jump us. I hope.

But how long can I continue to travel with this Seeker? she wondered. Sooner or later we'll have to part company. I can't allow him to follow me all the way home. I can't risk him finding out what I am, or who and what my parents are. He's a Seeker, and no matter how personally friendly he might be, he's still part of the established order of Free Council and 'hoods. That automatically makes him a potential enemy.

A slice of the sun threw its light westward across the Plain. She saw the tops of the tall grass brighten suddenly. Again she stood and searched the area for sight of the killers. Nothing.

She gazed down at the sleeping Seeker. Time to

wake him. A pity, though. He looks so peaceful. And so . . . so interesting. No, that's not the right word. She shied away from that line of thought, afraid where it might lead. This is a potential enemy, she reminded herself.

As she leaned down to shake his shoulder, a new thought entered her mind. Is he an enemy? Would the fact that I'm a Keeper turn him against me? If he knew I'd escaped Mother Elena, would he hand me over to the head of the next 'hood we passed? Suddenly, looking at his face, it all seemed so unreal, so unimportant. Not really knowing why, Yolan laughed.

Edwyr's eyes opened at the sound. A wide grin covered his features as he stood and stretched. "Now that's the way to be awakened," he yawned. "In the middle of the Plain. Hunted by eight armed Ronin. Huddled all night on the ground. And the girl wakes me with a laugh!"

Yolan laughed again. "Pretty silly, huh? I guess I should be solemn, wake you with a hesitant touch and immediately bring you up to date on the current status of our critical situation."

He nodded sagely. "Oh, yes. Most proper. But somehow, for a day as beautiful as this one, I think your method a lot nicer." He grinned again. "I'll contribute some fresh Ken-cow cheese they gave me at the Brotherhood I stayed at the other night. What have you got to add to our breakfast?"

Mumbling, she rummaged in her pack. "Uh, would some not-so-fresh ken-cow cheese do?" They both laughed. "Let's eat mine first. It's older and yours will keep longer."

They ate quickly, in a relaxed silence. Toward the end of the meal, Yolan began to feel uneasy again. "Something's wrong," she muttered. Cautiously,

Edwyr lifted his head and looked eastwards. After a few seconds, he sat down with a grunt.

"I can see them off to the east. They're just standing there, waiting for us to make a move." He looked at her quizzically. "How did you know?" She shrugged.

"Anyway, they're still on our trail. Look, Yolan, how fast a pace can you keep? Last night, when we were looking for a place to stay, you were going pretty strong. Could you keep that up all day?" She shook her head no. "Ummmmmm. About half that pace? Good. We won't outrun them that way, but they'll have to move out to stay with us. Maybe they'll figure it isn't worth it after a day or two."

He looked down at the ground as if deciding what to say next. "I know you don't want to answer this, but could you give me some idea of where you're heading? As far as the territory of the PlainsLords?" Stiffly, suspiciously, Yolan nodded. "Good. Then we can stay together at least that far. Let's see, I make that at least three days at our present pace."

Edwyr hesitated again. "Look, Yolan. Once we get there, we'll have to split up. I . . . I have to do something. It's a little risky. And frankly I can't have anyone else along. So, if we don't lose the Ronin by then, there's a 'hood not too far from where we'll be entering the grazing lands and you can . . ."

"No," the young woman interrupted, "I . . . I can't go to any 'hood. I mean I . . ." confused, she let the sentence hang.

"Can't?" Edwyr asked with a slight frown.

Yolan stood suddenly. "We'd better be moving. I'm not going to any 'hood. When we reach the Barrier Hills, we'll split, Ronin or no Ronin. O.K.? I'll just have to take my chances."

"But that's stupid," Edwyr said. "If they follow

you, you're as good as dead!" He didn't know why, but suddenly it mattered very much. "You'd be safe in the 'hood. If they follow me it doesn't matter. I can outrun the whole lot of them. Or outfight them if I can't."

"No!" Yolan replied, too forcefully, too sharply. "No 'hood! No more discussion. Let's move. They're coming." She waved a hand toward the distant figures of the Ronin, who were indeed moving toward them.

Without further comment, Edwyr slung his sword over his back, stowed his food in his front pocket, and then hitched the skirt of his robe up for running. When he turned to Yolan, the young woman was ready to go.

They trotted side by side at a steady pace. For at least an hour, Edwyr was silent, his brow furrowed as if thinking something through very carefully. From time to time, Yolan would give him a covert glance, but she refrained from breaking into his reverie.

Finally he laughed and turned a smile in her direction. "O.K. No 'hood. For whatever crazy or sensible reason, no 'hood. But I'm not leaving you until we're through the Barrier Hills. And I'm not leaving you with eight killers on your trail."

"How are you going to stop them?"

He grinned broadly. "Oh, something will come up. One or two might drop out of the race here and there. Yes, something will come up. I can almost guarantee it."

They travelled in silence again. Yolan kept glancing over at Edwyr, however, a look of indecision and longing on her face. "Uh, Edwyr," she began eventually, "I'm sorry to be so mysterious and such a problem. Really, I am."

He waved his hand in dismissal. "As to being a problem, you're not. Any more than I'm a problem to you. Look, you have your mission, I have mine. To be honest, it's a good thing we fell in with each other. Gods, girl, there were a dozen Ronin in those hills! Either one of us alone would have been killed! No, you're hardly a problem.

"As to mysterious . . . yes, I admit you are a bit of that. Though even there, maybe you overestimate things. I know you're running from someone or something. Don't bother to deny it. Since you don't want to go near a 'hood, it obviously has something to do with them. I think the story about looking for your parents is true, but it's strange. Why should you have to 'look for' your parents? Or your own home?

"So the mystery isn't total. I know you're running. I suspect you've done something to offend the 'hoods.

"Yolan, you don't have to tell me anything you don't want to. But just understand that I'm not a spy for the Free Council, the 'hoods, or anybody else. I really find it hard to believe you've done anything terrible, like murdering someone. Whatever you've done is probably a lot more important to you and whoever's after you than it is to anyone else, let alone to me. I honestly don't care. But I have to tell you, it'd be a lot easier to know as much as possible about each other if we're going to work together under conditions of rather extreme stress." He glanced back over his shoulder. In the distance, the eight figures followed soundlessly. "And that," he nodded, "is what I call 'extreme stress.' Take your time to think about it. But when we rest for lunch, I'm going to bore you with some facts about me. Maybe this evening, you'll return the favor?"

Not replying, the young woman ran on, her eyes fixed on the ground, her brow creased with a frown of uncertainty and confusion. Inside was a growing yearning to share some of the burden she had carried alone for so long.

*   *   *

Yolan was more than ready to stop and rest by the time the sun stood overhead. There was no question she was in excellent physical condition. But she'd never had to keep up such a grueling pace for such a long time. There were several unexpected blisters on her feet, and her legs throbbed with weariness. During the last hour or so before stopping, a twinge in her right knee had been growing into a sharp pain. The final half hour had been uncomfortable, to say the least.

Lying sprawled in the grass, she was almost too tired to eat. Propping herself up on her left elbow, she nevertheless accepted the piece of ken-cow cheese and strip of dried meat Edwyr handed to her. The Seeker, apparently not the least phased by the morning's run, smiled compassionately as she complained about her various aches and pains.

The meal was finished swiftly without any conversation. Then Edwyr stood and helped her to her feet. "We might as well rest by walking slowly. If you just lie there, your muscles will tighten up in no time flat. Then starting again will be twice as hard. We'll just sort of meander along, and you can sit down from time to time if you want. Just don't stay in one position too long. Best to keep the blood flowing in your legs to get rid of that fatigue you built up in the muscles this morning."

With a groan, Yolan began hobbling along next to the young man. Looking straight ahead, he began speaking softly about himself and his own past. She didn't pay terribly close attention to the words. She wasn't as interested in the facts of his life as she was in the general feeling she got for his voice and manner. The words, after all, could lie or be inaccurate. But the way he felt about them, how he presented them, what they meant to him . . . those were keys to his character, things he could not fake.

In any case, it was all pretty much what she had expected. An ordinary life, unexceptional in any way. Loving parents, happy childhood, early training in the nearby Brotherhood, bright promise of a good student, further studies, finally the Way of the Sword. All the way through it, one fact stood out: Edwyr was truly dedicated to the Way of the Sword.

If the tale itself was unremarkable, the way he told it was very revealing. Every word seemed to glow with a personal sense of joy. Edwyr loved and cherished the little things: the way a tree lizard sang, the fragile beauty of a water lizard's nest, the taste of fresh ken-cow cheese after a day of fasting, the feel of cool water in a dry throat, the heft of a good blade, the exhilaration of running across the Plain.

She remembered an instance only this morning. They had been running along when suddenly Edwyr had stopped and cried out. Startled, she had turned to stare in the direction he was pointing. She had noticed nothing but the endless Plain, the tossing grass, and in the mid-distance, a large swarm of Darters. They were strange creatures, insect-like in many respects, but with nervous systems highly developed to include something that might almost be called a brain. They flew in groups, never alone, and had six overlapping, semi-transparent wings. It was their flight pattern that gave them their name. The swam would hover, almost motionless, over one spot. Then, without warning, the entire group would dart off in some direction to a new spot where they would resume hovering once more. Their path was a wild, unpredictable zig-zag across the face of the Plain. But the creatures were always in perfect alignment, perfect timing with each other.

As they had watched, the swarm had darted off northward about a quarter of a mile, then directly back towards them, and finally southward out of sight. In their last move, the sun had hit their wings at just the right angle, and the entire swarm had burst into a mass of twinkling diamonds of light. Yolan had never seen that happen before and had been struck by the sudden beauty of it.

When she had turned to say something to Edwyr, his face had positively glowed, his eyes bright and joyous. No words had been necessary. And she had understood about the Bright Eye, too.

As she listened, fascinated and drawn into the story of Edwyr's life in spite of her intention to remain aloof and watchful, she began to reach a preliminary understanding of this man who walked beside her. His tale was constantly sprinkled with good humor and a very calm ability to recognize and laugh at his own foibles. Warmth and compassion were there in plenty, making the steel at the center of his character softer, yet somehow stronger at the same time. She knew Edwyr would cry over something sad, but never waste a second over foolish, maudlin sentimentality.

He was open and fair. He did not judge. He didn't demand explanations, reasons, justifications. He looked at an action or a person, observed the results, and modified his picture of the world to fit what he saw. He assiduously avoided preconceptions of what "ought" to be. Rather he viewed a thing as it was, naked, standing alone in the light of itself. She thought of the lies she had told him and quailed inwardly.

But what a beautiful way to view the world! Every-

thing was always so fresh for him! So . . . so itself!
Each experience was eternally new, pregnant with
unexpected potential, like the sudden sun flashing
from the wings of Darters.

Reaching back into the memories of her own childhood, she recalled moments from the past when the
same wonder had filled her world. The touch of a leaf,
the pattern of sunlight on a rock, the lacy shadows cast
by the four moons. What would it be like, she wondered, to see the world that way every day?

Edwyr's tale had reached his years of training in the
Way of the Sword now. Yolan concentrated carefully
on his words, hoping that something he would say
might provide the clue she needed to tell her how far
the Seeker could be trusted and whether or not she
dared reveal her true identity.

"We go through four phases in our training," he
said. Their pace had picked up slightly from a fast
walk to a slow jog. Occasionally Edwyr would cast a
quick glance over his shoulder to keep check on the
Ronin who were still far off in the distance behind
them. "Everyone goes through the four, although not
in exactly the same way. They're not quite as neat and
clearly defined as they seem when you just talk about
them. There's a lot of overlap, a lot of moving from
one to the other, and the chronological sequence is
fuzzy at best.

"The first one is known as 'Sword, not Seeker.' In
this phase, the Seeker is totally dedicated to the
sword as a physical thing, a weapon whose techniques
he has to master utterly. All a Seeker's energy, all his
concentration, all his ability must be focused on the
sword. Everything else is excluded. During this time
we train very hard. We rise about four in the morning, eat, and then do small tasks for the Master;

chopping wood, weeding the garden, sweeping, washing, cleaning. We use this time to think about the techniques we're working on and to calm our minds so we can focus our concentration later.

"When the chores are done, we go to the practice yards and begin with basic techniques, cuts and blocks mainly, but footwork and body movement too. Once the Master is satisfied with our performance, (by the way, when he isn't you sometimes stay with basic techniques all day long!), we begin doing combinations of cuts and blocks. All told, the session lasts until noon or a little beyond.

"After a short, light lunch, we're back in the yard again, this time doing 'kata,' complex practice forms that are really formalized, mock combats against an imaginary opponent. The katas are a way to teach us to combine isolated individual techniques or short combinations into larger, more complicated sequences.

"Finally, in the late afternoon, we have practice combats with light wooden swords. We wear specially padded robes, but you still get a lot of bruises, and you learn to avoid the opponent's blade, even if it's only a wooden one!"

He paused for a moment, a musing smile on his face. "Those are good times, Yolan. Simple times. There's only you and the sword and your need to master it. It's hard work. At times incredibly hard. And painful, too. But there's a clean joy in it that you've never felt before. And never feel again," he finished with just a hint of sadness in his voice.

"The second phase of the training actually starts while you're still engaged in the first. We call it 'Seeker, not Sword.' We have a chant. Supposedly Jerome got it from his Master, who got it from his

Master, who got it from his Master, and so on all the
way back to Nakamura who brought it from Earth. It
goes like this:

The Sword is the Mind.
When the Mind is right,
    the Sword is right.
When the Mind is not right,
    the Sword is not right.
He who would study the Sword,
    must first study his Mind.

That's really what the second period of our training is
all about: the Mind and knowing it. The physical part
of the Seeker's life stays the same. But now rather
than turning outward to the sword, concentrating all
his energies on it and on mastering it as a physical
weapon the student turns inward, into his own mind.
Everything changes. Everything stays the same. You
still swing the sword in the practice yard, but now you
watch the motion of your mind instead of the motion
of the blade. A kata is no longer a physical exercise,
but a spiritual one, a form of moving meditation.

"The object of this phase is to calm the mind even
when the body is in motion. Walking, eating, fighting, running, all become moments of quiet and meditation.

"When the Master thinks you've achieved at least a
good start in mastering your mind as well as the
sword, you begin the third phase. It's the hardest and
most difficult of all. Many can't pass through it. They
fail. They break down, go mad, commit suicide, return home. We call this phase 'Not Seeker, not
Sword.' A Seeker's first Satori comes now. He goes
'unsane' and the universe disappears. Everything he
knew crashes down around him in rubble. And he has
to rebuild it all, completely on his own." Edwyr shook

his head in a self-deprecating manner. "Oh, all that sounds so silly, so foolishly mystical! Mumbo-jumbo about vast Nothingness, universes disintegrating! It's all such rubbish! Don't believe a word of it!" He turned his head sideways until his eyes met Yolan's. "It's rubbish, but not because it isn't true," he said solemnly. "But because the words are only words after all and don't mean what I want them to mean." He grinned broadly as an idea struck him. "It's sort of like trying to describe the taste of a ground-apple by letting you suck on the pit. It might give you a vague idea, but only a taste of the real thing will make you understand."

Yolan nodded. "I think I see. But what's the last stage?"

"Ah, the last stage! We call it 'Seeker and Sword.' It begins when the Master decides you know enough about yourself and your sword and throws you out and sends you on your way. It ends when you die. You live it every day and every night. After all, what good is all that practice, all that meditating, all that work, if you don't use it? Why bother with Enlightenment and Satori if they have no practical purpose in everyday life?

"So the last phase, Yolan, is right here, right now. It's running next to you on the Plain. It's enjoying the texture of dried meat, the slight sourness of cheese. It's watching Darters and feeling the warmth of the sun on my head. It's seeing the shadows of the moons and pressing back against the earth before I go to sleep."

They trotted along in a companionable silence. Finally Yolan looked over at Edwyr from the corner of her eye. "Is that it?" He shrugged. "I mean, what about doctrine? What about the Way and the words of

Jerome? Or the teachings the 'hoods beat into our
heads? What about the Dream of Nakamura the Free
Council talks about?"

Edwyr threw back his head and laughed, loud and
long. Yolan was so astonished by his reaction that she
stopped dead in her tracks and stared at the Seeker.
Controlling his hilarity, Edwyr also halted and turned
to face her. "Doctrine?" he chuckled, "Words?
Teachings? The Way of the Sword has nothing to do
with things like that! This is the Way of the Sword!"
And he stepped up to her, grabbed her under her
arms and swung her wildly around, laughing uproari-
ously the whole time.

When he finally put her down, Yolan was so utterly
non-plussed that she couldn't think of anything to say
or do. She simply stood and stared in open-mouthed
wonder at the young man. Seeing her look, Edwyr
glared back, stuck out his tongue, crossed his eyes
and stuck his thumbs in his ears, wiggling his fingers
at her. Then he laughed anew at her startled reaction
and pulled at her arm to get her moving again.

After a few moments of chuckling, he said, "Yolan,
Yolan, the Way of the Sword has nothing to do with
doctrines and words and teachings. It's an attempt to
cut through all that, to cut through to the basic ground
of experience that underlies all those things, the place
from which all knowledge, understanding, and
creativity spring.

"It's not knowledge as such, or even the knowable,
we Seekers seek. We aren't trying to understand this
or that, or even this *and* that. We're trying to understand what it is to understand.

"The universe is just too vast a place to be comprehended by piling one bit of information on
another. Very soon a person has to form generalized

theories about the myriad bits of information, theories that organize, include, and exclude various parts to make sense of the whole. And a point comes when the theories become theories about ideas rather than about things. They become more and more complex, more and more abstract, and move further and further away from the original perceptions that provided the bit of information they were built on or explain. Eventually the ideas take on more reality than the thing itself.

"But the ultimate ground of all this is still the original experience. And that original experience, shorn of all theories, stripped of its words and meanings, is the source of knowing. When it's perceived in its purity, it becomes the source of knowing about knowing. It reminds us how we know and what it means to know. We find in it the broad lines of all there is to know. It's the final theory about theories, the end point toward which all knowledge is striving. And it gives us a fixed, sure base, a clear pattern, that shows us the way to all future knowing.

"Doctrines, teachings, even these words I'm using right now to explain this to you, have nothing to do with the Way. The Way is totally personal and subjective. It must be directly experienced or it has no meaning. It can't be taught, only learned. Each must walk it for and by himself."

"But," Yolan protested, still dazed by what Edwyr had said and done, "the 'hoods, and the Great Way that Jerome taught, and—"

The Seeker waved his hand in dismissal. "A sign post isn't the destination. A map isn't the territory. Words and ideas come into play only after the original verification by personal experience. They're simply an attempt to objectify the original experience so that it might be shared with others. But they're always crude, unsatisfactory, inaccurate, and downright misleading.

"And doctrine is the worst of the lot! The only possibly adequate form of communication about the Way would be illogical, paradoxical, poetic. It would try to strip the usual way of thinking and perceiving from the mind and throw it back on itself and its original pure contact with the world. It would try to make you 'unsane.' The Koans used in some of the Ways of the Home World were like that. As is Nakamura's Koan and the ones left by Jerome.

"But doctrine does just the opposite. It unifies, rationalizes, organizes, numbers, orders; it imposes oh, I don't know what all sorts of distortions on experience." Edwyr snorted. "There are those in the Free Council, the Great Way, and the 'hoods who would feel very comfortable if they could limit the meaning of the Way to what Jerome 'said.' But the Way isn't what Jerome said. It's what Jerome did."

Yolan's mind was racing furiously. From what the Seeker had told her, at least from what she'd been able to understand, he seemed to hold the whole institutional structure of the Great Way in good humored contempt! It hardly sounded as if he was one of Andretti's men! She decided to probe the question more directly. "But then you don't have any relationship with the 'hoods or the Free Council at all? You're completely independent?"

"No and yes," he answered. "Once you decide to seek the Sword you owe allegiance to no man or institution or doctrine or philosophy. 'Owe' is the operative word there, by the way. We can choose to serve anyone or anything we want. I spent two years as one of the companions of the last Way-Farer. But it was completely voluntary. I could have left at any

time. Right now I'm supposed to be on a mission for
the Free Council. But in fact, I'm not doing it for
them at all, but strictly for my own purposes." He
looked sideways at her with a sly smile. "And it has
nothing to do with you."

Then he's not an enemy, she thought, and a strange
thrill of secret pleasure coursed through her. He's
exactly what he appears to be and I can like and trust
him if I want to. I can even tell him who and what I
really am.

The idea warmed her. She felt as if a great burden
was slowly lifting from her back. No need to lie any
more, she thought. No need to lie.

And as she ran across the Plain by the Seeker's side,
she silently pleaded with the vastness, "Oh, let it be
true. Let it be true!"

XVII

The sun lay dying in the west, already half-eaten by the horizon. In the east, three moons stood high in the evening sky. Their dim glow mingled with the last of the daylight to give the Plain a long, drawn-out twilight.

For two hours the runners had kept up a punishing pace, trying, before darkness fell, to put as much distance as possible between themselves and the killers who followed. Alone in the waving sea of grass, they finally stopped on the crest of a long ridge that gave a good view back along their trail.

Yolan slumped to the ground, her exhaustion so palpable she could feel it clinging thickly to her limbs. Her legs throbbed with a bone-deep agony, her lungs ached with a pulsing pain that shot to her head, and her feet felt raw and brutalized.

Edwyr stepped to her side and grabbed her arm. "Up," he commanded sharply. "Walk. In a circle. Cool down slowly. Get your system back to normal gradually." Her head whirling, focus wavering uncertainly, she obeyed, clinging feebly to his arm. After a few circles, she was able to continue on her own.

While she walked, the Seeker stood and peered eastward through the gathering gloom. Finally satisfied, or perhaps simply giving up, he turned to her and announced, "I can't see any sign of them. Our burst of speed probably took them by surprise."

"Took me by surprise," she gasped, still short of breath. "Didn't think I'd make it." For several moments she circled without speaking, sucking great chunks of air into her lungs. Then, in a voice hopeless with fatigue, she muttered, "Doesn't make any difference. They're still there. Our trail will be clear for days. Damn grass! They'll follow us forever. We can't outrun them. At least I can't. Tomorrow they'll catch up. Or maybe the next day. Then they'll attack. They'll never give up. Never."

Edwyr found himself groping for words to try to cheer her up. "You're doing fine. That little run gave us a good lead on them. You can sleep easy tonight, get a good rest. We're safe enough."

"Huh!" she interrupted with a snort. "Safe enough! If they snuck up tonight and murdered me in my sleep, I'd never even know it."

"They won't catch up tonight," he replied firmly. He looked at the sky. "Light's failing pretty rapidly now. Three moons. Two in a little while. That's not really enough to track by, even in the grass. No. You can sleep soundly tonight, Yolan. And be plenty rested up for tomorrow's run."

She groaned. "How many more days of this agony do we have left? I'm almost beginning to think it'd be better to let the Ronin kill me, quick and clean, than let you do it slowly and painfully by running me to death."

Edwyr smiled wryly. She must be feeling better, he thought. Her sense of humor's back. "You can sit down if you want." She slowly lowered herself to the ground. "How many days?" he continued. "Oh, I think we'll get to the Barrier Hills sometime late tomorrow. Actually, we're going a lot faster than I'd figured on. Or I should say, *you're* going a lot faster."

"Tougher than you thought, am I?" she replied with a toss of her head. "Couple more days training like this and I'll give you a race. Don't laugh! I'd give you a good run for it! Ohhhhhh," she moaned theatrically, rubbing her legs, "that word. 'Run.'" Pulling off her low boots, she began to check her feet. "Crippled," she muttered. "This crazy Seeker has crippled me for life."

Grinning, he began to set out their very frugal supper. "Not much food to fuel the machine. You're going to lose some weight this trip."

She looked up, exaggerated anger on her face. "Are you suggesting I'm fat? First he maims me and now he heaps insults on my head! Just you wait 'til I get my bladed staff out. I'll make you eat those words!"

"Uh, no, no . . . I . . . didn't mean it that way . . . I . . . " he stammered, flustered by her reaction and uncertain how much of her anger was real.

She looked down her nose indignantly at him. "Well! I should hope not!" Then, unable to keep up the pretense any longer, she smiled suddenly. "Although, to tell the truth, I did put on just a teeny bit of weight sitting around that dumb Sisterhood."

"So you really were at a Sisterhood," he said as he passed food to her. "Do you feel like telling me why you left? And don't bother with that story about somebody being sick."

"Well," she began between mouthfuls. "I left in a hurry." Her expression was one of deep consideration, her brows knitted as if she was pondering a decision. Deciding, her face cleared and she brought her head up and looked the Seeker directly in the eyes. "Edwyr," she said softly. "I'm not an ordinary Sister."

"Yolan, you're not an ordinary anything."

She smiled. "Thanks. But I meant more than that." She was quiet again for several moments, her eyes averted, as if organizing her thoughts.

"Edwyr, I'm a Keeper," she announced finally, her gaze boring into his once more. "My mother is, too. And my father's an Artisan." Her expression became expectant and she watched him closely for any hint of a reaction to her statement.

The Seeker nodded slowly, thoughtfully, his face unchanging. "Ummmmmm. So. That explains several things."

Yolan asked, "Like what?"

"Like 'angiosperms' and 'gymnosperms' for one thing. No Sister knows things like that. Did the 'hood find you out?"

"Oh, they knew my mother had trained me. They were trying to undo my education and convert me to the Great Way. I let them think they'd succeeded. I thought I had them fooled. But I got careless. Like I did with you. And a little bit arrogant, I'm afraid.

"You know, it'd all make a lot more sense if I just start from the beginning." And for the next hour, Yolan recited the story of her life, from her parent's expulsion from the Home Valley to the moment she met Edwyr.

When she finished, there was a long period of mutual silence and musing. Relieved of the oppressive burden of secrecy she had carried for so long, Yolan let her mind drift and listened to the soothing whisper of the wind in the grass.

Eventually she became aware of Edwyr's gaze. He was carefully and slowly scrutinizing her features as if trying to read some message written there. Gently, he spoke. "And you were worried I'd turn you in to the 'hoods if I knew who you were?" She nodded. "And you really believe Father Andretti and the Free Council would have punished you?"

She snorted. "Look what they did to my parents."

"Hmmmmmm. Things have gone even further than Father Johnston thought," he murmured half to himself.

"But Yolan, the things Mother Elena said about the dangers of science are true. You realize that, don't you? The Home World was destroyed by technology . . ."

"Oh, Gods! You're as bad as the rest of them! You're not thinking! This isn't the Home World and we're not the technologists of Earth. What we Keepers and Artisans are proposing has nothing in common with what they did. We don't even share the same basic values. Damn it, damn it, damn it!!! Before you even hear what we have to offer you close your ears with horror stories about the past! We know what happened on the Home World. We're aware of the dangers. If anything, we're more worried about them than you are! Why won't you listen?!" Yolan was panting with anger and frustration. Edwyr could see the beginnings of tears in her eyes.

"All right, Yolan," he said simply, "I'll listen."

A look of mixed gratitude and disbelief swept rapidly over her face. "You'll listen? Just like that?"

"Not 'just like that.' I've spent two days with you. We've fought Ronin together. And I've paid close attention to everything you've said or done. I know you're no fool. But more important, I know you're not evil or vicious or petty. Anything you have to say, anything a person like you could believe so deeply, has to be worth listening to, even if I don't agree once I've heard it. Fair?"

"It's the fairest thing I've ever heard from anyone even remotely associated with the hierarchy of the Great Way." Eagerly, she arranged herself in a more comfortable position. Her face was alive with excitement at the prospect of actually talking with someone about her beliefs. This is important, she told herself. This isn't just another teaching session with sympathetic settlers already interested in what I have to say. Chants won't do here. It's got to be my own words. And they've got to be convincing!

"First of all," she began, "we don't deny or reject Jerome or his ideas, no matter what Andretti says. After all, it was Jerome who encouraged Mother Cynthia and the original Keepers in the first place! He gave them the Medallion. He suggested they go to the Flagship and collect data from the computer. The whole thing was his idea!

"So we have no quarrel with Jerome. Our problem is with the way Andretti and the Free Council interpret Jerome. We just don't agree with their version of the Great Way. And we base our disagreement on the ideas of Jerome himself!

"Jerome talked a lot about 'Oneness', Edwyr. I don't even pretend to understand all the fine points of the Way, but I learned enough from Mother Elena to know that somehow Jerome realized that all things come from, and return to, the same source. So each of us really is one with the World. And all things in the World really are one with us. Everything we do affects the World in some degree. And everything that happens affects us in return. I guess at least part of following the Great Way is coming to understand that and learning to live accordingly."

"Yes," the Seeker agreed. "In Satori, you actually experience the Oneness you're talking about. It's a blending, an intertwining. It . . . it . . ." he laughed and shrugged helplessly. "I guess it just can't be explained. So 'Oneness with the World' is probably as good as anything."

"Right. But there's another kind of Oneness Jerome talked about. Or maybe 'balance' is a better word. Anyway, he recognized that human existence isn't just a purely physical thing. At the very least, it's got mental and artistic and spiritual aspects as well.

They're all twisted together, but a person isn't really and truly 'human' in the fullest sense unless he develops all sides of his nature. If any one aspect is out of sync with the others, if one becomes overpowering or dominant, the result is an imbalance, a lop-sidedness, a warping of the person." She gave a self-deprecating little smile. "I don't think I'm explaining this too clearly."

"You're doing fine," Edwyr smiled back encouragingly. "you're describing what we call 'Harmony': Oneness within that mirrors the Oneness without. It comes when all aspects of a person's nature are in balance. And it's crucial for following the Way." He paused for a moment. "Yolan, if I read you right, you're about to say that the Great Way as it's currently being practiced is lop-sided. That it overdoes things in the spiritual direction and ignores the physical and mental and artistic too much?"

Yolan looked surprised, then pleased, that the Seeker was following her argument so closely. "That's exactly my point!" she said eagerly. "The Free Council keeps saying the Keepers want to introduce a materialistic technology on Kensho and that that's directly contrary to Jerome's emphasis on the spiritual aspects of the Way. They claim a return to materialism, any kind of materialism, will cause endless desire for material things, block all progress in the Way, stop our developing an immunity to the Mushin . . . oh, all kinds of assorted horrors.

"But we believe that's all nonsense, Edwyr. And we think Jerome would agree."

Now it was Edwyr's turn to look surprised. "How do you come to that conclusion?"

"By sticking with Jerome's own ideas," she answered firmly. "Edwyr, as I already said, Jerome was the one who encouraged the Keepers in the first place. And we're convinced he did it for a very good reason.

"Look, we know Jerome started out seeking the answer to Nakamura's Koan because he realized mankind was stagnating under the rule of the Grandfathers. We were more or less safe in the 'hoods and on the 'steads, but we weren't expanding or making any progress. Kensho had regressed to a very primitive social and economic level and wasn't developing at all. Nothing had changed in five or six generations.

"Finding the answer to the Koan and breaking the hold of the Mushin was the first step. The second step was opening up the rest of the planet for colonization. That got us physically away from the mind leeches and allowed us to increase our numbers dramatically. Before, we were always just on the edge of possible extinction. But now . . ." she gestured widely at the Plain as if to indicate all the thousands who dwelt on it.

"O.K. There've been a lot of changes since Jerome's day. And the first steps of his plan are complete. But just travel around some time. Check on how the average 'steader or settler lives. Look at the tools he uses. Or go to a 'hood. See what kinds of production techniques they use to make those tools.

"What you'll find, Edwyr, is a world not one bit advanced over the one Jerome left. Three generations, and not one bit advanced. And if Andretti and the Council have their way, in three more generations it'll still be the same!"

"But we're making progress in the Way . . ."

"Are we?" Yolan countered aggressively. "Are we really? Are we so much more advanced, so much further along the Great Way than we were a generation ago? Is everyone in the hierarchy, everyone on the Free Council, really and truly enlightened? Are they all immune to the Mushin? Or what about Mitsuyama and the PlainsLords? Are they even following the Way? Are they developing as Jerome intended?

"I'm sorry, Edwyr, but everywhere I look, all I see is growing conflict, disintegration, backsliding, and regression. Damn it, we're *not* progressing! We're stagnating again!

"The Keepers don't think Jerome meant it to be this way. We believe there was a third step to his plan, a step that's never been realized. And we're convinced that's why he sent us to the Flagship."

Edwyr looked and sounded astonished. "Are you saying Jerome wanted you to use the information in the computer to reintroduce technology on Kensho? Is that what you mean by a 'third step'?"

She nodded confidently. "Once the Mushin were under control and the population large enough to make extinction unlikely, the next logical step was to move forward and improve the standard of living. There's no good reason why Kensho has to remain a marginal agricultural economy forever, you know. And there are plenty of good reasons why it shouldn't.

"Right now, most 'steaders and settlers spend nearly every waking hour grubbing out a meager living. It's their sweat that supports the 'hoods, the Free Council, and the whole damn hierarchy. But aside from a little training as children, they never have enough time to really follow the Way themselves.

"Jerome knew technology could change all that. It could free a lot more people to follow the Way. And that's why he sent us to the Flagship. To bring back the knowledge necessary to reintroduce technology.

"But it wasn't just a rehash of the Home World methods he hoped for. No, he expected us to develop a new kind of technology."

"New?" he questioned. "New in what way? What do you mean?"

"I mean a technology that fits in with the rest of his plan. One that's appropriate to the Great Way and our needs here on Kensho. It has to be a technology that'll provide each and every one of us with a decent, becoming existence. But it has to do it without destroying our world and our humanity in the process."

"But how is that possible?" he muttered in bewilderment. "On the Home World . . ."

Yolan pushed his words aside, relentlessly pressing her argument home. "Forget Earth! They didn't have the Way. They saw things in a completely different light. They never really believed in Oneness with the world. Nor did they ever truly understand the idea of Oneness within themselves. Their technology simply reflected their values; it was their values that destroyed their world, not their technology!

"But our values are different. We *do* have the Way! Thanks to the Mushin, we have to practice it for our very survival. It colors and shapes our every thought and action. So any technology we develop will have to incorporate the values of the Way if it's to have any viability on Kensho at all.

"Look, Edwyr. Jerome taught us the inter-relatedness of Each to Each to All. So any technology we create will have to be nondestructive of the environment. You don't tear your world apart if you're conscious of your Oneness with it. You learn to work with the world, in harmony with nature.

"And if you honestly believe in inner Oneness, in Harmony, you don't build a system that puts people on assembly lines that take away all meaning from their work and their lives. Instead, work becomes a way for a person to develop his character. It gives him an opportunity to express himself and provides an outlet for his creativity. It puts him in touch with his fellow men by giving him a chance to produce things that fill their needs as well as his own. The emphasis shifts from 'product' to 'person.' And tools that enhance an individual's ability to work take the place of machines that merely displace him by taking over the truly human part of his task."

"But where does a technology like that go, Yolan? How far can it develop? Can it really accomplish this 'third stage' you believe in?"

She shrugged. "I don't know the answer to your first question.

"Nobody knows, because nobody's ever tried it on a world-wide scale before. It certainly wouldn't take us down the path Earth travelled. So if you're worried about the Message and catching up with the Home World, I can't offer much help.

"But I do think it'd accomplish what Jerome had in mind. And maybe a lot more.

"There is one thing I am sure of, though. Wherever our kind of technology leads us, it'll always be firmly based on the ideals of the Way and the vision of Jerome. It won't destroy Kensho and it will provide for human dignity and creativity."

For a long time, Edwyr sat, considering everything Yolan had told him. Finally he spoke in a soft, warm voice. "I'm impressed. I never guessed the Keepers's vision was so . . . so beautiful." Yolan smiled slightly in response, but didn't answer, realizing he had more to say and not wishing to interrupt now that her story was told.

"But I'm worried," he continued. "Not about what you said or about the intentions of the Keepers and Artisans. I'm worried about the others. Let's face it. You're right when you say not everyone nowadays holds Jerome's ideals in as great esteem as you do.

Once you've introduced technology, how will you keep it true to the Way? How can you keep other people from misusing the things you create?"

"You mean people like Mitsuyama?" she asked. He nodded. "I can't guarantee it. But then not everybody within the Great Way sticks to it, either. Can you guarantee that somebody like Andretti won't twist the words of Jerome to his own ends? Maybe we should abolish it because it might be turned to evil!"

Edwyr smiled patiently. "That's not an answer, Yolan."

"Then here's one," she snapped. "If you suppress technology just because it might be turned to evil, it'll appear eventually anyway. It's only human to want a decent living. And only technology can provide it. The pressures will grow and grow. That's what Mitsuyama really represents. He's just the first. There'll be more. And when technology finally does break through, it'll be from outside the Way and as its enemy!"

The Seeker smiled again. "That's still not an answer. A threat, yes. And probably true. But not an answer."

For long moments Yolan stared at the ground. Then she sighed, the tension draining from her frame. "Yeh. I know what you're saying. You know, it's funny. When I was at home, when I was around Keepers and Artisans and was learning to be a Keeper myself, I never questioned the rightness of what we were doing. It was just so obvious! We were following the Way, doing what Jerome wanted. I don't think my mother ever once mentioned the idea that anybody here on Kensho would even think of misusing our knowledge. That was the way things had been on the Home World, but not here on Kensho.

"Mother Elena was the first who ever raised the

question with me. I never let her know it, but it's
bothered me ever since." She glanced up at Edwyr,
her expression mutely pleading for understanding. "I
really want to find the answer. I feel there is one. At
times I can almost reach out and touch it. But then it
twists away just at the last moment."

She was silent again, her expression closed, her
attention turned inward. "I guess," she muttered
softly, "we all just thought it would happen naturally.
Just a result of the Way and men adapting to life on
Kensho. It seemed to be the inevitable direction the
human race was heading, the path the Mushin were
forcing us to follow. But now with Andretti and Mitsuyama . . ." Her voice faltered. "There are times,"
she started up again, a hint of wistful regret tinging
her words, "when I almost wish we'd never penned
up the Mushin."

The Seeker glanced at her sharply. "What do you
mean by that?"

"Well, look. Exposure to the Mushin produced
Jerome. And Chaka. And Obie. The Mushin used to
act directly on almost everyone, weeding out the
weak and those who weren't capable of following the
Way. Now only a few experience them. Oh, I know
we all study the Way. But sometimes I wonder if
that's really changing mankind as much as the Mushin
did originally. Maybe we're just fooling ourselves
when we think we're still developing. I mean, Andretti studied the Way all his life. But is *he* the
direction we're heading now? Gods! If he's the best
the Way has to offer . . . ! Or Mitsuyama. Would
anybody with a mind like his survive if the Mushin
were still loose? Out there beyond the Barrier Hills
nobody can force him to study the Way, and there
aren't any Mushin to expose his evil thoughts."

She shook her head sadly, dejectedly. "I don't

know, Edwyr. I just don't know. I *feel* we're right. I *feel* that the answer to the doubts you've raised is right there in plain sight. But I can't point to it.

"That doesn't mean I don't intend to go on seeking it, though." A note of determination added firmness to her voice. "And it doesn't mean that I intend to give up being a Keeper just because I don't have the answer to every question.

"Edwyr, we can't reject all the good that technology, our kind of technology, can accomplish just because it *might* be used for evil. Giving in like that would be a terrible defeat for our race and for its future on Kensho. It'd be like admitting we're incapable of improving ourselves or our society. It'd be like saying that our only hope lies in withdrawing to some mountain top to live in poverty and ignorance. I can't accept that. I refuse to believe that evil always and inevitably wins in the confrontation with good. Good and evil aren't absolute forces, independent of us, Edwyr. They come from within us. We create them. If evil triumphs, it's because we allow it to. And by the same token, good can be the victor if we care enough and work hard enough to assure it. It's up to us."

Silent, wrapped in her own thoughts, Yolan stared into the dark. Unwilling to break into her reverie, Edwyr lay back and looked up at the sky. One of the moons had already set. Another was near the horizon. The third had moved only slightly westward. And a glow at the eastern edge of the Plain promised the arrival of the fourth. Behind the moons, the stars shone faintly. Off to the east, below the horizon from where they now were, the Fixed Stars, the Arks and the Flagship, kept bright, steady watch over First Touch.

Carefully, Edwyr calmed and cleared his mind. Then he let Yolan's words roll through his consciousness. Here and there they struck responsive chords with his own ideas. In other places they seemed fuzzy or mismatched. But on the whole, they fitted well.

Could Father Johnston have known about the Keepers, he wondered. Could they actually be a part of the Plan?

An unexpected thought entered his mind. It was one of Jerome's Koans. "As the Ronin strikes, oh, how beautiful the constant stars!" He had repeated it thousands of times, contemplated it, even used it to achieve Satori. But now, amazingly, he saw it in a new light! Could he have been misinterpreting it all these years?

"As the Ronin strikes . . ." could stand for any kind of danger. . ". . . oh . . ." directed the attention to . . . ". . . how beautiful the constant stars!" which might very well refer to the Arks and the Flagship! They were "constant stars," always in stationary orbit over First Touch! Was Jerome trying to hint that help against enemies might lie in the Flagship? Perhaps in the computer on the Flagship? Was the Koan Jerome's way of pointing to how useful the material gathered by the Keepers would be to those who followed him on Kensho?

And Jerome's other Koan! "A sword in the scabbard is a treasure beyond compare." That could mean that the data in the computer was a treasure beyond compare! After all, Jerome had found the sword of Nakamura on the Flagship! In a sense, the ship had been the sword's scabbard for centuries. And the ship was also the scabbard for the knowledge the Keepers had collected.

Stunned, Edwyr lay for a long time trying to assimilate these new ideas. At the first opportunity, he knew he would have to spend several days in deep contemplation to work it all out.

But even now he knew that what Yolan had just told him changed everything!

XVIII

Long, long ago the pressure became too great and the Plain broke in two. The western half tilted upward along its eastern edge and a sudden range of jagged hills was born. Stretching north and south for over a thousand miles, they were nowhere more than five or six miles wide, nor greater than 200 feet high. Nevertheless, their sheer steepness, especially along the eastern face, made them an effective barrier to travelers.

Time and several rivers had created a few passes. One, the broadest, lay far to the north where First River cut its way toward the setting sun. A second, twisted, abandoned by the stream that formed it, bisected the hills at about their half-way point. Two more were located many miles to the south. Most travelers took the easy routes to the far north or south. The only real advantage to the Middle Pass, as it was called, was the fact that it was the most direct path to the grazing lands of the PlainsLords. Since that was no advantage at all as far as most people were concerned, it was seldom used.

The soldier who lay on the crest of the hills near the mouth of the pass gazed with bored eyes across the Plain. He'd been there for four hours, ever since noon. And in all that time he'd seen nothing more interesting than a flock of Darters. If it wasn't for the fact that the Groupleader was such a bastard he would have dozed at his post. But the son-of-a-bitch had a nasty habit of sneaking up on sentries and Gods help the poor soldier who wasn't awake and doing his job.

He rolled on his back for a few minutes and stared up at the sky just to break the monotony. Shit, he

thought, what a stupid way to spend a week! Sittin'
out here in the middle of nowhere waiting for some
bastard who never comes. Wouldn't be so bad if old
Group would let us just sit. But no, the bastard makes
us drill like always. Hell, he makes us drill more.
That's a fact! Shit.

Turning back on his stomach again, he glared eastward. Bet this son-of-a-bitch we're rotting here for
went north like everybody else. Travelers never
come this way. Shit. Least if we were back at Base,
we'd have women. Like Janie. Or that new little one I
met just before leavin'. Bet she's already tied up by
some guy now. Damn. Another miss.

A small dot appeared on the horizon. He tensed,
then relaxed. Probably just another bunch of Darters.
Maybe a lost ken-cow. He looked again, straining to
see more. Now there were two dots. No doubt about
it. Two. Couldn't be Darters. Flocks never got that
close.

He watched for several more minutes. Two dots.
Almost figures. Tiny, but not ken-cows, not Darters.
We're only waiting for one man, he remembered. But
there isn't any good reason a man can't travel with
someone he met on his journey. Lot safer that way.
Could be our man, he decided. Too bad about his
companion. Tough shit, fellow. That's the way it goes.

Coming at a run, he estimated. Better get my ass in
gear and get down to report to Group. He'll want to
get the men set in position, just in case it is the right
man. Poor bastard won't know what hit him. Just
chop-chop from eight of us. Won't be much left. And
that's a fact.

He rose and left at a trot. If he'd stayed for just a few
more minutes he would have seen eight new dots
appear on the horizon.

* * *

The Ronin had been closing the gap all afternoon.
Yolan simply couldn't keep the pace today. Not after
yesterday. Edwyr looked sideways at her drawn face.
She was on the verge of utter collapse.

Up ahead the Barrier Hills loomed into the sky.
They really weren't all that high, but in the midst of so
much flatness, they seemed towering mountains. He
could see the break that indicated the mouth of Middle Pass. Well done, he congratulated himself. Right
on the button.

He glanced at Yolan again. The time for action was
coming soon, he realized. I've got to get rid of at least
two of the Ronin and make sure the other six take out
after me. It's her only hope. He had a vague plan in
mind. Somewhere in the twisting pass ahead he
would double back and ambush the last two Ronin,
then lead the rest on a merry chase eastward while
Yolan escaped through the pass to the west. It might
work. It *had* to work.

The Keeper stumbled and almost went down,
Edwyr grabbed her by the elbow to steady her. She
turned a bleak, empty smile in his direction. He
nodded toward the hills and said, "We'll rest soon."
Yolan simply gave a quick glance back at their pursuers and didn't bother to answer.

Edwyr copied her motion. The Ronin were closer.
All day they had been driving the two before them,
creeping nearer and nearer. The Seeker had pushed
Yolan as far as he dared. She simply didn't have any
reserves left. There would be no more bursts of
speed.

He estimated the distance left to the pass. Then he
figured on the lead they had over the Ronin. About
two and a half to three miles. They might catch us
somewhere near the western mouth of the pass, he
realized. Or on the Plain on the other side. That gives

me just enough time to try my plan. Somewhere in the middle would be best. Hide Yolan, then double back. When she hears the commotion, she can take off westward.

He turned it around and around in his mind. Any way he looked at it, it was still a long shot. Would it be better if they just made a stand and fought it out? Eight to two? And Yolan barely able to lift her weapon? The long shot was better odds.

As they came to the slight upgrade leading to the mouth of the pass, Yolan's breath began to take on a sobbing quality. She sucked the air in huge, quavering gasps. "Not much further," Edwyr urged her. "Just a little way." It was like talking to a child. Yolan was just a machine now, unthinking, merely repeating motions in a hopeless, mechanical way. She staggered slightly on the uneven ground and the Seeker held her arm again, supporting her, ready to drag her if necessary.

At first the walls of the pass were sheer and offered no place for doubling back, much less concealment for an ambush. It'll get better in the middle, he reassured himself. Just around the next bend, it'll widen out a bit. It took a full mile before his prediction came true. And then another mile passed before conditions really looked right.

He was about to stop when Yolan suddenly pulled back on his arm. At first he thought the Keeper had fallen. But as he turned to face her, he saw she was on her feet.

Her chest heaving with the effort to breathe, she had a wild, frightened look on her face. Clearly she was struggling to bring her gasping under control so she could talk. Her free hand waved emphatically toward the west. "Bad," she managed to croak.

He pulled gently at her arm. "Come on," he urged.

"Just a little further. I have a plan."

"No!" she shook her head emphatically. "No. Wrong. All wrong."

"What do you mean?" he asked in perplexity.

"Danger. Ahead. I can sense it. Wrong."

"Ahead? You sense danger ahead? Is it the Ronin? Gods, they can't have gotten ahead of us!"

"Not . . . not Ronin," she answered uncertainly. "Different. But danger."

For a second, Edwyr considered. Her sense was usually very accurate, even if he didn't understand it. But danger ahead? What? Or who? He looked at her, a question in his glance. "To the east?"

Yolan nodded. "Still there."

"Which is closer?"

She nodded to the west. He quickly calculated. The Ronin would be just about entering the mouth of the pass now. Make that two miles back. About fifteen minutes. Say the new danger was a mile or so ahead. They just had time to check it. "O.K.," he said. "Let's go see what this new problem is. Tell me when we're close." The woman nodded and they set off again.

In about a mile and a half, she pulled at his arm. "Close. Just ahead." The floor of the pass was wider here, maybe 500 yards across. Just ahead, it narrowed suddenly as a hill thrust out a steep shoulder from the north side. The remaining gap was perhaps 200 yards. wide. Perfect spot for an ambush, Edwyr thought.

Leaving Yolan walking in a slow circle to cool down, Edwyr quickly scaled the shoulder of the north hill and peered over the top to its western slope. For several moments he saw nothing. Then, suddenly, a flash of light, the merest flicker of sun reflected from metal, shone from behind some low shrubs. In an instant, Edwyr saw the whole plan.

There were eight of them, hidden and waiting.

Anyone coming around the shoulder of the hill from the east would run right into the middle of their group. They'd be on him in a flash, before he even had time to unsling his blade. And their swords were already drawn, ready to slash and kill. He shuddered. Yolan's sense was inexplicable, but invaluable.

Carefully, he scrambled back down to the waiting Keeper. Two sets of enemies! The eight ambushers were in all likelihood Mitsuyama's men. I should have known he'd try again, he silently cursed. He shook his head grimly.

Wait, though! The Ronin and the PlainsLords were hardly allies! And the enemy of my enemy can turn out to be my friend, he reminded himself. Provided they're handled right! Of course! he almost chortled out loud. Mitsuyama has provided me with exactly the ambush I was looking for!

He reached the Keeper and hurriedly bustled her off to a spot of concealment with instructions not to reveal herself no matter what happened. Satisfied she could not be seen by anyone coming from the east, he set off at a run down the pass toward the Ronin.

He was hoping to find them just inside the pass, at the narrowest, most twisted point. That way the pass itself would act to screen the first yells of the Ronin from the ears of Mitsuyama's men. If he ran the killers hard enough, he figured they'd stop screaming almost immediately to conserve their wind. The quieter they were, the better.

As he came around a particularly tight bend, he suddenly came on them. In mutual surprise, Edwyr and the eight stopped dead in their tracks. Then, with a fierce shriek of blood lust, the chase was on. The Seeker turned and fled. The killers responded as he had expected, straining to keep up with him, eager to strike, silently conserving their precious breath for running. Aside from the pounding of eight pairs of feet, and the labored gasping of eight mouths, the pursuit was as quiet as death itself.

The adrenaline flooding his body, combined with his calm, clear state of mind, gave Edwyr a sense of euphoric floating. There was joy in this race, joy even in the thought of possible death. Death held no fear for the Seeker. Long, long ago, he had learned to confront it. Now all that counted was living and enjoying the moment. If death came, it came. There was nothing more to be said.

He slowed his pace just slightly to tease the killers who panted behind him. Sensing a chance to close for the kill, they put on a new burst of speed. The lead Ronin was no more then 15 yards behind him now and he could feel the tingling pressure of excited Mushin. They were hungry and eager for a feast. I'll give them more than they bargain for, he thought grimly.

Another minute and he rounded the last bend. Dead ahead was the hill that thrust its shoulder southwards, narrowing the valley. He headed straight for the spot, hoping the Ronin would continue their silence.

They did. As he raced through the gap, he could see the men who lay in ambush leap to their feet to attack. But he was going much faster than they had anticipated or had any reason to expect. Before any could strike he was past them and heading swiftly westward.

They had no chance to pursue, for no sooner had Edwyr swept by than the Ronin poured around the hill. There was a brief moment of dead silence and mutual astonishment as the two groups faced each other. Then the air was split by the hideous screech of the Ronin and the startled bellows of the ambushers as the two sides closed in combat.

It was a wild, bloody melee. Every man hacked at anyone who came within sword's reach. Naked blades flashed in the sun once, and then flashed no more, but shimmered instead with red gore. The clash of metal on metal, the dull thunk of metal on flesh, was nearly drowned out by the cries of agony or shrieks of victory. The battle swirled over the fallen, and more dropped to the ground, some instantly dead, others writhing or crawling, clutching their hacked bodies to keep them from falling apart.

Edwyr stood some hundred feet off and calmly watched the mutual slaughter. He looked on as dying men became feasts for the frenzied Mushin and met their ends in raving madness. There was nothing new here. In fact, it was as old as mankind. Death was never pleasant. And violent death, made even more violent by the Mushin, was no sweeter.

With a final, mingled scream of one man dying and another victorious, silence fell over the pass. Carefully, his own sword drawn, Edwyr approached the last standing figure. It was a Ronin, his back turned, swaying slightly as if deeply exhausted. The man turned and with a shock the Seeker recognized the leader of the killers, the one he had spoken with before.

The two stood several yards apart, slowly eyeing each other with appraising looks. Then the Ronin spoke. "Totality is sated. I am wounded and exhausted. There is no power left. It would be an easy kill." His voice was soft and sibilant. "But it would be wasted. Totality is sated."

For a moment longer, he stared at the unmoving Seeker. Finally he shrugged. He began to wipe his gory blade on the shabby skirt of his robe. While he worked he glanced out of the side of his eye at Edwyr and muttered. "This one is strange. He does not attack. Totality cannot read him. He is not there."

Finishing his task, he thrust the sword back in its scabbard, ignoring the fact that Edwyr's was still drawn. "This one will not attack. Why? Will this human let a Ronin live?"

"This human does not like the idea of setting so many Mushin free to roam around on their own, Ronin. Out here on the Plain, people aren't so well protected against them. The Way isn't practiced by everyone. And many who do practice it are weak in its disciplines. No, best not to kill you. Alone, you're no threat. The mind leeches will stay with you. They're sated now, as you say. You'll be a long way from here before they become a problem."

"No," the Ronin shook his head. "There are too many for one Mind Brother. Too many. We were 12 once. Now we are one. Totality is too great a burden for one."

Edwyr was startled and disturbed by this news. "You mean you can't hold them all?"

"Totality is too great for one Mind Brother," he affirmed.

They stood looking at each other.

The Ronin muttered to himself. "But this one can carry some. Yes. This one can be Mind Brother to Totality. This one is not here, but he can carry. This is strange. But this is true."

Edwyr stared blankly at the killer. "Me? Carry Mushin?"

"Yes," the other nodded. "Yes. Totality will divide. Each half will be weaker. This subunit can control and carry one half. This other one can be Mind Brother to the rest. Yes."

The Seeker's mind raced as he tried to make sense of what the Ronin had said. Too many Mushin? Yes, that did seem logical. This had been an unusually large pack of Ronin. If the ratio of killers to mind leeches was similar to that in the foothills, then there would be a large number of Mushin accompanying the group. And since the practice of leaving one Ronin alive to carry the group's Mushin had been developed for dealing with smaller numbers, it probably wouldn't work here. The Ronin leader's claim that there were too many for him to handle alone seemed likely to be true.

But that implied that the man actually had some control over the mind leeches! That they didn't control him! What had he called himself? "Mind Brother?" What in the hell could that mean? Edwyr remembered their first encounter. At that time, both he and Yolan had noticed that the Mushin seemed to be in some kind of order. Could it be that the Ronin were able to organize the invisible creatures? Or were they automatically structured by being a Totality?

Come to think of it, weren't the 'hoods in the Home Valley actually doing basically the same thing? Their way of tying the Mushin to the 'hood, by keeping them fooled and fed through the careful release of emotive energy, was clearly a form of conscious control. Was it possible that the Ronin had developed a similar form of control naturally? Gods only knew they'd had some ten generations of extremely close contact with the mind leeches to accomplish it.

But that meant that intimate contact with the Mushin wasn't necessarily or automatically destructive! For the fact was that the Ronin had not become extinct! Even though their major source of recruitment had been cut off by the spread of the Great Way and the penning of most of the Mushin in the Home Valley, the Ronin had not disappeared! Could it be that the killers had managed to establish some kind of mutually beneficial relationship with the mind leeches? Had they become symbiotes?

The very idea staggered his imagination. It was simply too huge, too contrary to everything he had ever heard or thought, to allow him to deal with it immediately. The whole proposition would have to be examined carefully, slowly, and a lot more data gathered, before it could be evaluated intelligently.

In any case, there was a more immediate problem. The extra Mushin couldn't be allowed to run free, spreading the Madness and death wherever they went.

He calmed his mind and considered the problem. The truth was that he could carry some. Before entering the Way of the Sword, he'd spent a novitiate period in one of the 'hoods in the Home Valley. There he'd participated in the care and feeding of the captive mind leeches. He knew how to bind them to him.

What would playing nursemaid to a bunch of invisible Mushin do to his mission? It would definitely be distracting, but not fatally so. He hoped. Others were doing almost the same.

The Seeker nodded. Yes, it *could* be done. Because it *must* be done. "All right," he said to the Ronin. "I'll carry half."

The man smiled a strange, blank humorless smile. "Yes, this one can do it. Totality knows. But will this one keep the part of Totality he will carry? Will he isolate it, make it weak, divide it from itself?"

Edwyr blinked in confusion. "What do you mean? What is it you want?"

"This subunit wants nothing. Totality wants Totality. You will go your own way and take part of Totality with you. This is not good."

"You want me to go with you?"

"Totality wants it. But I see it is not possible. I will tell Totality." He began to mutter to himself. "Totality understands," he said after a few moments. "But will you return those you carry? You will not take them to captivity?"

"Return them? How? Where?"

"Ahhhh. Yes. To me. Or to some other Mind Brother. Our Totality is already so small, so weak that any loss is too great."

Edwyr snorted. "I'm not very likely to go searching for a bunch of Ronin to return some damn Mushin! I value my skin too much for that."

"But we will not hurt this one," murmured the Ronin softly. "No. No. We wish it no harm. It is helping Totality. It would be a good Mind Brother. Even though we cannot see it," he finished in a mutter.

The Seeker looked at him with frank curiosity. "You're actually offering me safe conduct to return the mind leeches to the first Ronin I meet?" The man nodded. "How can you guarantee it? How do I know they'll honor it?"

"Totality wants it. All subunits will want it and obey."

Edwyr's jaw dropped in astonishment. "You . . . you . . . are you saying you can communicate with all the other Ronin?" There was a firm nod for a reply. The Seeker gasped.

Again he stood immobile, his mind turning a whole new set of data over and over. If the Ronin controlled the Mushin, or at least had developed some sort of stable and mutually beneficial relationship with them . . . and if they could use the Mushin to communicate with each other in some fashion . . . An incredible idea suddenly occured to Edwyr and a whole piece of the Plan, a part previously unresolved, fell into place. "Do you . . . can you control the Ronin? I mean, can you keep them from attacking?"

"Attack is not necessary. This subunit does not attack you. If it is not in Totality's interest, this subunit will not attack."

"What about in your own interest?"

The Ronin looked briefly puzzled. "Own? This one is a subunit, a Mind Brother."

"But you wouldn't attack unless it would be beneficial to you and the Mushin?"

"Yes. That is true."

A thrill of excitement ran through Edwyr. It might work! And if it did, it would solve the biggest problem in the Plan.

"Ronin," he said sharply. "Tell Totality this. I will return the part I carry. I will return them to Ronin who will come to First Pass in one month at the time of the three moons followed by one. You will lead those Ronin. There will be many of them. They will stay on the mountains at the sides of the pass.

"I will do more. I will do things which will be very beneficial for Totality, which will increase its size and strength. But Totality must agree to withhold attack, before and after. You will watch me and follow my lead. It will be good for Totality. This I promise."

The Ronin looked puzzled at first. Then, with a shrug, he began to mutter silently to himself, a sign Edwyr had come to recognize meant he was conferring with the Mushin he controlled. After a few moments, his expression changed to one of surprise followed by pleasure. He spoke. "Yes. This subunit will do as you say, human. Totality agrees. Yes. Much benefit will come.

"But, if not, human, the agreement will be broken and Totality will attack. Not you. You are a Mind Brother. But others, any who are with you."

"Agreed. If I don't deliver what I promise the deal's off. Even for me. O.K.?"

"Yes. Now we will pick up our burdens."

In less than half an hour, the Ronin had limped back down the pass towards the east. Edwyr, tightly holding a pack of sluggish Mushin with his mind, was already growing used to the situation. The killer had made a few very useful suggestions on how to be a Mind Brother and Edwyr had found them easy to put into practice. Now, when the invisible creatures were sated, was a good time to try things out and he experimented as he walked slowly back to where he had left Yolan.

He found her, sound asleep, huddled against the boulder she had hidden behind, and decided to make camp there for the night. Understanding that sleep was better nourishment for her condition than kencow cheese, he ate a quick supper and then settled down to develop his abilities as a Mushin herder.

Several hours later, as two moons stood high overhead, he felt secure enough in his control to sleep. He looked over at the soundly slumbering Keeper and smiled. Tomorrow they'd part ways. Perhaps forever. He had new allies in his quest, but failure was still possible. And death.

Yet he knew that if he survived, he'd find her again. They'd only travelled together for a few days. But it had been long enough to show him the journey was worth continuing.

BOOK VII

JIMSON

XIX

The sword sliced a glittering curve in the air, and with a ringing clash met another blade and stopped it. For a moment both blades paused, clinging together as if stunned.

"Well blocked, Lord" panted Jimson. He stepped quickly back, moving slightly to the right. "But I still think two hands are stronger than one. I can break through."

Mitsuyama smiled grimly. "Prove it, renegade. A one-handed sword is lighter, faster. And my arm is strong. Come. Try to break through. Let us see the color of your blood!"

The two men circled each other warily, looking for openings. Jimson feinted a cut to the wrist. With a grunt of surprise he barely evaded Mitsuyama's swift counter. Damn! he thought. That cursed sword of his is quick! But he's got to be weaker. Especially against head cuts. What if I strike overhead, catch his sword near the hilt, and then grab his wrist with one hand while keeping the pressure up on my sword with the other hand? I should be able to twist the thing right out of his grasp!

Action followed thought. The ex-Seeker feinted low, then stepped in, aiming a sweeping slash at the PlainsLord's head. Again the other man's blade rose to block. But this time, as the two met and paused, Jimson stepped in and grabbed for the wrist as planned.

With a grip like steel, he twisted Mitsuyama's whole arm to the left. His voice heavy with his effort, he gritted out, "I told you two were stronger than one! I win, Lord!"

Mitsuyama laughed harshly. "You spend all your time on one hand and don't even know what the other is up to. Look at my other hand!"

Jimson glanced toward his own right side. There, firmly pressing an iron dagger against his ribs, was Mitsuyama's left hand! The renegade paled. "You're *dead*," hissed the PlainsLord, his eyes glittering with triumph.

As Jimson's grip loosened, Mitsuyama stepped back, laughing viciously. "You trust, renegade. You trust appearances. Because you only see one hand fighting, you assume only one hand is fighting. Fool! Be very happy we only play with practice blades. And remember the lesson for the future!" With a last snort of a laugh, the Supreme Lord of the Plains spun about and stalked toward the shade at the edge of the practice yard.

I'll remember, Lord, Jimson thought as he wiped his brow. When the moment comes, I'll remember, and there'll be one less trick you can use!

There was a sudden commotion at the eastern end of the yard and a guard from the gate came loping up to Mitsuyama. Jimson hurried over to see what was happening. As he got there, the man was repeating his message in a low voice.

". . . he says eight swords, my Lord. Wants to return 'em, he says. Says they're yours."

Mitsuyama shot Jimson a sharp glance. "Would you recognize the swords of that patrol you sent out?"

"The one we sent to the Barrier Hills?"

"Yes."

"Uh, well, I'd know the Group's sword. I might know some of the others. Certainly I would recognize the general pattern of our swords—and there aren't eight of them missing."

The PlainsLord gazed musingly at the ground.

Without looking up he asked softly, "Sentry, what's this man look like?"

"Oh, he's youngish, my Lord. Dressed in a plain brown robe. Carries a sword slung across his back, he does. Dusty. Been travelling a while, I'd say."

Jimson and Mitsuyama exchanged a meaningful glance. "He couldn't . . ." began the renegade.

"He did," finished Mitsuyama. "Sentry, take a squad. No, take two. Bring the traveler here, to me. Now."

"Lord, is that advisable? If he really . . . I mean, eight men . . . He might be dangerous." Jimson frowned as he spoke.

"They attacked him. I know it's hard to believe, but somehow I know he's not dangerous unless provoked." The PlainsLord took a new towel and began drying his forehead and neck again.

The disturbance around the gate increased as the two squads of Avengers, swords drawn, entered with a lone figure in their midst. Every idle person in the yard moved as close as possible to see what was causing the commotion. Before the little knot of soldiers was half way across the open, sun-drenched space, a fair-sized crowd had gathered.

"I don't like this," muttered Jimson to his Lord.

"Agreed. But," with a shrug, "we must make do with circumstances." Mitsuyama refused to crane his neck to catch a glimpse of the brown-robed figure. He stood stolidly, his arms crossed on his chest, his glance straight ahead.

The two squads stopped directly in front of him. The leaders parted, leaving clear space between the PlainsLord and the man in their midst. Standing there, a slight, distant smile on his lips, a bundle of swords over his shoulder, stood Edwyr.

The Seeker inclined his head slightly toward Mit-

suyama. "Lord William Mitsuyama, Supreme Lord of
the Plains, I assume." His tone was light, almost
bantering. He looked at the mob surrounding him, at
the soldiers with their drawn swords forming a tight
wall, and at Jimson and several others who stood next
to the PlainsLord, their hands on the hilts of their
weapons. "You're well protected. Were you expecting an army?"

Mitsuyama instantly liked this cool young man who
stood amidst a sea of enemies and joked. What a pity
he's an enemy instead of an ally, he thought. I could
use a few like him! Did he really kill all eight? Best not
even ask. No need to dishearten my mighty warriors
with the news that one young Seeker of the Way of the
Sword is worth eight of them!

"You've brought me something?" he asked, indi-
cating the bundle over Edwyr's shoulder with a flick
of his eyes.

The young man looked at his burden almost in
surprise. "Why, yes. So I did. Some men of yours left
these lying about. I thought you might want to give
them to their next of kin." Carelessly, he dropped the
swords to the ground in a clattering heap. "No sense
in wasting good metal. You can always make them
into plows."

"And whom am I to thank for this generous gift?"

"Ah. Edwyr. Just Edwyr. Oh, yes. I'm a Seeker of
the Way of the Sword."

"Lord," interrupted Jimson, his voice breaking in
anger. "Lord . . . all eight of them. Good men. I—"

A harsh hand motion from the PlainsLord chopped
the renegade's words off suddenly. "The man is our
guest. He came upon some of our soldier's weapons
and was kind enough to return them. That is all." As
he spoke he kept his eyes steadily on Edwyr's. "He'll
be our guest for a while. Yes, our honored guest.

Perhaps he can tell us news of what is happening to the east. We hear so little, out here beyond the Barrier Hills.

"Of course," he continued off-handedly, "you'll have to give up your sword. It wouldn't be hospitable to let you carry it around. You're quite safe here. Kindly give it to my man," he indicated Jimson, "and he'll take care of it for you."

Complete silence fell over the courtyard. For several moments Edwyr stood there, unmoving. His gaze was locked on Mitsuyama's, but he was keenly aware of the growing tension all around him. Finally he shrugged and reached slowly up to unsling his sword from his back. Every hand tightened on sword hilt as he brought it around to the front and slipped it over his head. With a mocking smile he laid it at his feet and stepped back two steps. "Do you think your man has strength enough in his legs to come and get it? I doubt your highly nervous friends would allow me to approach you with a sharp stick in my hands, much less a sword."

Mitsuyama made a small motion with his hand. Jimson stepped jerkily forward and snatched up the sword. The renegade's face was stiff with his effort to control his emotions, but his eyes burned with anger as he stared at the Seeker. Eight men! he thought. Eight of my best! You've got a lot to answer for, Seeker!

The other man simply cocked his head to one side and calmly returned Jimson's glare. Yet there was something in his gaze, something indefinable, that chilled Mitsuyama's man to his very core. He shuddered as he stepped backward toward the protection of the circle of men. There's something wrong here, he told himself. This man is more than he seems. He has an air, a . . . a feeling about him that doesn't ring

true. What could it be? he wondered. I almost recognize . . . something . . . He tore his eyes from Edwyr's and turned to hand the sword to Mitsuyama.

Drawing the sword part way from its scabbard, the
PlainsLord looked it over. "Hmmmm. Nothing special. A thoroughly ordinary weapon. Obviously, then,
the skill lies with its wielder." He shoved it back with
a snap and handed it to Jimson. "Put it in the 'guest
armory' while Edwyr is visiting us. Now show him to
his room." He turned back to the Seeker and inclined
his head slightly. "We'll talk later." With that he left
the circle guarding the lone figure and strode across
the yard.

Jimson bowed mockingly to Edwyr and said, "This
way, honored guest. Follow me."

"Certainly," the Seeker replied softly. "I'd rather
have you leading than behind my back."

The renegade's face went rigid at the remark. He
spun about with a curt, "Come," directed at the two
squads of soldiers. "Bring him." They began to troop
obediently after Jimson, with Edwyr in their midst.
He walked freely, untouched, with an empty space of
several feet between him and the surrounding
guards.

On the north side of the courtyard, at a point ap-
proximately equidistant from the two gates, they entered a door guarded by two men with drawn swords.
Inside, they followed a hallway that ran straight before them. Halfway down it, they turned right into a
branching corridor. After passing several closed,
barred doors, the side-hall ended at a final door next
to which stood another sentry. At a signal from Jimson, the man lifted the heavy bar and swung the door
open. The renegade bowed the Seeker into the room
which lay beyond.

The room was about twenty feet square. The flat white walls were bare and windowless. The only light came from a skylight set some fifteen feet overhead in the ceiling. It was barred with a heavy iron grill. Here and there, brackets were set to hold torches, but they were presently empty.

In each of the two far corners were pallets for sleeping. Set into the walls at the head of each were screens which slid back to reveal recesses for storing clothing and bedding. Against the right-hand wall was a low table and two cushions. A folding screen stood by the left-hand wall and just visible behind it was a chamber pot.

Standing in the middle of the room was a small, slender man who looked startled and frightened. His narrow face had a pinched, unhappy look, and his eyes held a wild, hunted glare. The robe he wore was dirty and rumpled, while the greying hair on his head stood out in unruly clumps and tangles. He shifted nervously from foot to foot and muttered uncertainly as Edwyr walked in and looked around.

"Carlson," sneered Jimson, "allow me to introduce your new room-mate. He's a Seeker. Edwyr. And I think he'll be staying for a while. Just like you." With a harsh laugh, the renegade slammed the door shut. The bar thudded into place and the two within the room could hear Jimson giving orders to put a double guard on the door.

"My," Edwyr laughed lightly, "one of us must be terribly valuable to be guarded so slosely. Carlson? Have you no other name?"

"Eh? What?" the little man said, turning suddenly from the door as if noticing Edwyr for the first time. "Oh, I'm a Keeper. Or I was a Keeper. Now I'm a prisoner. No, no. I'm a fool, that's what I am. And a coward!"

"A Keeper?" asked the young man. "I didn't know any had joined Mitsuyama."

"Joined?" snorted Carlson. "Ha! Never joined. Taken. Forced. Kept captive: Never joined." He began to hum tunelessly, his eyes wandering around the room. His gaze fell by chance on Edwyr again and he started. "Seeker? Eh? What's a Seeker doing here? Are you really a Seeker? Or just another spy Mitsuyama's sent to try and make me tell things! Oh, damn, damn, damn, if only I weren't such a coward! But I know what they'll do to me! Jimson's explained it, yes, in graphic detail!" He shuddered, his eyes tightly closed.

"Weapons-technology, that's what he wants! Not interested in plows or quantum theory." He brightened visibly and fixed Edwyr with a sharp stare. "You interested in quantum mechanics, young man? Carlson knows it. There are only two Keepers in all of Kensho who know it and Carlson's one of 'em." His eyes went blank again when the Seeker failed to respond. The humming started up once more, interspersed with muttered "damns."

For a few moments Edwyr stood still and watched Carlson. Then he moved toward one of the pallets. The Keeper stepped quickly in front of him, grasping his wrists with surprisingly strong hands. "Escape! Take me with you! We've got to warn the Keepers! Everyone! Mitsuyama's raised an army. Thousands of men! Millions! He's got battle lasers! Bombs!" He turned away, the words tumbling from his mouth in a ceaseless flow.

"Death, destruction, that's what he wants from us. Our Knowledge twisted and distorted to kill. So he can rule. He cares nothing about progress. Ha.! I'll stop him!" He twitched around again, facing Edwyr, his eyes wide and fearful, his mouth slightly flecked with spittle at its corners. "We've got to escape! Got to warn Kensho! The Message! They're coming! We must defeat Mitsuyama!" Mumbling incoherently, he stumbled over to one of the pallets and collapsed in a heap.

Edwyr walked slowly over to the huddled little man and knelt beside him. He reached out and touched Carlson on the shoulder. The man's head jerked up and he stared at Edwyr for a moment. Then he clutched gratefully at the young man's extended hand. "Save me, Seeker," he pleaded. "Save us all. Gods! I'm going insane and I know it! Nothing to read, nothing to do! I've repeated my chants until I don't hear them any more. And they keep asking me and asking me. And I don't know what to tell them! The Flagship didn't tell me or anyone else about weapons. It knew better."

"Tell me about quantum theory, Carlson," Edwyr said simply.

For a brief second, the Keeper didn't know how to respond. Tears came to his eyes and he let go of Edwyr's hand to brush them away. "I . . ." he began haltingly. "Yes, Seeker."

The Keeper began speaking in a faltering, whispery voice. But as he talked and chanted, his tone became firmer and his gaze brighter. He sat up straight and pride filled his tiny frame as the words poured ever more fluidly and surely from between his thin lips. By the time the light was dimming in the room, he was a man transformed.

When the sound of the bar on the door being raised interrupted his flow of words, he merely snorted in irritation at the impertinence of the soldiers who entered with two bowls of food. Jimson accompanied them and stood, his arms crossed over his chest, his face dark with a scowl, watching the two as they ate.

Carlson threw several irritated glances in his direction and finally burst out, "Why the hell don't you get out and let us eat in peace, renegade!" The effect on the other man was amusing. His jaw fell in utter amazement. "Yes, you, Jimson! Out!" the little man demanded. With a look of confusion and bewilderment, Jimson meekly obeyed.

Carlson chuckled, hugely enjoying the man's discomfort. "Been wanting to do that for a long time!" he crowed. "Damn, but talking to a real human being's done me a world of good." He cocked his head to one side and looked quizzically at Edwyr. "You're not one of them, that's for sure. So you must really be a Seeker after all. Fear. Fear and loneliness, that's what gets me. Sometimes it's so bad, I . . . ah . . . but you're not one of them. You're a prisoner, just like me. I . . ." He paused for a moment, shaking his head sadly. "I'm not well, Seeker. I'm more than a little crazy. But I still know my quantum!" he proudly announced. "Still the best on Kensho, by damn!" He chuckled again. "You really interested? Or just trying to humor a crazy man?"

"Both," Edwyr responded. "I just met a Keeper myself. So I'm interested in Keepers in general, I guess. And you needed a bit of humoring."

The small man's interest was aroused. "Keeper? You met a Keeper? Where? Who?" he demanded eagerly. "No!" he instantly contradicted himself, "Don't tell me a thing! Those bastards might be listening! No, nothing. A Keeper!" He muttered happily under his breath, casting brief grins in Edwyr's direction from time to time.

When they finished their meal, Carlson took both bowls and went to the door. Beating on it with his fist and kicking it with one foot, he set up a terrible racket, yelling for the guards to open up instantly.

The door swung back and the two soldiers standing there looked confused and nonplused. The Keeper thrust the bowls at them and shooed them out with angry arm wavings.

Once the door was closed again, he stood glaring at it for a moment and then burst into peals of laughter. "Ah . . . ah . . ." he finally gasped, "I've been . . . wanting to do that for a long time! Bastards! Keeping a Keeper!" He swung around to Edwyr, his face suddenly sober.

"Not very stable, am I? Too manic now, too depressed earlier. More than a little crazy," he mumbled. He came up to the Seeker and placed both hands on the younger man's shoulders, looking long and deep into his calm eyes. "But you don't despise me for it, do you? No. And no pity, either. Good. You accept me. That's what I need, a little touch with reality. Seeker, you've done me a world of good. Now it's my turn to help you."

Tugging gently at Edwyr's hand, he pulled him toward the center of the room. He looked furtively all around the empty room, then gave the young man an appraising glance. "Now, I know you're not here by mistake. Oh, no, not likely. You're much too smart for that. No, you're here for a reason. And I'll wager that reason has something to do with the current crisis. Maybe even with the missing Sword of Nakamura? Don't tell me," he whispered hoarsely, "they might be listening."

Edwyr looked the Keeper steadily in the eye. "You're not far from right," he said. "But let's just say I'm here for the future of Kensho."

"Just so, just so! Good. Hmmmmmmmmmm. And I wish to help you. No, it's plain to see you're not one of those Free Council scum. No. You have a friend who's a Keeper. Yes, and now another one. Carlson as well. So. I know many things, Seeker. Many things. They think I'm crazy. They say things in front of me, believing I can't understand. Ah, and they think I'm hard of hearing, too. But I hear, I hear!

"I can tell you many things. Many things. I know all about the Avengers. How they are armed. Their tactics. And I know his plans. Yes, from what I've heard and guessed, I know many things. Come closer, lad and I'll whisper them to you. They might be listening, you know. But what I have to say should get into the right hands. It must! Otherwise there's no stopping Mitsuyama!"

As the room became darker and darker, Carlson muttered and murmured his knowledge into Edwyr's ear. Much of it was merely corroboration of the rumors the Seeker had already heard. But a great deal was new information, some of it quite useful.

Most interesting of all were Carlson's descriptions of Mitsuyama. Edwyr carefully probed the Keeper's memory for recollections of the PlainsLord in action. Combining these with what he had already heard and his own recent observations, he was able to build up a fairly accurate picture of the man's character and motivations. It was a complex portrait of a complex individual. He wouldn't be an easy man to deal with under the best of circumstances. And if the Plan was to succeed . . . well, the critical need for achieving Identity was clearer than ever.

Carlson also told him a great deal about Jimson, including his background as an ex-Seeker of the Way of the Sword and his role in the creation and training of the Avengers. The Keeper's sketches of the other PlainsLords, while brief, revealed that the Council was not completely dominated by Mitsuyama and that there were indeed discontents and disagreements even within this inner circle. Edwyr got the distinct impression that the individual Lords were not on the best terms with each other, and that without Mitsuyama the Council would disintegrate into bickering disunity.

Finally finished, the little man sat back and gazed quietly into the dark, his mind and body appearing calm and relaxed for the first time since Edwyr had met him. It's been a long, long while since he's been able to do what he loves and is trained for, the Seeker mused. But now he's performed his Keeper's role again, gathering and passing on information, and he's happy. Not to mention a little saner than he was a few short hours ago.

This is the second Keeper I've met, he thought. And if they're all like the two I know, the Free Council's fear of them is sadly misplaced. Rather than being the natural allies of Mitsuyama and the harbingers of the evils of Home-World technology, they seem far more likely to be the staunchest friends and supporters the Great Way has on Kensho! Still, he admitted to himself, the possible misuse of what they offer bothers me. Even more so after what Carlson has revealed about Mitsuyama's intentions.

His mind turned to the problem of the PlainsLord. Time was running out. The crisis was fast approaching. If anything, everyone had underestimated the power and determination of Mitsuyama. And such a mistake could prove fatal. I must achieve Identification with Mitsuyama, and soon, he calculated. Jimson, too. The man was a previously unknown factor, but obviously could end up being an important one. If possible, it would even be wise to attempt Identification with a few of the other PlainsLords. Perhaps their mutual suspicions could be exploited.

What he needed was a chance to be with the Supreme Lord of the Plains someplace where there weren't too many other people around. Identification wasn't easy under the best of circumstances, and with a crowd of minds in the area, it was almost impossible. Maybe he'll come here to talk with me, he hoped. Then it would be simple. Perhaps he'll even bring Jimson with him and I'll be able to get them both!

But that wouldn't give me access to the other Lords, he realized. Is there any way I can get them all together? He estimated that in total they numbered no more than ten or twelve individuals. Indentification would be possible in a group that size. Not easy, but possible.

Of course! A Council meeting! The perfect place! But how in the world was he going to gain admittance to a Council meeting? There must be a way . . .

For a moment he was distracted as the Mushin he held with his mind stirred restlessly. He quieted them quickly and efficiently. Thank the Gods for the few extra days of practice I had in handling them while I was all alone on the Plain, he thought. There was more to it than he'd realized at first. Actually, the mind leeches had proven quite useful, especially when he left them just a little bit hungry. Then they acted as a warning system, alerting him to the approach of other minds. The invisible creatures were capable of spotting a food source long before Edwyr could hear or see it. All told, they'd helped him avoid three moving patrols and several hidden sentries. He imagined his unexpected arrival had caused considerable consternation!

Now, though, there were just too many unprotected minds around. He couldn't afford to leave the Mushin even slightly hungry. He'd have to keep them as quiescent as possible. That would take energy, he knew. It would even interfere with his ability to achieve Identification. But there was nothing he could do about it. I'll just have to make the best of it, he sighed. Can't have the mind leeches attacking people, not even these people.

Wait a minute! A new idea slowly dawned in his mind. Carefully he thought it through. Once I've achieved Identification, my next goal is to escape and return with the information so it can be used for the Plan. But as long as I'm locked in a windowless, guarded room in the middle of Mitsuyama's fortress, there doesn't seem to be much chance of accomplishing that.

But if I can use the Mushin to . . .

For a long time, he sat still as a statue. Finally, completing his scheme, he moved slightly, turning his head to seek out the dim figure of Carlson. The man had gone to sleep some hours ago and now lay peacefully at rest. Edwyr let his gaze drift around the room. It was bathed in the soft glow of the moonslight which seeped in through the grille of the skylight. Everything was still. Aside from the gentle breathing of the captive Keeper, the only sound he could hear was an occasional rustle as one of the guards changed his position on the other side of the barred door.

Time to rest, he told himself. Carefully checking the Mushin to make sure they would remain quiet until the morning, he lay down on the other pallet and was almost instantly asleep.

XX

Three days slowly passed. Edwyr filled his time with meditation, exercise, planning, and listening and talking to Carlson. The little man was delighted to have an audience. He spent many happy hours chanting and discussing the fine points of quantum theory. Edwyr was surprised to find that after a while he started to understand what the other man was saying. He even began to discover parallels between some of the Keeper's ideas and his own. Although there was no way of knowing how far those parallels could be carried, they indicated that perhaps his world view and Carlson's were not that far apart after all. At times, despite differences in both method and vocabulary, he almost had the feeling they were discussing two different maps of the same territory.

Their relationship quickly matured into one of mutual liking and respect. The only friction between them came when Edwyr spoke out loud about knowing things Lord Kondori would find interesting. Then Carlson would flutter his hands in agitation, hop nervously from foot to foot, mutter dark warnings about spies and listening guards, and urge the young man to whisper. The Seeker responded by smiling slightly, nodding good-naturedly, and stopping, only to do the whole thing over again in a few hours.

On the morning of the fourth day, Edwyr awoke to the sound of feet and cursing overhead. He looked up at the skylight just in time to see two soldiers covering it with a tarp. They were wet, as was the floor directly below the opening. It was raining outside.

With the skylight covered, the room was plunged in gloom despite the hour. The two guards who

brought breakfast were damp and grumpy, refusing
to respond to the Seeker's cherry "Good Morning."
When they closed the door again, Edwyr could hear
them exchanging angry words. He crossed the room
quickly and pressed his ear to the rough wood. As
near as he could make out, they were arguing about
which one had a better claim to the attentions of a
certain young woman named Beth.

Carlson and he had hardly finished their meal when
the door swung open again. Jimson entered, looking
grim. Following him were two squads of guards with
their swords drawn. He scowled at Edwyr. "Come
along, Seeker," he commanded harshly. "The Council wants to talk to you. Don't try to escape. I've got
orders to cut you down if you do. And I'd love to carry
them out," he finished with a wolfish grin.

With a shrug, Edwyr walked to the door. Before
leaving, he turned back and waved a casual goodbye
to Carlson. The Keeper was trying hard not to show
how distressed he was. Bravely he waved back and
called out, "Don't tell 'em a thing, Seeker!" as the
door thumped shut.

They came to the main hall and turned right, away
from the door that lead to the courtyard. The corridor
continued for a short way and then ended as another
one capped it. Edwyr caught a glimpse of stairs leading up to the roof on his right, but the guards took him
in the opposite direction.

After passing several ordinary halls branching off to
the left, they finally turned into an unusually broad
one. Halfway down it, they halted in front of a pair of
heavy doors set into the right-hand wall. Four sentries stood at attention on either side.

Jimson turned to Edwyr. "This is the Council
Chamber, Seeker. When you go in, act courteously
and carefully if you want to come out alive. No tricks,

no fast moves, don't even breathe heavily. There'll be a guard on either side of you and one behind. They'll all have drawn swords and orders to kill if you so much as twitch." He looked at the sentries and motioned for them to open the doors.

As Edwyr entered between his guards, his sharp eyes swept the Council Chamber. It was a large room, plain and stark. To his left sat Mitsuyama, slightly elevated on his cushion. To the right sat the rest of the Lords, hard-looking men, for the most part middle-aged or older. Directly ahead was an empty cushion behind a small table.

He immediately picked out the hawk-like features of Lord Kondori, the old man's eyes glittering at him with keen interest. D'Alams sprawled on his cushion, fat and seemingly indifferent. Most of the rest talked quietly among themselves. But a few gazed at him with open curiosity. A quick head-count indicated a total of fourteen people in the room, including the guards. Good, he thought, Identification is possible. But whom shall it be? Mitsuyama is clearly the most important. Then possibly Jimson. Of the other Lords, Kondori is necessary. And D'Alams. What about Odobe, the huge, shrewd-looking black man lounging so casually toward the rear? Yes, he's clearly a force here. Any others? Perhaps Dembo. Let's see how things go first.

As the guards took Edwyr across the room to the empty cushion, Lord Kondori scrutinized the young man with avid eyes. Why did you try so hard, and so crudely, to attract my attention, Seeker? he wondered. Such an obvious ploy, loudly saying you knew things I wanted to know. Of course I have spies among the Avengers. And naturally some would be on guard duty over you. Did you really think I didn't know about you the moment you arrived? Or that I'd let William keep a monopoly on you and your knowledge?

While Edwyr sat on the cushion and the guards placed the table over his crossed legs, effectively locking him in place, Kondori's gaze drifted to Mitsuyama. *Annoyed, aren't you William? I can tell by the tight way you're holding your mouth. Perhaps even a bit angry? Good, good! I knew forcing you to produce your little secret would upset your smug equilibrium! As long as you're involved with your projects, and as long as I can keep you off balance with these petty annoyances, I can work on my own schemes unhindered by your insatiable curiosity. Yes, yes,* he nodded to himself, rubbing his hands together, *my schemes, my schemes!*

Looking back at the Seeker, he saw the young man was finally in position, with a guard on either side and one standing directly behind. *No matter how dangerous he is, he's neutralized now,* he thought. *He can't even get up without knocking over that table. Good, good. It's time to start this farce.*

Fixing Mitsuyama with a sharp stare he said dryly. "Let's get on with it."

The Supreme Lord bowed his head sarcastically in recognition. "Be my guest, Lord Kondori. In light of your expressed interest in this Seeker, yours shall be the very first questions."

The old man rose and walked over in front of Edwyr. "Young," he muttered loud enough for all to hear. "Young for one so . . . so talented. At least if what we've heard about the eight is true.

"You're a lucky young man, Seeker. I was all for torturing you to get information we seek. But others protested." He waved his hand in disgust toward the seated Lords. "Weak," he murmured under his breath.

"Yet, seeing now how young and strong you are, perhaps they were right after all. It might take too long. You might even die silent and thwart us. But," he continued, his voice dropping to a threatening hiss, "there's always that option open to us if you fail to cooperate."

Edwyr didn't bother to answer. He was concentrating as hard as possible on the old man. Now! he thought and reached out with his awareness. Kondori's eyes blinked and he swayed uncertainly for just an instant. Then everything was normal again and the Seeker was smiling up at him. "Ask away, Lord. What I know is yours."

"Andretti," Kondori rasped out, shaking his head slightly as if to rid himself of a momentary dizziness, "will he fight?"

"Yes," came the prompt answer.

The old man's eyebrows raised at the readiness and obvious honesty of the answer. "He's willing to shed blood to maintain his power?"

"Yes. But he sees it as defending the Way against you."

"Of course, of course, but no matter. He'll fight, as I've been trying to tell these fools all along.

"Now, the Sword. Did he steal it?"

Edwyr looked surprised. "What makes you think he'd do a thing like that?"

"Oh, I don't, I don't. But others do. Just answer my question, young man!"

The Seeker shrugged. "To the best of my knowledge, the answer is no, he didn't steal the Sword. He sent us out to look for it. His concern was very real, and I don't think he could have fooled us on that. No, he didn't take it."

Kondori paused to cast a triumphant glance at

D'Alams. "Ha!" he snorted. Turning back to Edwyr, he smiled slyly. "And have any of you found the Sword, Seeker?" He shot a quick look at Mitsuyama from the corner of his eye. "Is it here, for example?"

"No, no one's found it that I know of. I'd be surprised if they did. And it's not here. I knew that before I came."

The old Lord had obviously not been expecting that answer. His mouth fell open in amazement. "Not . . . here?" he gasped, his eyes turning in astonishment to look at Mitsuyama "Then . . . we . . . you didn't . . ."

"We don't have the Sword, Kondori," the Supreme Lord said quietly. "We never did. Nor did we have it stolen by someone else."

"Then we won't have it at First Pass?" mumbled D'Alams in bewilderment. "But . . . but . . ." his jowls jiggled in dismay, "if we don't produce the Sword . . . we can't get the people to . . ."

"We'll fight for the right to rule," replied Mitsuyama simply.

"Fight?" boomed Odobo. He stood and strode forward. "Fight? Is Andretti ready for us, Seeker?"

The young man nodded. "Very ready." His eyes narrowed as he focused on Odobo. The huge man blinked twice and shook his head.

"I . . . well, damnit, then, it'll be a bloodbath!" Odobo turned and jabbed his finger at Mitsuyama. "You've known this all along! You've let us think we could win this thing peacefully!"

Mitsuyama nodded calmly. "I wasn't sure until just recently. But I've always assumed Andretti wouldn't step aside without a struggle." His voice became harder, with a vicious edge to it. "And you've all known it too! What the hell do you think we've been training an army for? Parade ground maneuvers? To pass in review before the Free Council? As an honor guard for Andretti?

"Fools!" he spit the word out contemptuously. "There never was any choice! A few of you dreamed of it. But the reality has always been the same. If we wish to rule, we must rip power from the Free Council's grip!"

"But the Mushin," wailed D'Alams.

The PlainsLord shifted his focus to Edwyr. "Answer that idiot for me, Seeker. You understand. I don't intend to destroy the Great Way. Just rule it and the 'hoods."

Edwyr looked at D'Alams. The fat man was so upset, he didn't feel a thing as the Seeker's eyes bored into his. The slight displacement the other's mind suffered was lost in the man's own confusion. "Lord Mitsuyama," he began to explain, "means that the people in the 'hoods will stay at their jobs, holding the mind leeches, no matter who rules Kensho. I think his estimate of their dedication is accurate. Even without the Free Council, the task would continue. Jerome so ordained it."

Mitsuyama acknowledged the Seeker's comment with a sardonic nod. "Thank you. You have more sense than all of these put together. You're quite certain Andretti will fight—but can he put up much resistance? Surely you Seekers won't fight by his side?"

"No, we won't. But he'll put up quite a 'resistance,' as you call it, just the same. From what I've seen of your Avengers, I'd judge it a close contest."

"Ah, yes, I'd forgotten you've had experience with our soldiers. So then, my Lords, you see I *am* justified in my actions! Andretti *will* try to impose his rule by force!"

Dembo stood to speak to them all. "Yes, my Lord! I know Andretti better than any of you. I've been with the man many times, talked to him, dealt with him. He's a fanatic. He's capable of doing anything for the Great Way." He rounded suddenly on Edwyr. "And you and all the rest in the 'hoods aid and help him to force all of us to follow the Great Way! If you had your say, you'd condemn all of us to walk the path you follow!"

"I ask no one to do anything. And as for forcing anyone to follow either the Sword or the Great Way, that's clearly impossible. The Way is the way to self-awareness. Each person must walk it on his own. It can't be taught, only learned.

"True, the ultimate goal of the Way is the freedom of every human being on Kensho. But that can't be forced. Jerome found it, but only for himself. The Great Way, even the Way of the Sword, is nothing more than a pointing in the right direction. Each individual must achieve his own freedom, must arrive at the beginning, back to where he was born, on his own. Only then, only when each has transformed himself, will all be transformed."

Dembo sneered. "Very nice. Very pretty, Seeker. But you tend to ignore what Andretti is actually doing."

"Andretti represents Andretti. He is doing what Andretti is doing. It may or it may not have anything to do with the Way. Each individual must judge that for himself."

"But the President of the Free Council will not *let* every one judge for himself," Dembo said triumphantly. "He seeks to impose *his* judgement on all of Kensho. 'Steader, settler, Seeker, Sister and Brother, PlainsLord, all alike must bow to him. But we cry out 'No! We will not be forced!' Can you deny the right-

ness of our position? With your own mouth you've
said the Way doesn't force us. You've claimed all of us
must judge for ourselves. The only conclusion I can
draw from that is that Andretti *does not follow the
Way!*"

"Father Andretti understands what he is capable of
understanding. There's more in the Way than he'll
ever know. More than you, little puppet, will ever
comprehend." Edwyr smiled as he spoke, but
Dembo still flushed strongly with anger at his words.
"I can't talk with you about something you can't even
conceive of. Cut your strings, come with me and
follow the Sword. Then we might speak and exchange
something meaningful. But now . . ." he shrugged.

"Then talk to me, Seeker," hissed Jimson, his eyes
bright with hatred. "I've walked your precious Way. I
know more than Dembo or Kondori, or D'Alams, or
any of the rest!" The ex-Seeker stalked forward, con-
fronting Edwyr. Dembo, Odobo, even Kondori,
moved out of his way, drifting silently back to their
places to watch.

The Seeker returned the renegade's glare with a
solemn stare. His eyes widened slightly and Jimson
blinked, momentarily disoriented. He shook his head
once and began pacing back and forth in front of the
seated man. "You lie," he said with contempt, "because the Way is a lie! An utter, malicious deception!
A false face on the rotten features of a corpse!

"Tell them, Seeker," he gestured widely at the
seated Lords, "tell them the truth about what the
Way teaches those who walk it. Tell them of the
Nothingness that underlies the reality we cling to.
Let them hear of the bottomless, empty abyss the
mind and soul fall through for all eternity. Explain to
them the death of all that is and the birth of unending

hopelessness." His voice dropped to an intense, hoarse whisper that filled the room. "Tell them of the Void!"

Edwyr shrugged. "The world may very well be Nothingness," he answered quietly. "But anyone who doesn't call this . . ." he struck the table with a resounding slap . . . "a table, is a fool." Mitsuyama scowled. A smile of almost-understanding flitted briefly over Kondori's lips. Odobo looked puzzled. The rest stared blankly at the Seeker.

Jimson snarled, "But where then is hope, Seeker? Where then is the reason for virtue, for love, for decency, for honesty? If everything is Nothing, what reason is there for even living?"

"After the rain there'll be a beautiful rainbow. Let's all go up on the roof and watch it."

The ex-Seeker stopped dead in his tracks and swirled to stare at Edwyr. For a moment he stood in uncomprehending silence. Then he muttered angrily, "You play with me, you bastard!"

The man seated at the table shrugged again. "What else are words good for with you, Jimson? You throw them at me, I catch them, and throw some back. I can't prove there's a reason for living by discussing it with you any more than I can verbally prove the existence of atomic particles. If you don't or can't experience it yourself, and if you refuse to accept my word for my experience of it, what have we really to say to each other?"

"You're no better than anyone else! You eat and shit and sleep like all the rest of us! And you're just as evil as any of us!

"Yes! Evil! You pretend to be perfect, but you can't be, no matter how long or hard you try. There's a rotten worm in you just like there is in all men! And all your meditating and sweating and following the damn Sword won't root it out. So what sense is there to your labors? None! None at all!"

Edwyr sighed. "Perfection isn't our goal. Freedom is. And to be free, you must be able to be evil as well as good. You're right, Jimson, when you say that the dark demon rides me the same as it does other people. I never said it didn't. The demonic in us is always there, as is the angelic. Neither can be made to disappear. And it's a serious mistake to try to smother one with the other. That kind of suppression is exactly what the Mushin find so attractive about us. Because it just leads to greater and greater pressure building up.

"No, Jimson, there's no way to shake the shadows from the human soul. The choice between good and evil is always there, always will be. It is, in a very real sense, what makes us human.

"All we try to do is to cease clinging to either one."

"But evil is stronger than good!" Jimson crowed triumphantly. "It's the ultimate Nothingness, utter destructiveness! It reflects and mirrors the true nature of Reality! There can be nothing mightier than evil, for evil is final!"

The Seeker smiled gently, sadly. "Ultimate? Final? Show me the evil in a growing tree. Put the evil of a burning star in my hands and let me hold it. Jimson, Jimson, there's nothing final or ultimate about evil or good. They're ours, they come from within us. The universe doesn't impose either on us. We impose them on ourselves and on each other."

"Then it wouldn't be evil for me to kill you?" Jimson leered.

"From my point of view, of course it would be. And I'd fight to stop you. But from the standpoint of the First River, it couldn't matter less."

Before Jimson could say anything in reply, Mitsuyama interrupted. "If I were to give Jimson permission to cut you down with his sword, right this instant, how would you meet your death Seeker? Unarmed, helpless behind that table, how would your years of labor and study prepare you to die?"

Edwyr's face blanched, a look of utter terror filling his eyes. His expression twisted into one of piteous pleading. Both hands thrust out in supplication. "Please," he cried brokenly, "Please spare my life! Ahhhh! Ohhhhh! It hurts! It hurts!" He writhed for a moment and fell forward on the table with a thud. After a moment of breathless stillness, he sat upright again and gazed about with calm indifference.

The PlainsLord's face grew dark with sudden anger. "Do you dare to mock me?" he growled.

"No, my Lord," the young man replied. "I'm merely pointing out that you misinterpret the purpose of the Way.

"The freedom we seek through the Way is not freedom *from* the world. It's freedom to be truly in and of the world. The Way doesn't provide an escape from the pain of life or the horror of death. When you stub your toe, it hurts, no matter what your philosophy. And the far more frightening agony of death is always there regardless of what you believe.

"The Way simply teaches us to accept death as much as we accept life. By clinging to neither, we are no longer bound by them. It's not that they cease to matter—that would be a horrid perversion and inhumanly cold—it's just that they no longer rule and suffocate us.

"If I meet my death more calmly than another, it's not because I fear it any less. Nor because I place a lower value on my life. Nor again because I've found some magical way of transcending both. The real reason is simply that I've learned . . ."

"Be silent!" roared Mitsuyama. His face twisted
with rage, he lunged to his feet and stood glaring
furiously at Edwyr. "I've heard enough of your mystical gibberish!" His eyes swept contemptuously over
the other Lords. "Can't you see what he's doing, you
fools? We bring him here to question him and all he
does is confuse us with his cursed philosophy! The
philosophy of that damned traitor, Andretti! We'll
learn nothing from him!" His head snapped back to fix
Edwyr with his stare. "Just what the hell are you up
to, Seeker?" he asked, his voice husky with barely
controlled fury, his hand moving automatically to the
dagger at his waist. The young man's eyes locked
briefly with his. Mitsuyama stiffened suddenly as if
jolted.

Then, without warning, his control crumbled and
he ripped his knife from its sheath. In total silence, he
strode swiftly to stand in front of the Seeker. With a
savage grimace slashing his face, he lifted the blade
high and stepped forward, bringing it down in a
blurred arc.

With a crash, it struck the table top, sinking into
the wood almost up to its hilt.

For an instant, the two men's eyes met. Tearing his
gaze from the Seeker's, Mitsuyama whirled to Jimson. In a cold, emotionless voice he ordered, "Take
him back to his cell. At sundown we'll see how well he
meets his death!"

XXI

Carlson paced in tight, nervous circles, wringing his hands and muttering anxiously to himself. "What's going on? When are they coming back? What's going to happen to us? Why . . . ." The worried litany rolled on and on with only minor variations.

A sudden noise from the door startled him into motionless silence. Someone was lifting the bar! Momentarily confused, dreading whatever was about to happen, he stood in the middle of the room, rooted to the spot.

The door swung open and Jimson strode into the room, smiling maliciously. Edwyr followed almost immediately behind, an amused expression on his face, looking for all the world as if he'd just returned from a short stroll around the courtyard. The two soldiers who were guarding the door finished off the procession, entering somewhat uncertainly. Beyond them, filling the hallway, were the two squads that had accompanied the Seeker to and from the Council Chamber.

Ignoring the little Keeper, Jimson turned and bowed mockingly to Edwyr. "I'll be back to get you just before sundown. Until then, just relax and enjoy yourself." He straightened up, his face becoming hard. His glance went past the Seeker to the two guards. "Be careful," he commanded sharply. "He's a tricky bastard. If anything goes wrong, you'll take his place in the execution circle." With a final, triumphant glare and a vicious bark of laughter, he strode from the room.

One guard backed out while the other pulled the door shut. Just before it closed, Edwyr caught the

man's eyes and asked in a husky voice "How's Beth?"
They both reacted just in time to catch the Seeker's
wink.

The door shut with a thud and the bar dropped into
place with a dull crash, as if slammed down in anger.
In two swift steps, Edwyr was at the door, his ear
pressed to the wood. Carlson, his voice trembling,
started to ask what was going on, but the young man
held his finger to his lips, signaling for silence. After a
few moments of listening, he seemed satisfied and
stepped back into the middle of the room.

"Carlson," he whispered, a slight smile playing
about his lips, "they're going to execute me at sundown."

The news hit the Keeper like a physical blow. He
sagged. The Seeker shot out a hand to steady him.
The little man's mind reeled, thought following
thought in a chaotic tumbling. They're going to kill
him! I'm such a coward. My knowledge—what'll happen to my quantum theory? I'll go crazy! No, I'll fight!
Oh shit, I'm afraid. I'm such a coward. Oh, help, help!

Edwyr shook him gently. "Carlson! Carlson!" he
whispered urgently. "This is no time to fail me! I need
your help. We're going to get out of here. Now!"

Carlson's eyes focused on the young man's face.
"Out?" he croaked weakly. "Out? How? There's no
way out!" Despair swept up like a great wave in his
mind. But he fought it, struggling to concentrate on
Edwyr. "Out," he muttered. "Yes, Out!" Blinking,
pulling himself together, he stood straighter, touching the Seeker's hand where it supported his arm.
"What do I have to do?"

"The sleeping pallets; rip off the covers and tear
them into long strips. Tie the strips together to make a
rope."

The Keeper blinked at Edwyr. "Why? We can't

make a strong enough rope with that. There's no place to climb to, anyway."

Edwyr winked. "I know that, and you know that, but *they*" he gestured toward the door, "won't even think of it. Just trust me and do it." The older man turned with a shrug and went to his task.

Crossing again to the door, Edwyr listened. When he turned back into the room, a wide grin stretched across his face. Confidently, he stepped over to the wall and examined one of the empty torch holders. Gripping it carefully, he began to pull steadily and slowly. After a few moments of straining, the holder ripped out of the wall with a small crunching sound. Holding the piece of metal in his hand, the Seeker returned to the door to hear if the guards had noticed the noise. No, he realized, they're too busy arguing to hear anything but a loud noise. I'll give them that in a few minutes.

He hefted the metal torch holder in his hand. One will do the trick, he decided. Quickly he went to Carlson's side and worked with the man to prepare the "ropes" of torn cloth.

In less than ten minutes they had finished. Edwyr carefully tied the rope to the torch holder and swung it around a few times to get the feel of it.

"Now comes the tough part. You're going to have to be an actor. And you're going to be in danger, physical danger. Can you do it?"

The little man blinked and swallowed nervously. "I . . . I'm a coward, Seeker. I admit it. I'm scared. But . . . , yes, I'll do whatever you say. I don't know what you're up to. You've never really told me, you know. But I trust you. I know it's important. I'll help. But I'm scared!"

Edwyr smiled and patted him thankfully on the back. "Good. And if it makes you feel any better, I'm

scared, too!" He looked up at the skylight.
"Hmmmm. Tarp's still there. Probably still raining."
He listened carefully for a moment. The sound of
drops could be heard. He nodded. "Hope the tarp's
not too tight."

Turning to Carlson he said, "This whole thing has
to happen quickly or it won't work. I'm going to try to
catch this torch holder in the grill. That'll make a nice
racket. Then you scream, "Help, he's getting away,"
or something like that. Cry out and fall down on the
floor. O.K.? And keep your mind as blank as possible.
Pretend like you're in a 'hood in the Home Valley. No
matter what."

Carlson nodded, his face a mixture of hope and
fear. To escape! he thought. To be free again! He
watched anxiously as the Seeker began to swing the
holder around and around. "Hope I make the first
throw," he heard the young man mutter. Suddenly
the holder was flying through the air. It hit between
two of the bars in the grill, pushing the canvas up,
then fell back around one of the bars with a ringing
clang.

Edwyr dropped the cloth rope and leapt for the
wall behind the door. Taking his cue from the young
man's motion, Carlson shrieked out, "Help, oh help!
He's escaping! Gods! Help!" Then, with a bellow like
a man hacked by a sword, he fell heavily to the floor.

The door literally flew open. The two guards, their
swords drawn, rushed into the room. They stood for a
moment, transfixed by the sight of the rope leading
upward. As they hesitated, Edwyr kicked the door
shut. The two spun around to face him.

From his position on the floor, Carlson watched the
whole thing happen. The young man never moved.
The guards began to step toward him, but suddenly
went rigid. Edwyr called out "Beth!" in an intense

whisper. A mutual shiver briefly shook both their
bodies and then with a mindless, wordless howl, the
two men fell on each other, hacking and stabbing.
Carlson felt the burning sensation just long enough to
identify it. Mushin! He clamped down on his mind,
forcing himself to go limp. Mushin?

Almost instantly he heard the Seeker call out urgently, softly, "Carlson, it's ok! It's over!" Gingerly,
the little man extended his awareness. The mind
leeches were gone! How . . . Did I just imagine it?

Edwyr was leaning over one of the fallen guards,
prying the sword from the man's rigid death grip.
"We're free?" Carlson muttered in an awed tone.
"Not quite," the young man replied, "But we're on
our way!"

Carlson got to his knees. He was about to stand
when the other guard, blood pouring across his
wrecked face, suddenly lurched to his feet. Edwyr's
back was turned to the man. Stunned, unable to even
yell a warning, the Keeper watched as the ghastly
figure raised its sword to strike. But he's dead,
Carlson's mind cried, unbelieving. He's dead!

Without thinking, the little man launched himself
from his kneeling position straight at the guard. His
aim was bad and instead of hitting the man, he thrust
himself between the arching sword and Edwyr's
back. The slam as the blade hit his body knocked the
air out of him in a shocked grunt.

The Seeker spun around, sword in hand, and swept
the guard's head off with a single stroke. Not even
bothering to look at the cumpling body, he knelt
quickly beside the fallen Keeper.

Gently he turned Carlson over, as much to hide the
gaping, blood-pumping wound as to see the man's
startled, pasty face. Carlson's eyelids fluttered open.
Grotesquely, a bloody froth bubbling from his lips,

the little man smiled. "He missed you," came the
bare whisper. "Good. Get going, Seeker. No time to
waste. I . . . I . . . No coward. Thanks." His eyes
closed again. Edwyr gazed down at him for a moment.
Tears filled the Seeker's eyes and he brushed at them
with his sleeve. "Shit," he cursed softly. "Oh, shit."
Then he stood and went to the door. Pulling it open
he stepped out into the corridor.

XXII

The five bodies lay stretched out in the courtyard, the two soldiers who had guarded the door to the Room, Carlson, and two sentries Edwyr had cut down as he made his escape across the roof of the stronghold.

Mitsuyama nudged Carlson's stiffening form with his foot. "Now I've lost my Keeper as well as my Seeker," he murmured in a musing tone. Jimson followed as the Supreme Lord of the Plains walked down the line, looking at each body in turn. The renegade's movements were tense and jerky, as if he was straining against invisible bonds. When the Plains Lord reached the end of the line, he turned and stood silently, gazing searchingly at his lieutenant.

He spoke eventually, his voice quiet and almost velvety in its calmness. "Jimson, explain to me how one man, unarmed, locked in a room, can escape from the very heart of my fortress."

Jimson bowed his head slightly. "Lord, I don't know. He's tricky, we know that."

"Oh, yes, tricky. Very tricky. But that's not an answer, renegade."

"Lord, the fault is obviously mine. I underestimated the man. I should have posted more guards at both ends of the main corridor. Even some at the bottom of the stairs. Punish me as you will, Lord. But first let me go and bring him back. While we stand here, he escapes. He's already got a start of several hours and he runs like—"

Mitsuyama held up his hand. "Jimson, how do you intend to catch a Seeker who has several hours headstart on you? Will you grow wings?" A hint of sarcasm edged the PlainsLord's words.

"Striders, Lord." The ex-Seeker's response was neutral and emotionless. The implications were so obvious sarcasm was unnecessary. Mounted striders were Mitsuyama's own innovation.

The PlainsLord smiled coldly. "Thank you for the reminder. Arrange it." He turned to leave, then stopped and turned back again. "Ah, yes, Jimson. Don't bother to bring back the whole Seeker. Just his head will do." For a moment he paused, as if just remembering something else. Then, "If you miss him, don't come back at all."

Jimson bowed low. Without another word, he spun on his heel and walked briskly off to begin the pursuit. As Mitsuyama watched him stride off, he remembered something he had once said to Miriam. A conviction grew within him that he had indeed been right and that Jimson was going to meet his fate on the Plain. Whatever it might be.

The bipedal, reptiloid Striders were swifter than a man on foot, covering perhaps twice as much ground in a day, even when carrying a soldier and his equipment. But they were difficult creatures at best, cantankerous, undisciplined, and very stupid. Even after two years of training, they were unable to recognize their riders and it took two men to hold their heads while a third mounted. The last men into the saddle in any group had to be extremely quick and agile, and even then luck had a great deal to do with it.

The Striders' own nature was the major problem, however. They were solitary animals, predators and eaters of carrion that wandered alone on the vast sweep of the Plain. The only times they ever came together were to mate or fight. The chance of a dozen being in the same place at the same time was, under natural circumstances, extremely unlikely and definitely unpleasant. To keep things from dissolving into a bloody melee, the Striders had to be blindfolded most of the time and carefully blinkered the rest. They could only travel in line abreast so that chances of them seeing each other would be minimized.

Damn things are almost more nuisance than they're worth. Not very comfortable, either, Jimson grumbled as he shifted his weight to ease the rubbing on his right inner thigh. *We'll have to make camp pretty soon, can't run them in the dark. Damn! If only it didn't take so long to get the creatures ready and on the trail! We lost another hour.*

Every hour counts, he realized. *Edwyr was undoubtedly heading at top speed for the pass through the Barrier Hills.* Jimson looked up at the rapidly darkening sky. *Overcast still, even though the rain's stopped. Good. A dark night. He'll be able to walk, but not run. I'd love to catch him out on the open Plain, just ride him down and slice him to ribbons!*

He snapped his attention back to the present. *Time to call it a day,* he decided. Up ahead he could see a slight rise. *Good spot to make camp.* He raised his right hand, covered with a white glove to be easily visible to the other riders. When all the men had their hands in the air, he made two circles over his head and then brought his hand down, pointing at the rise. The others repeated his gesture and began to slow the pace of their beasts as they approached the campsite.

It took a full hour to picket, feed, and bed the Striders down for the night before they could attend to their own needs. *I wonder,* Jimson thought wearily, *if the Flagship still has any viable fertilized horse ova?*

Edwyr walked on for about two hours after darkness fell. Eventually he came to a small stream and a grove of stunted trees. Feeling his way carefully to avoid low-hanging branches, he found a smooth spot not far from the water. There was no food, of course, but the water was cool and refreshing.

The pass was the best place to head for, he decided. *I don't know this territory, so there's no sense in taking any chances. Of course, the pass is exactly where Jimson, or whoever they send after me will go, too. My only hope is to beat them there in any case, so it doesn't make any difference.* He tried to remember where the 'hood nearest the other side of the pass was. He seemed to recall it was to the north, about half a day's journey. *If the pursuit becomes too hot, I'll just head there and lay up for a few days until it cools down. Even the Supreme Lord of the Plains won't attempt to attack a 'hood just yet.*

He laid back and stretched out. No stars, no moons, just the dim shapes of the treetops against the lighter black of the sky. *Beautiful in its own way.* He moved his head from side to side to see what effect a change in angle would have on the shapes and patterns. *Lovely.*

Carlson entered his mind. Edwyr remembered how the little man's eyes had glowed with hope at the idea of freedom. And then the fierce pride, mingled with pain, that had filled them as he lay dying on the floor. *It had taken so little to change the Keeper from a mumbling, frightened, half-crazy old man into a proud warrior willing to die for his cause,* he mused. *Just a sense of purpose had been enough, a mere whiff of the idea that he and what he did mattered in the world. How many other people are slowly going crazy simply for lack of a purpose?* he wondered. *And how much raw human power could be generated just by* giving them one? He paused for a moment, regarding the idea with awe. If you gave them the right purpose, a human, constructive one, they could accomplish incredible things! And with the wrong one, they could be equally as destructive! Was that really what this confrontation was all about? Was that what would be decided at First Pass?

He let the idea run through his mind for a while. Then he closed his eyes, slept.

Far across the Plain to the east, a good ten-hour run away, another pair of eyes closed. All day long they had gazed expectantly westward, searching for sight of a single running figure. Finally, when the fall of night had made further looking futile as well as impossible, the watcher had left the ridge of the hill and descended to the floor of the pass. There, hidden in a fold between two hills was a rough camp.

After a brief meal, the watcher settled back and looked up at the night. Perhaps the runner would come tomorrow. Yes, that seemed possible. And I'll be ready and waiting.

A slow smile spread across the watcher's face. Ready, waiting, and totally unexpected. Somebody was in for a real surprise!

The smile faded as the eyes drooped shut. Sleep came quickly.

Edwyr cast a quick glance back over his shoulder. Damn! They're still gaining! Looking ahead to the Barrier Hills, he estimated the distance. I just might make it. Without a yard to spare, though. Not much time to pick a place to make a stand, either.

The afternoon was already nearly gone. The day had been a hellish one, with a hot sun burning the clouds away around noon, turning the Plain into a steaming torture. About the same time, he'd caught his first glimpse of the pursuers from the top of a long ridge. Ten of them, all mounted on some kind of creature! It could only be Jimson and some of the Avengers on those lizards Carlson had told him about.

At that moment, the race began. Edwyr knew there was no sense in holding back any reserves for later. If he didn't get to the hills before they caught up, there wouldn't be any later. Out on the Plain, with nothing to cover his back or flanks, they'd cut him to pieces. But in the hills perhaps, just perhaps, he could hold them off. It was worth a try. And it was his only hope.

He could make out the break in the line of hills which indicated the position of the pass. Good, I'm dead-on again; I just might make it. As he ran, he tried to remember possible places to make a stand. The site where the soldiers and Ronin had massacred each other was too far. They'd catch up long before then. The problem was that the hills on this side weren't as sharp or as steep as on the other. Well, he decided, I'll just have to pick the first thing I see and make do.

Carefully he checked himself over; still capable of a fight. If they do catch me in the open a lot of those Striders will still go home riderless.

The men on the Striders began to yip and shout battle cries. He could pick out Jimson's voice, urging them on. He gave them a glance, then estimated the distance to the pass. I'll make it! Without slowing his pace, he unslung his sword from his back. Holding the scabbard in his left hand, he forced a sudden burst of speed.

Feet pounding, lungs pumping furiously, he sped between two low hills. Nothing there. No place to stand. Need at least one side covered. He ran on.

Behind, the sound of the gaining Avengers grew louder. The rasping of the laboring Striders was clear and he could almost feel their hot breath on the back of his neck. He repressed an urge to whirl and fight on the spot.

The path through the pass took a twist to the right. As he came around the shoulder of a hill he heard his name urgently called out. The shout had come from the left. There, in a fold between two hills he saw something that almost made him stop dead in surprise.

Yolan! With her bladed staff! And in a place where the pursuers could only attack from the front! Not questioning his luck, he dashed over to her.

"You do show up in the strangest places!" he panted as he spun around at her side to face Jimson and his men.

"Huh," she snorted back with a huge grin, "Took you long enough to get here. I've been waiting two days."

"Didn't know we had a date. Last I saw, you were heading north to find your folks."

"Found them. Stuck around for a couple of days before I realized I wasn't needed and that I had better things to do anyway." She pointed at the soldiers, milling about in confusion as they dismounted. "Friends of yours?"

He grinned. "Oh, they're just following me around because they're worried about the state of my health."

She looked him up and down with mock seriousness. "You look pretty healthy to me."

"Right. That's what they're worried about."

Yolan laughed. "Can't you stay out of trouble?"

"Seems to me the last time we met in some hills, it was you in trouble."

"Yeh. Well, turn-about's fair play."

The Avengers were ready, strung out in a line, with Jimson at the middle. They approached cautiously, almost gingerly. Word about the eight must have gotten around, Edwyr thought.

About ten yards off, Jimson raised his hand to call a halt. They all kept their swords nervously on-guard. Edwyr's was still sheathed. fastened now at his waist in its proper place.

An arrogant sneer on his face, Jimson looked them over. "Well, well," he commented harshly, "you've invited a friend. Won't you introduce me to her, Seeker?"

"Do you want to meet him?" Edwyr asked Yolan in a loud stage whisper.

"No," she whispered back. "He smells."

The renegade's face froze, but the red crept up his neck. For the space of a breath, no one spoke. Then he grated out, "Very well, then. I'll introduce myself more forcefully after you're dead, Seeker. And so will all of my men." He shot an order to the line on either side of him. "Don't kill the girl. We've got better uses for her!" The men growled appreciatively as Jimson leered at Yolan.

She laughed in his face. "The only thing any of your scum will ever use me for is a simple way of committing suicide!"

With an abrupt gesture, Mitsuyama's man motioned the line forward. Slowly they approached, still hesitant but eager for the girl. Closer and closer they came, until only five yards separated the two groups.

With a sudden mutual yell, Edwyr and Yolan sprang to the attack. The Seeker's sword flashed from its scabbard so swiftly no eye could follow it. His battle cry froze everyone but Yolan both by its unexpectedness and its sheer volume and ferocity. Yolan's blade shot out faster than a striking snake.

In an instant, two Avengers were down and the rest backpeddling as quickly as they could. One of the fallen men was bubbling his last gasps through a ruined throat. The other sat stupidly staring at the stump of his right hand as it splashed his lifeblood all over his dirty robe.

Before the eight survivors could respond, the two attackers were back in position. Jimson cursed fluidly, viciously. He glared at Edwyr. "That's your last trick, you bastard!" He spun on his men. "No retreat, you fools! We outnumber them! Get behind them and cut them down, you lizard-loving cowards!" The men hesitated again, eyeing Yolan's bloody blade and the Seeker's glistening sword.

Seeing their uncertainty, Edwyr spoke in a low, intense voice. "Yes, come and die. Ten left home. Only eight now. How many will ride back again? Who'd like to be the first?"

The seven soldiers stared at him, their eyes bulging, torn between their fear of the death he held in his hands and their fear of Jimson. The renegade growled threateningly at them. A few stirred slightly as if to respond.

"Wait!" Yolan suddenly called out. They all turned their eyes on her. "Your wives and sweethearts are waiting at home. Think for a second! It's not worth it. If your leader wants Edwyr so badly, why not let *him* fight? Let them battle it out, man to man. If the Seeker wins, go back home, alive. Together you can figure out a story that'll save your skins. Hell, you can even come out heroes! And if your man wins, well, then you've got what you came for. And more." She smiled invitingly at them.

Several of them mumbled under their breaths,

thoughtful expressions replacing their worried looks.
Jimson literally exploded. "You stupid bastards!
Don't listen to that bitch! Attack! Now!"

One of the men drew himself up decisively. "Aye,
that's fine for you to say, Jimson, sir. But it's us as got
to do the dying. Why'nt you fight him yerself, like the
little lady sez? Us'll see he don't pull no fancy stuff."

"Bascom," Jimson said coldly, struggling mightily
to control his fury, "Lord Mitsuyama's orders are to
kill this Seeker. And we will kill him. Now."

Bascom returned Jimson's glare. "Not I, sir. If us
don't kill him, he don't kill us. I gots a woman and
kids, sir. The man's willin ta fight you alone, fair like,
man ta man, an I'm all for it, I am. Yer so Gods-a-
mighty good with yer sword, Jimson, sir. Sure yer not
atremble of him?"

Stunned, the renegade's eyes swept his men's
faces. Their looks were hard and cold. He saw no
yielding, no compassion, not even a liking in their
eyes. All those harsh punishments that Mitsuyama
made me carry out, all that brutal discipline; they
blame me for it! They hate me! Only fear keeps them
in line—and now they fear that damn Seeker more
than they fear me!

There was only one thing he could do and he knew
it. He spun away from them and glared at Edwyr. "Do
you really dare to face me?"

Edwyr smiled slightly. "Hardly daring."

Jimson bared his teeth in a feral grin. "Don't bother
trying to bait me, Seeker. I'm not some fool to be
rattled by mere words." Edwyr stood in a relaxed
stance, his sword not even on guard, calmly watching
the renegade. Jimson took two steps forward and
stopped. "I'm going to kill you," he hissed. "How
does it feel to know you're about to die, Seeker? To
see the endless abyss yawning at your very feet? To

realize your whole life has been a foolish chasing after something that never existed?"

The renegade laughed, a nasty, jeering sound that grated on the ear. "You don't see it, do you? No, you won't understand what I'm saying until the very last second. Until it's too late!" He laughed again, a raw, slightly mad quality tinging his cruel humor. "As your guts spill out on the ground you'll know!

"I saw it all years ago! I saw the world for what it is, the emptiness, the hopelessness, the falseness. And I knew what I had to do! I knew! I left the Way and sought the only things that really matter. I sought power and pleasure! Yes, Seeker! Power! The ability to bend others to my willing! To make them do what satisfies me! And pleasure, too. The pleasure of taking and using. I'll grasp it all, hold it, suck all life from it and then discard the husk as I reach for more!"

The renegade's eyes had taken on a wild glow, his breath was coming in excited, panting gasps, and a light sweat covered his brow. "And now it's almost in my grasp," he continued, his voice dropping to a husky, trembling whisper. "All the power, all the joy and pleasure, everything, almost there, almost in my hand. Only you and a few others stand in the way. And you won't be standing long."

A look of pity hung like mourning on Edwyr's features. "Poor renegade," he said softly. "You've spent so much time scrambling after your joy and happiness, you've never had time to find it. You snatch a quick bite from one Ko pod only to drop it hurriedly for the next so you won't miss anything. And you miss everything.

"What can I say to you, Jimson? The Way isn't an attempt to search for happiness or power or anything else. Its only goal is to show you what's already there, to get you to open your eyes so you can experience the

joy that's all around you, so you can participate in the
power of the whole universe. The Way is living, not
looking for life."

For a second, something soft and yearning shimmered just below the surface in Jimson's eyes. He
wavered slightly. Then, with a snarl, the coldness
slammed down again and his glance was one of pure
hatred. "You never miss a chance to preach, do you,
you little bastard? Well, your talking days are over!
Meet your death!" He moved toward Edwyr, his gaze
intent, his lips curled back to show his bared teeth.

The Seeker raised his sword as the other came
within striking distance. "Yolan," he said, "watch the
others. This is between Jimson and the universe. Best
they don't get involved."

Edwyr stood ready, his right foot slightly in front of
his left, the two of them about shoulder width apart.
His left heel was slightly off the ground, the weight of
his right foot on the ball. The tip of his sword was
pointing directly at his opponent's throat. Edwyr's
eyes were locked on Jimson's, his gaze boring intently
into the other's as if trying to read something written
inside the man's head.

For several moments, the two of them stood like
statues. Each man was taking stock of the other,
trying to find weakness in his stance or grip or sword
position or something, anything, that would give an
opening for an attack. Apparently, neither could find
what he was looking for because Jimson finally moved
slightly to the left. His feet slid along the ground,
never losing contact, the balance always staying on
the balls and slightly forward. The Seeker matched
the other's movement to perfection, returning the
situation to what it had been before.

Jimson moved in slightly, lessening the gap between the tips of their swords to about 18 inches.

Edwyr held his ground, but rose just slightly up on the balls of his feet as if coiling to strike. The renegade stopped.

Yolan watched in fascination. She could feel the tension between the two men building until the very air around them crackled with repressed violence. The only sign of the strain each of them was undergoing was a slight beading of sweat on their upper lips, and in Jimson's case on his forehead as well. She shot a quick glance at the Avengers. They were huddled in a tight little group about ten yards away, their eyes wide and their mouths hanging open. The scene unfolding before them held the seven men in complete, absorbed thrall. If Edwyr won, however, there was no telling what they might do. Attack was as likely as retreat. If Jimson won, she knew exactly what would happen. And she was determined not to be taken alive.

If Edwyr won. How could she doubt it? The two men were circling now. Every second seemed to stretch out to eternity. It should be over by now, she thought. He should have won. If he wins. Could he lose? She forced the idea from her mind. When he wins. Yes. When.

Suddenly Jimson moved in a lightning-quick cut for Edwyr's wrists. The Seeker stepped back, parrying the stroke with a slight flick, stepping back in with a counter to Jimson's wrists. The renegade easily parried. "Elementary, Seeker. Baby stuff," he muttered.

Edwyr stepped forward and feinted for the wrist, then went for the head. Jimson wasn't fooled and easily blocked the head cut, replying with a slash at the Seeker's wrists once more.

The two antagonists began to circle again, eyeing each other carefully. Jimson's face was set in a tooth-baring grimace. With a scream he lunged forward, aiming two quick slashes at Edwyr's head, followed by a cut at his chest. The Seeker absorbed all three attacks without bothering to counter.

Sweat was pouring from Jimson's face now and Edwyr's eyes were looking pinched with the strain. The duel couldn't last too much longer. The renegade decided to take the initiative and press the attack. He stepped in with a swipe at Edwyr's wrists followed by a slash at his head. The swords clashed again as Jimson tried to knock the Seeker's aside to provide an opening. He feinted at the head, then struck for the chest. Stepping back, he swung at the head twice in rapid succession.

The tempo began to pick up as the two of them swirled and slashed at each other. The sheer volume of Jimson's attack seemed to be wearing down the other man. Or perhaps he was just tired after such a long run across the Plain. Step by step, the renegade appeared to be driving the younger man backward.

Finally, after a flurry of blows, Jimson struck Edwyr's sword with a mighty blow, forcing it down and over to the right. It was the opening he'd been waiting for! He sprang in, his sword carving a whistling arc that would end at the other man's head.

But Edwyr's sword did not stay down. Nor did he back up and block. Instead he stepped in and jabbed the point of his blade into Jimson's throat just below the chin. The point sliced through and burst out the back of the head in a spray of blood.

Jimson sagged, the sword falling from his grip, harmlessly striking the ground behind Edwyr. His arms fell to the Seeker's shoulders as if he was trying desperately to hold himself up. The only sound was a whistling gurgle as his last breath fled his body. The sword ripped from his throat as he twisted to the earth. There was no life in his gaze even as he struck.

A profound silence settled over the little group. For a timeless instant they all seemed outside the normal flow of the universe. Even the endless breeze held its breath.

Then Edwyr shattered the stillness with a cry so full of fear and horror it shocked the gaping soldiers into instant action. "Run!" he shrieked, "Mushin! Run!" In a mad panic the seven Avengers fled, leaving their Striders, their swords and their dignity behind.

Yolan walked over to Edwyr and watched the last of them disappear out onto the Plain. Then she turned and looked at him oddly. "There actually were Mushin," she said. "I felt them myself."

He nodded. "Yes. I'm carrying a pack of them. Have been since the last time we met. Never told you before. Didn't think there was any reason to." He shot her a quick, slightly worried look. "Bother you, does it?"

The Keeper shrugged. "I guess not. It's just . . . strange. They can't get loose, can they?"

"No. They're under control."

"Ummmm," she replied. She reached out with her foot and gently prodded Jimson's body. "That was pretty spectacular. Was he really good, or were you just playing with him?"

"Playing? No, not playing. I was just waiting for him to kill himself. All I was doing was following his lead, moving with him." He gestured vaguely with his right hand to emphasize his inability to explain exactly what he meant. "I didn't really do anything. He did. It's . . . that's just the way it is."

He knelt and turned the renegade over. "Pity," he muttered. "Wish that hadn't been necessary."

"Pity?" the young woman snorted. "Just as well pity killing a viper or a stink lizard!"

"No. There's more to it than that. Jimson wasn't all

bad. There was good in him, too. Or at least a capacity for good."

"Yeh, sure. And vipers eat insects. But that doesn't make their bite any less deadly."

He shrugged. "Jimson wasn't a lizard. He was a person. And I think people need a sense of purpose in their lives. Without it, they go crazy with despair. The trouble is, any purpose will do, even an evil, destructive one. All that really matters is somehow counting in the scheme of things." He reached out and gently closed Jimson's eyes against the glare of the late afternoon sun. "If all of his energy and ability had been used for a good purpose . . ." He sighed, letting the sentence drift off, incomplete.

With a fluid motion, he stood and began to wipe his sword blade on a piece of cloth he took from his front pocket. His voice was brisk and businesslike as he spoke. "Better clean your weapon." He shot a glance at the sun. "We should be moving out. I'd like to get to the other side of the hills before dark. Tomorrow we have to get an early start. It's a long way back to First Pass. The meeting's less than a month away and we've still got a lot to do!"

" 'We'? What makes you think I'm going with you?" she asked, her eyebrows arching to accentuate the questioning tone of her voice.

Edwyr gaped at her. "I . . . well . . . that is . . . I assumed . . ."

Yolan laughed at his confusion. "Don't ever assume anything! But, yeh, I guess I might as well see this thing through. I still don't understand what's going on or what you're up to, but I admit I'm curious enough to want to find out.

"And besides," she continued as she began to clean the blade of her staff, "Mitsuyama wants you dead. Knowing the way that man hedges his bets, I wouldn't be the least bit surprised if he's already sent another bunch of men out after you—just in case Jimson blows it." Her gaze drifted thoughtfully toward the west. "No, I don't believe you've seen the last of him or his Avengers," she murmured.

Turning back, she threw him a quick little grin. "So the way I figure it, you're going to need all the help you can get just to stay alive long enough to reach First Pass!"

BOOK VIII

FIRST PASS

XXIII

It had been raining for two days. The air was filled with the gurgle and splash of water falling from rock to rock or seeping reluctantly toward the lowlands. Clouds, dark with rain still unshed, seemed to lower almost within reach as they flowed eastward, twisting and turning to avoid mountain peaks, flowing steadily where First Pass cut its narrow way through the Mountains.

I hope it clears tomorrow, Andretti thought as he looked westward. There was nothing to see. Even the near foreground was hazy behind the misty veil of the steady downpour.

Rotten weather. Rotten time for it to happen, too. Damn! It's been impossible to get much information on Mitsuyama's movements for two whole days. The rain hides him as effectively as the night cloaks a thief. It's almost as if the weather were on his side, as if he'd planned this! Hold it, he cautioned himself, that's foolish. Let's not give the man more than his due! He's a clever, canny opponent. But he doesn't have any supernatural powers.

And yet . . . Well, just how had the PlainsLord spirited away the Sword of Nakamura? And how had he kept it so well hidden all these months? Even from the Seekers. He shook his head. I had some hope they'd find it, but no, not even a trace. Not even a hint.

But he's got it, I'm sure he does. Where else could it be? And I wouldn't be the least bit surprised if he reveals it during the special meeting to legitimate his attempt to take over Kensho! He snorted. If he's fool enough to bring it here, he'll not have it for long.

Even if I have to use force, I'll bring it back to the
Brotherhood where it belongs!

Burke stood a little behind Father Andretti, watching the older man rather than the rain. Nervous, he
judged. The pressure's beginning to tell. Good, good.
It's all to my advantage! The less in command Andretti is the more in command I am.

The little spy crossed his arms smugly across his
chest. My men are ready, he thought. It hadn't been
possible to make sure all the Faithful he'd brought to
First Pass were loyal to himself. But those in key
positions were. The Group Leaders were. I've got
'em all where I want 'em! Andretti, Mitsuyama, the
'hoods, the PlainsLords, the 'steaders, settlers . . . all
of 'em will soon know you can't play around with
Burke, oh no! Just a little spy, am I? Just a sneaklizard, eh?

Well, my fine Free Council President and Supreme Lord of the Plain, I'm smarter than both of you!
What would Andretti think, for instance, if he knew
that *his* chief spy was also Mitsuyama's main source of
information? Ha! Or what would that lizard-loving
PlainsLord say if he discovered that *his* pet informer,
the man always cloaked so carefully against detection,
was none other than the head of the spy ring the Free
Council employed? He rubbed his hands together.
Not much longer, just until tomorrow, and you'll all
know about Burke! And you'll all bow down to me!

Because I know the final secret! I know that the
Sword of Nakamura is gone, gone forever! It has to be.
There's no other explanation. I've looked
everywhere, had my men searching. I figured it out.
Andretti thinks Mitsuyama's got it. Mitsuyama thinks
Andretti's got it. Only I know neither one of them has
it! The Keepers don't have it either. That was just a
silly rumor to throw both of them off the track.

No, I figured out what happened. Some madman stole it. Some Mushin-crazed idiot. And he fled into the mountains with it. Yes. And fell into some crack or starved in some cave. So it's gone. Forever. That has to be it. Nothing else makes sense.

For a few moments he gloated silently, his eyes drifting off to stare at the rain. *I've got 'em all figured, I've out-thought 'em all.* He frowned slightly. *Except those damn Seekers. What the hell was that all about, all that running out on the Plain and everywhere around the Home Valley? Andretti still thinks they were hunting for the Sword. Huh! I know better than that. They didn't even bother to look! Strange, that's what they are. I'll get rid of 'em first thing when I'm in charge. But what were they up to?*

He dismissed them with a shrug. *Doesn't matter. There aren't more than twenty or thirty of them. Not enough to cause any real trouble. Creepy though,* he shuddered. *I swear they're creepier than ever. Something about them. . . .*

Andretti motioned for him to come up. "Burke," he began softly as the spy reached his side, "send your men out again. I must know what that devil's up to. Rain or no rain, I must have an accurate count of his numbers and dispositions. Find out if that mounted column is coming here in a single body or going somewhere else, too. I don't like that one, Burke."

Burke nodded. "Me either. Those lizards are big and mean looking, Father. Wouldn't want to face one, myself. I'll send four of my best men out soon as we get back to camp. I'll have word by nightfall, latest."

The older man looked down at the spy. "The men, are they ready? Do they thoroughly understand the situation, the plan I drew up? Timing is crucial, Burke. Crucial."

"Aye, sir, they understand. They know what to do.

And when to do it."

"Good. A great deal is riding on them and their performance. Perhaps the whole future of Kensho." Andretti waved Burke away and stood gazing thoughtfully westward for several more moments. Then he turned and began slowly walking back to join the small knot of Council members that had accompanied him to the meeting site.

When he reached them, he stood in silence for a few seconds, scanning their faces, one by one. Finished with his scrutiny, he raised his palms to the falling rain and shrugged. "It's in the hands of the Gods now. Tomorrow will decide. Let's go back to camp and get into some dry clothes. If any exist."

As a body, they walked eastward back to their tents.

Lord William Mitsuyama looked at the bedraggled, sodden figure that was dripping water all over the floor of his tent, and wished for the hundredth time that Jimson was still alive. Damn! The man was dangerous, even deadly. But at least he was competent!

The march to First Pass had been a nightmare of confusion from the very first moments. The Striders had proven almost impossible to manage in such numbers. More than seventy of the creatures in one place! The stink alone was enough to make you gag! But the noise! . . .

And now the cursed rain! Three days of slogging along through it. Not even sure if they were going in the right direction half of the time. Eventually they'd had to move back to the main trail and follow it rather than move cross-country. If we have any element of surprise left at all, it's because Andretti's spies hate the rain more than we do!

"Well, Dembo, how is the ex-diplomat making out as a leader of men?" he asked the wet man. "Is everything in order?"

"Lord, everything's in order. At least in as much order as it'll ever be in." He sighed hugely. "Being a general, even a junior one, isn't must fun in weather like this. Especially since you expect us to be with the troops all the time."

Mitsuyama raised an eyebrow. "Complaining? My, my Dembo. Yours but to serve, not to question. Like a good soldier. We're a small army, a close one. No more than fifty all told in the main party, including the Lords. Two more columns of fifty each on the flanks. And a mounted reserve of another sixty-five."

"Sixty-two," corrected the other man. "Two more of those damn lizards died and one ran away."

"Casualties are to be expected in warfare."

"Before the battle?"

"The battle, Dembo, began a long time ago. Now we're merely approaching its climax. And in any case, a few lizards more or less shouldn't make any difference. I expect I won't even have to use the beasts."

"I pray you won't." Dembo shuddered. "I don't trust the disgusting things. Just the idea of one of them behind me, with those teeth . . . ugh! If they can't even tell their own riders, how will they know I'm on their side?"

Mitsuyama chuckled dryly. "Then be sure to win quickly so they won't be required, Dembo. Now, are all the men in place for the advance tomorrow morning?"

Dembo nodded. "Yes, sir. The main body, weapons strapped on their backs and hidden in the baggage, will move off at dawn. We figure they'll get to the crest of the pass about an hour before mid-day.

The meeting officially starts at noon, so that gives time to settle in.

"At about the same time the main group arrives, the two flanking columns will advance to the western mouth of the pass. We'll send word back as soon as the meeting starts and then they'll move forward, on opposite sides of the valley, to a point about a mile beyond the second bend. That puts them, oh, a fifteen minute run from the meeting site. The lizards'll wait at the mouth of the pass and the men will mount up at the same time the flanking columns move up."

"Good, good. See that it comes off smoothly, Dembo."

"Yes, Lord. I'll do my best."

"Do better than that. Now go."

As the man left to go out in the rain again, Miriam appeared from behind a curtain that divided the tent in two. She moved quietly to stand behind her husband, putting her hands on his head and gently rubbing his temples with her fingers.

He sighed. "I almost wish . . ."

"Don't say it, William. We're better off without Jimson. You were right the first time. He and the Seeker were meant to cancel each other in the equation."

"But we only know that one half of the equation was cancelled. For all I can discover, the balance was never achieved. The damn Seeker may still live."

"Surely one of those two groups caught up with him and the girl and cut them down, William. No doubt they had a merry chase of it and that's why they haven't reported in yet. They could be on their way here right now."

"Yes, yes, I suppose you're right. And I'm not sure it matters in any case. But I'd dearly love to kill that Edwyr with my own hands. What a pleasure!"

"When you're Supreme Lord of Kensho," she crooned, "you'll be able to kill anyone you want, Lord. Edwyr, Andretti, Dembo, anyone."

"Not anyone, no. Just a few. The dangerous ones. Those who would stand in the way. Anyone who cooperates is safe, my dear. As long as he cooperates."

"And the Keepers?"

"They'll play their part. Oh, I might have to make an example of a few to show them I mean what I say."

"Don't forget how stubborn old Carlson was, William. One or two examples might not be enough."

"Then to hell with them. We'll create our own Keepers and send them up to the Flagship ourselves. We'll have the Medallion once Andretti's out of the way."

Her hands slid lower and worked on his neck. He let his head roll loosely forward. "Ummmmm. And what do you want, my dear?"

For a moment, she was still, even her hands stopping their motion. Then she began kneading his muscles again as she leaned her lips close to his ear and whispered, "Everything, William, everything."

The ceaseless sound of the rain trying to wash away the world invaded and enfolded the tent and the people in it.

XXIV

The morning hardly dawned at all. Low, sluggish clouds plodded across the sky, cutting off all view of the surrounding peaks. The world seemed to be folding in on itself, narrowing down its existence to one tiny valley lost amid the mist-shrouded mountains. First Pass felt more isolated and bleak than ever.

Andretti had all his men in place by ten o'clock. The Free Council took up a position on a slight rise near the center of the pass. On the right and left flanks, reaching almost to the walls, were Burke's picked members of the Faithful, the delegates chosen by the 'hoods, and those 'steaders Andretti felt could be relied on. Extending westward from the ends of his lines were the rest of the 'steaders, the representatives of the settlers, and a number of on-lookers who had come to satisfy their curiosity or simply to be present at what everyone felt would be an historic event. Mitsuyama and the other PlainsLords would make up the fourth side of the rough rectangle.

At eleven, Burke's runners brought news that Mitsuyama was near at hand. A few moments later, a light drizzle started. Andretti raised the hood on his robe with stoic resignation and stood in the midst of his host, peering through the misty rain for a first glimpse of his enemy.

It was a good fifteen minutes before their sodden banners became visible. On a sunny day, the arrival would have been a brave show. The brightly colored flags of the four Great Clans would have rolled and snapped in the breeze. The devices of the individual clans that made up the Great Clans would have fluttered gaily. But the rain, growing heavier now,

smothered everything beneath its dripping weight.
The banners hung limp and motionless, their hues
muted by the gloom.

A stony silence greeted the newcomers as they
moved into their alloted position. Andretti watched,
soberly estimating their number and strength.
Burke's information is accurate, he decided. We're
equal. So training, discipline, and timing will be the
decisive factors. He looked over at Burke, who stood
hunched miserably against the downpour. The little
man felt his stare and turned to acknowledge it. Andretti moved his head in a prearranged signal. The
spy nodded his understanding, then scuttled off on
his errands.

In the middle of the PlainsLord's line, Dembo
stood next to Mitsuyama and covertly pointed out the
figure of the President of the Free Council. "That's
him," he murmured, "right at the front of that group
on the rise. The tall, heavy one."

"The others?"

"Members of the Council. Olson's over on the
right. Dubrow is behind him. It's a little hard to
identify them with their hoods up, but as near as I can
tell, they're all there. The good Father must have
done a lot of fence-mending to get them all to support
him like this."

The Supreme Lord of the Plain nodded and concentrated his gaze on Andretti. His eyes carefully
scanned the other man, missing nothing. He appears
to be calm, Mitsuyama thought, as if meetings like
this were an everyday occurence. But there are
plenty of little hints that his coolness is feigned, a
mask to hide his true feelings. See how he picks at the
seam of his robe with his left hand? Or how he shifts
his weight unnecessarily and constantly looks here
and there? Signs of a tightly controlled nervousness,

an underlying uncertainty. Yet his face is quiet, grim, determined. He may be unsure of himself, may even be afraid of failure. But he'll never back down, never retreat an inch. He's every bit as stubborn and fanatic as I've always thought. Which means there truly are no alternatives. We will fight. Blood will flow.

Completing his assessment of Andretti, he allowed his gaze to drift down the opposite line of men. They looked, at first glance, much like any group of 'steaders—with a Brother or Sister thrown in here and there. But a second glance by a knowing eye revealed that these were no cloddish farmers. Trained, every one of them. My spy was right, he decided. Andretti's packed the meeting with the Faithful, undoubtedly those loyal to himself and the Council.

He sensed more than saw the figure that moved to his side. Looking from the corner of his eye, he found the hooded form of Miriam. He didn't like having her here, this close to the enemy, but she had insisted. And, in all truth, he was glad to have her sharp mind near him at this moment. At least if things got bad, there would be time to send her to the partial safety of the reserve columns.

For several moments the two of them stood there, scanning the line of men that faced them. Then she spoke, quietly, almost as if talking to herself. "You were right to bring the reserves and the Striders, William. We may need them."

"Ummmm. Yes. Do you see the other one anywhere? The Seeker?"

She looked again, slowly, for several long minutes. "No" she finally responded. "Can you spot any Seekers at all?"

He shook his head. "Of course Andretti might be holding them in reserve."

"Would they follow his orders that faithfully?"

"No," he said slowly, evaluating the possibility, "no, I don't think so."

"Then they aren't here. They've refused to play his game."

Thoughtfully he gazed up at the walls of the pass. "Perhaps they're playing some game of their own." He turned to look for Dembo. The man was right behind him. "Dembo, have the runners from the two columns reported yet? It nears noon."

"No, Lord. But I expect them any moment."

"Don't 'expect' them. Send two men to find out where they are."

"Yes, Lord."

William turned back to his scrutiny of the Free Council's forces. The ground to the right was rougher than to the left. And Andretti's line there was more uneven, seemed less firm. Was it deliberate, a trap, a planned weakness? It would certainly be harder to attack there, in any case.

What about the center? A drive there would have the most immediate effect, especially if it managed to reach the members of the Council and particularly Andretti. Of course, there would be the danger of flanking movements. But if we timed it right, we could actually turn that against them! If we allowed a flank attack, even invited it, and tricked Andretti into committing his forces to it, we could fall on them from behind with our spare columns. We could literally flank the flankers! It's risky, and requires perfect timing, but it's certainly an unexpected maneuver, the kind that wins battles and makes men rulers of worlds! We'll want a tighter formation. Have to pull in the ends of our line a little. That'll give us more concentrated strength and act as a lure at the same time.

Gesturing to Dembo, he began to organize the attack plan.

Andretti watched the huddle between Dembo and his master with interest. Decided something, he guessed. Probably his attack plan.

A hand touched his sleeve. He turned his head to his right and found himself looking into the cold eyes of Father Olson. "Let's quit stalling and get this thing going, Andretti. I don't like the looks of it one bit. So let's get the unpleasantness over with as soon as possible."

" 'Unpleasantness'? Don't be coy, Olson. It's a battle and you know it."

"There's no fight until it's started."

"It started when William became Supreme Lord."

"I still have hopes we can head it off short of a battle."

"That's wishful thinking of the kind Johnston used to specialize in."

"I'd rather not fight."

"I'd rather not lose!"

The two men glared at each other for a few moments. Eventually, though, Olson backed down with a sigh. "All right, Tomas. But let's get on with it. It's near enough to noon to begin. Everybody's here. Even the rain is letting up."

In surprise Andretti looked up. The rain had indeed slackened to a drizzle while he had been concentrating on other things. He returned his gaze to Olson. "All right," he nodded curtly. "You were chosen to speak for the Council in this matter, since I'm ineligible as an interested party. Start it."

With a curt nod, the other man turned and strode between the lines. An immediate hush fell over the pass. As Olson spoke, he turned back and forth to address everyone.

"Let the meeting begin. Who is entitled to speak for the people of Kensho? Let them step forward. Who will speak for the Sisterhoods?"

"I speak for the Sisterhoods," responded a slender, greyhaired woman. "I am Mother Carol, of the Sisterhood at RoundHill, chosen by all to speak for all. Nine others are here as my conscience and guide." She stepped forward, her glance strong and challenging.

"Who will speak for the Brotherhoods?"

"I speak for the Brotherhoods," rumbled a deep, harsh voice. A large, totally bald man shuffled out. "Though I'll be damned if I know why," he quipped. "The fools trust me, or perhaps they picked me because I talk so damn much they figured they couldn't miss! Anyway, there are fourteen of us here."

"Who will speak for the 'Steaders?"

A middle-aged woman walked into the center. "I will," she said softly as she moved fluidly to join the group gathered in the space between the lines.

Olson continued the roll call, asking the person chosen to speak for each delegation to step out and join the rest of them. As expected, Mitsuyama was the speaker for the Council of Lords. Last of all, Father Andretti joined the group.

All told, there were nineteen of them. Together, they constituted the Council of the meeting, the body that would present the viewpoints of the delegations, discuss the issues, report back to their respective delegations, poll the members to ascertain their decision, and then return to announce the result.

They seated themselves in a tight circle as the rain stopped and began discussing the matter at hand: whether or not Father Andretti should be permanently invested with the title, duties, and powers of the Way-Farer. Relaxing somewhat, those in the lines

followed their example and sat down on the damp
ground. A few, like Dembo and Burke, remained
standing, stalking here and there, keeping their men
in order and on the alert.

Although the Council's discussion lasted for more
than two hours, and at times became quite heated, it
was evident almost from the first how matters lay. The
speakers for the 'hoods, the Faithful, and the 'steaders, were solidly behind Andretti. The settlers were
wavering, unwilling to commit themselves to either
side since they had to live between them both. The
PlainsLords, both the Council and each of the Great
Clans, were clearly and vociferously against allowing
the President of the Free Council to take up the
Way-Farership. Repeatedly, they pointed out that
Johnston himself had made no choice, that the Sword
of Nakamura was missing, and that they did not consider Andretti as representing their interests or those
of Kensho.

To the surprise of everyone, neither Mitsuyama
nor Andretti took any part in the proceedings. Each
man sat, silent and aloof, as if alone in the world.
Their gazes never crossed and neither one deigned to
recognize or even admit the existence of the other.

After going over the same ground for the seventh or
eighth time, Olson called for silence. His face was
grim and weary with frustration, his eyes haunted by
the shadow of the inevitable fate he wanted so badly
to avoid. He bowed his head for a moment, as if
gathering strength from the stillness he had called
into being. Then his head rose and he swept the circle
with his glance. "We've discussed this enough," he
declared bluntly. "There's no sense in endlessly repeating the same arguments. It's time to go back to
your delegations and report on these deliberations."
They all nodded bleak agreement. "May I remind

you," he continued, his eyes seeking out each one of them individually and fixing them momentarily with a baleful glare, "that a decision *will* be reached." His gaze locked with Mitsuyama's. "And that decision *will* be considered to be the Word of the people of Kensho." His head swiveled to Andretti. "And that all parties *will* comply with it, whether they agree or not."

Before anyone else could rise, the two antagonists stood as one man. All pretense at indifference was gone now as the two of them flung defiant, hate-filled looks at each other across the circle. Andretti spoke first, his voice husky with restrained emotion. "I understand, Father Olson. And I want to assure everyone that the power of the Free Council will be used to enforce that decision if necessary."

Mitsuyama sneered openly. When he spoke, his voice was soft, almost velvety, with a hissing sibilance that carried a greater threat than any raging bellow. "You'll need that power, Andretti. Oh, yes. You'll need it more than you can imagine!" With a snort of contempt, he turned his back on the President of the Free Council and stalked back toward his waiting followers.

In tense silence, the others stood and trudged slowly back to their delegations.

XXV

The discussion and decision within the delegations took less than three-quarters of an hour to complete. As the nineteen gathered again, responding to Olson's call, they came slowly, almost reluctantly. They seemed nervous and self-conscious, preferring to stare down at the ground rather than meet each other's eyes.

When they were all seated, Olson stood and swept the lined-up PlainsLords with his cold glare. They were all standing, motionless and silent. Only their eyes moved as they intently watched the isolated group between the lines. Turning to the other side, Olson saw the same thing.

For a brief moment, a flutter of fear ran through his mind. He could actually feel the pressure of all those eyes, was almost smothered by the sense of anticipation that rolled toward him across the empty space to where he stood. As he stared, their faces seemed to flicker in and out of focus, one moment becoming strange, alien, and hateful, the next transforming back into the ordinary men and women he had lived among all his life. Gods! he thought in a rush of despair, what kind of creatures are we? What sort of insanity is this? Why are we standing here, ready to strike out in mindless anger and destroy all we've built in the last three generations?

Jerome had once said that the Mushin only make us what we already are, he recalled. The Madness is really just what's already there, made more so. Which is why the Way seeks to change men rather than to destroy the mind leeches. Even our method of controlling the creatures in the 'hoods isn't meant to kill them. It merely keeps them at bay so *we* have time to develop.

But have we changed all that much? Have we succeeded in transforming ourselves in keeping with Jerome's vision? Isn't this very confrontation proof of our failure, proof that while we may have learned to control the Mushin, we still don't know how to control ourselves?

A realization dawned in his mind, an understanding so strong and vivid that he closed his eyes against the brightness of it. Even with the Mushin penned in the 'hoods, we're acting exactly the way we would if they were free! He opened his eyes wide and stared wildly about. The two straight lines, the eager, expectant faces, all this will disintegrate into a bloody turmoil, with men hacking madly at each other . . . exactly as if the Mushin had caused it! The Madness! his mind screamed. The time of insanity and death is back! First Touch has returned!

With a wrench, he brought himself back under control before his fear got the upper hand. Calm, he told himself. Panic won't solve anything. Keep a cool head. Maybe something will show up. A silent laugh, heavy with bitter resignation, welled up from the depths of his soul, smothering the tiny spark of hope he was trying to kindle. Why try to fool myself? I'm just one more helpless, ineffective human being caught up in something I can't control or understand. Nothing I do or don't do will make any difference; the thing I fear most is about to happen, whether I want it to or not. And I have the honor of starting it.

Where will it end? And when?

He spread his arms wide to gain everyone's attention. "The delegations have reached their decision. The people of Kensho have given their Word. Let those who speak for them pronounce it. Shall Father

Tomas Andretti, President of the Free Council, appointed Interim Way-Farer, be granted the permanent title, duties, and responsibilities of the Way-Farer? How say the Sisterhoods?"

"Yes," came the reply, subdued, but firm.

"The Brotherhoods?"

"Yes."

The vote went rapidly and without surprises. The split between the forces of the Free Council and the PlainsLords was clear and unmistakable. As the last voice, that of one of the delegates from the Great Clans, shouted its defiant "No!", a heavy silence settled over the throng.

Mitsuyama stood, raised his clenched fist. With a roar, his men ripped off their outer robes, snatching at the swords hidden beneath them, strapped to their backs.

Stunned, the other members of the little Council stood and fled back to their respective places. Andretti held his ground, with Olson standing uncertainly slightly behind and to his right. His face was twisted into a ferocious grin as he ran his glance over the sword-waving men opposite him. "True to form, William! I expected no less of a man who'd poison his father and steal the Sword of Nakamura! Monster! Do you think we'll meekly stand by and watch you destroy the Way with your miserable ideas, your sick, insane desire to bring the horrors of Earth to Kensho? Never!" He raised both his hands over his head, then brought them sharply down to his sides.

Behind him he could hear the answering shout of his own men as they pulled out their concealed weapons. Casting a quick look over his shoulder, he saw a bristling mass of bladed staffs and swords.

As he turned back to confront the PlainsLord again, he was surprised to find the man smiling. Before he could say anything, Mitsuyama spoke. "I'm glad to see I didn't underestimate you, Andretti. Not one little bit. It really would've been a pity if I'd had to kill you without any fight at all. History wouldn't have treated such a victory kindly, I fear. This is much better, much better!" A brief look of pity flashed across his features. "You really have many admirable talents. How sad you've used them so unwisely. And now you'll never have a chance to make all your errors good."

Andretti snarled his reply. "Don't try to be clever, sneaklizard! The time for witty conversation's over. Only one of us will leave this valley alive! And it won't be you!"

"How melodramatic," sneered Mitsuyama as he began to walk back toward his own men. "Get ready Mr. President of the Free Council," he called back over his shoulder. "I'll be over to personally cut your throat in about ten minutes!"

Burke could barely contain his excitement. For the hundredth time that morning he ran his eyes over his lines, checking once more to make sure his men were in their places. He nodded to himself, rubbing his hands with brisk delight. Perfect. Let the 'hoods and those I'm not sure about take the brunt of the fighting. We'll hold back, we will, waiting. Waiting for Mitsuyama to kill Andretti or vice versa. Waiting for the death of as many on both sides as possible. And then when they're weak and least expecting it . . .! Oh, yes! They won't be laughing at Burke any more!

Dembo was terrified. He gaped across the empty space at a man who was waving a bladed staff in his direction. He's looking right at me! he thought. He wants to kill me! Gods! I don't even know the man and he wants to stick that blade in my guts! His hands shaking, his palms slippery with sweat, Dembo

pulled himself together and glanced over at Mitsuyama. Will he order us forward, into *that*? he wondered, stealing another quick look at the enemy line,
alive with deadly metal.

Mitsuyama was about to lift his hand to give the
signal when an unexpected movement on both the
right and left caught his attention. From the mixed
crowd of 'steaders, settlers, and on-lookers who
formed the sides of the rectangle along the walls of the
pass, robed and hooded figures were stepping out and
striding rapidly to take up a position directly between
himself and the mass of the Free Council.

With a sudden shock, he recognized them, even
though their individual faces were hidden. The fluid
grace of their gait gave them away. Seekers! More
than 20 of them!

Quickly, breathlessly, he counted. Twenty-seven,
no, twenty-eight! All armed with swords, except one
who carried a bladed staff, and looked curiously out of
place. Damn! he cursed. Where in the hell did they
come from? What in the devil are they up to? He felt
Miriam's hand on his arm and looked down to meet
her questioning gaze. "Damned if I know," he muttered.

Andretti could scarcely believe his eyes. The Seekers! But they refused to join me! Have they changed
their minds? Surely they have! Gods, what luck! Now
I've got that bastard cold! he gloated triumphantly.
But why in the hell are they out there rather than in
our line? And why are some of them facing this way as
if we're the enemy?

The twenty-eight figures came to a halt in a roughly
oval configuration, half facing each of the two lines. In
the center of the oval, two figures stood together, one
intently scanning the crowd, the other casually leaning on a bladed staff. The first reached up a hand to

pull back its hood, revealing the features of Edwyr. A quick toss of the second's head, and Yolan appeared. The others followed suit.

Edwyr raised his hands to still the buzz of speculation that had sprung up. "This madness has gone far enough," he said into the silence. "Put away your weapons and go home."

"And leave Andretti as Way-Farer?" Mitsuyama cried. "Never!"

"Andretti isn't the Way-Farer," Edwyr replied calmly. "Johnston picked his successor before he died, and it wasn't Father Andretti."

Andretti exploded. "What kind of nonsense is this? Johnston picked a Way-Farer? What are you talking about? I was there! I saw no such thing!"

"It happened just after you left, though even if you'd been there, you probably wouldn't have known what was going on. The Way-Farer offered you a Ko blossom. You were so filled with yourself and your problems, you didn't see it for what it was. You rejected it."

"Of course! The Sword was missing, the Way-Farer was dying—and I . . . I was the only one who—"

"You rejected it. When you left, he turned and offered it to me. I took it for what it was, a Ko blossom given by a friend. Then he whispered to me."

"He . . . what did he say?"

" 'Mountains, rivers, earth, sky, the Ko, there is not a thing that is not real. The real aspect is all things.' I was overwhelmed. I'm told I cried, although all I remember is light filling my mind."

"Are you trying to tell me . . . ! "

"I'm trying to tell you that Father Johnston passed the Way-Farership to me when he handed me the Ko blossom. It was his way of transmitting the office. It was a test and a proof of my worth. Any one of us," he gestured at the others in the group, "any one of the Companions the Way-Farer gathered together during his last years, could have been chosen." His voice dropped in volume, becoming sad and somewhat regretful. "For whatever reasons, Father Johnston chose me. I am the Way-Farer."

"But the Sword," Andretti sputtered, "a Ko blossom isn't the Sword of Nakamura! How can you be the Way-Farer without the Sword?!"

"Is the Way-Farer no more than a man who carries an ancient sword?" Edwyr asked gently.

"No, but the Sword is missing, it's been stolen, it's . . ."

Edwyr smiled. "No, it wasn't stolen. And it's never been missing."

Andretti's jaw dropped. "Not missing?"

"No, Johnston took it out of the shrine himself and hid it when he felt death was near."

Burke pushed his way to the front of the line, his eyes wild with fury, spittle flying from his lips. "You lie! You lie, you rotten Seeker! Johnston never appointed you anything! Filthy lies! Burke knows, oh, yes! The Sword's gone! Gone forever! If you're the Way-Farer, if Johnston hid the Sword, where is it, eh? Where? You can't stop Burke with a cheap trick like that! Oh, no! You lie! The Sword's gone! Where is it, eh? Where?"

"Right here," the Seeker answered quietly. He reached inside his robe and pulled out the Sword of Nakamura, secure in its scabbard.

A cry of surprise and wonderment soared over the crowd. Andretti was almost frantic. Mitsuyama stood as if carved from stone, his mouth hanging wide in utter amazement. The shock was too much for Burke and the little man crumpled, unconscious, to the ground.

The President of the Free Council was the first to recover. "All right, then," he addressed Edwyr, his voice brittle with tightly controlled anger, "if you really are the legitimate Way-Farer, it's your duty to defend the Great Way against this rabble from the Plain."

"Defend the Great Way?" Edwyr replied with a slight smile. "I have no intention of defending the Great Way. In fact, I plan to completely dismantle it and the entire hierarchy that's been built up around it."

Speechless, Andretti stood staring at the Seeker. Several times he worked his mouth, but no words came. Finally he found his voice and said hoarsely, "You're insane! The Great Way is our only hope, now and forever. It's the only thing that controls the Mushin and stands between us and the Madness. Gods, man, it's the only thing that keeps riff-raff like that," he gestured contemptuously toward the PlainsLords, "from turning Kensho into another Earth!"

"On the contrary, Father Andretti, the Great Way is the main obstacle standing between us and our accomplishing the goals Jerome set for us."

"But we've already accomplished them! The Mushin are penned in the 'hoods, we've spread across the Plain, there are enough of us now to protect the race from possible extinction; all we have to do is stay loyal to the Way and everything will come out just as Jerome planned."

"It's the very successes you speak of, Father, that make the Way an obstacle to the realization of Jerome's plan. You, and others like you, have tried to institutionalize those achievements to preserve them for eternity. But they were never meant to be permanent. They were merely the first steps in a long

process, the beginning of an almost endless journey.
Jerome never intended the Way to become a gov-
ernment. Its purpose was to change men, not rule
them."

"But we *are* still changing! We're becoming more
immune to the Mushin in every generation."

Edwyr shook his head. "I'm sorry, Father, but
that's simply not true. Fewer people than ever practice the disciplines that Jerome taught us. The
PlainsLords don't even bother to pay them lip service
any longer. The settlers get a minimal education in
the Way, mainly because they want to stay on good
terms with the 'hoods for purely economic reasons.
Even in the Home Valley, the only people really
practicing what Jerome taught are those in the 'hoods.
And they use it mainly to control the Mushin."

"But that's what Jerome wanted! That's the whole
point to what he did! He gave us the Way so we could
free ourselves from the Mushin and live our lives in
peace. And the hierarchy of the Great Way has become the only thing that assures the continuation of
that freedom."

"Andretti, Andretti," Edwyr sighed, "the Way is so
much deeper than you know. Jerome didn't free us so
we could live out our lives in peace. He freed us so we
could continue the struggle to change ourselves and
adapt to Kensho and the Mushin. The peace was only
meant to be temporary, a breathing space to let us
prepare for the struggle ahead.

"And now the peace has lasted too long. It must
come to an end."

A rising murmur of confusion came from the crowd.
Cries of "What does he mean? What's he talking
about? End? End how?" could be heard.

"What are you up to, Seeker?" challenged Mitsuyama. "Do you have some crazy plan you're not telling us about?"

Edwyr laughed. "Yes, I do have a 'crazy plan'. Or I should say that we," he indicated the others in his group, "have developed a plan based on Father Johnston's ideas and insights."

"And you expect us to buy this scheme, just like that?" sneered the PlainsLord.

The Seeker shrugged. "It doesn't really matter whether you buy it or not, Lord. We've already put it into effect."

"What are you talking about?" Andretti demanded.

"I'm talking about the freeing of the Mushin."

For several long moments, utter silence filled the pass as the throng absorbed what Edwyr had just said. Then, as understanding came, a frightened whispering began to swell and grow until it became an avalanche of fear.

Andretti was screaming at the top of his lungs. "Free the Mushin? Are you crazy? You can't do that! It's . . . It's . . ."

"It's already been done!" Edwyr's shout cut through the babble, forcing everyone to stillness. "And that's another reason you all have to disperse and go home. The mind leeches will be swarming up here, right through this pass, out onto the Plain, in just a few hours. If you're still here when they come, you're doomed!"

"Bluff!" roared Mitsuyama, his face dark with rage. "You're lying! It's a total fraud!"

Edwyr smiled cooly. "No bluff, no fraud, no lie. Truth. In fact, since I thought some of you might not believe us, we've brought a few of the Mushin with us to give you a little taste of what's on its way." He spoke quietly to his followers. "Take those you

achieved Identification with. Focus the Mind
Brothers on them. Just briefly. Let them feel the
presence and the fear. That's all."

Instantly, Mitsuyama, Andretti, and numerous
other important individuals in the crowd went white
and rigid. One man fell to the ground, shrieking in
terror. The PlainsLord staggered, his face pasty with
sudden horror. Andretti doubled over as if struck in
the stomach. "Enough!" he whimpered, his voice
filled with anguish and pleading.

"I'm sorry," Edwyr said gently as those attacked
felt the pressure withdraw. "But you wanted proof."

"You've done it," Andretti muttered, shaking his
head in utter confoundment. Anger blazed up in his
eyes. "You're worse than Mitsuyama ever was! Do
you know how many people will die horrible deaths
thanks to what you've done? What kind of monsters
are you, anyway?"

A look of infinite sadness and compassion welled up
in Edwyr's eyes. "Yes, I know," he murmured. "I
know better than any of you exactly what's involved."
He shuddered. "I also know the alternatives. Still, it's
a burden I'd rather not bear. But the choice isn't
mine. I'm the Way-Farer. And this must be."

His face ravaged by anguish and defeat, Andretti
turned away from Edwyr. Head bowed and shoulders
drooping, he slowly began to shuffle off, back down
the pass toward the east. A few of the other members
of the Free Council joined him, but most of them just
milled about in aimless confusion, unable to decide
what to do with themselves.

Mitsuyama stood slumped in a dazed stupor, still
trying to shake off the effects of the Mushin attack.
Dimly, he was aware someone was calling his name
and pulling urgently at the sleeve of his robe. He

managed to focus his attention and eyes on the face of his wife.

"William," she was hissing, "William, snap out of it!" As she saw recognition return to his eyes, Miriam grabbed his chin in her hands and turned his head so he had to notice her.

"This is our chance, William," she said in a hushed but intense voice. "The Sword of Nakamura is right there, almost within reach. Take it William, reach out and tear it from the Seeker's grasp! Take it and become ruler of Kensho!"

"But—but . . . " he stammered, "you heard what he said. The Mushin are coming! We've got to run, run!"

She slapped him hard. "Come out of it, damn you! The Mushin won't be here for hours, if ever. If we act decisively now, we'll finish the whole thing in a matter of minutes! Andretti's people are so frightened they'll run at the first attack! I tell you now's the time!"

He stared at her wild eyes and twisted face with complete amazement. He looked over at the opposite line. She was right. Andretti's men were milling about in total confusion, not sure what to do next. He glanced quickly up and down his own lines. The men looked stunned, but at least they were maintaining some semblance of order.

Edwyr followed the exchange between the Supreme Lord of the Plain and his wife with great interest. Although he couldn't catch what they were saying, he watched with growing anticipation as the man snapped out of his daze and began to look around, shrewdly evaluating the situation. When he saw Mitsuyama's back straighten and his shoulders square with resolution, he realized he would have to

spring his last surprise. He didn't want to because it
was a little unpredictable. But . . . he shrugged and
spoke quietly out of the side of his mouth to the others
in the group. "Prepare to release your Mind Brothers
when I give the signal. It's time to keep our bargain."
They all muttered their understanding.

Moving from the center of the oval to the side
facing the PlainsLords, Edwyr called out, "Lord Mitsuyama!"

The man turned to look at him in surprise.

Edwyr took two more steps in his direction and
stopped, smiling grimly. "Lord," he said, his voice
low and hard, "before you make any decisions, there's
one more thing you should know."

A look of momentary confusion fled across Mitsuyama's face. He cast a quick sideways glance at
Miriam. "What should I know, Seeker?"

"That we are not the only ones here at First Pass."
Without waiting for any reply, Edwyr cupped his
hands around his mouth and gave a long, loud, ululat-
ing cry.

Instantly the call was answered. On both sides of
the pass, at the tops of the walls that hemmed in
PlainsLords, Brothers, Sisters, Councilors, 'steaders,
settlers, and Seekers, raggedly dressed men suddenly stood, waving their swords, setting up a fright-
ful animal howling.

A collective gasp went up from everyone. Like
wildfire, one word swept from mouth to mouth—
"Ronin!" Mitsuyama's face went pasty white. Miriam
shrank back with a little cry and covered her face with
both hands.

"There is no victory, Lord," Edwyr said softly.
"Only death."

Mitsuyama's glance turned and fell on the Seeker.